MW01148148

THE VITRUVIAN MAN

A Novel

David Aucsmith

Omnis fabula iter est—gratias ago hoc mecum susepisti.

This is a work of fiction. Though some characters, incidents, and dialogues are based on the historical record, the work as a whole is a product of the author's imagination.

Tera Nova Books, LLC
Seattle, WA
www.teranovabooks.com

Editors: Matt Bennett and Miki Hayden
Cover Design: Dee Marley at White Rabbit Arts, The Historical Fiction Company
Illustrations & Maps: David Aucsmith

Library of Congress Control Number: 2022923117

ISBN-13: 978-1-7349889-4-9

Printed in the United States of America

DEDICATION

To my mother, Mary Ammons, on reaching 90 years young.

ACKNOWLEDGMENTS

I owe a debt of gratitude to those who slogged through early drafts; my wife, Shana; the Saturday morning gang, Aaron Falk, Cecilia Austin, Jessica Cox, and Crystal Tankesley; and good friend, Dan Wachtler.

A warm thanks to Matt Bennett for story editing, and Miki Hayden for masterfully line editing the finished manuscript. The story is much better for their efforts.

I would be remiss if I did not call out Dee Marley with White Rabbit Arts at The Historical Fiction Company for the excellent cover design. It brings Vitruvius to life.

AUTHOR'S NOTE

Leonardo da Vinci's famous drawing *Vitruvian Man* represents his concept of ideal human body proportions. Its depiction of the human form inside both a square and a circle comes from a description by the ancient Roman architect Marcus Vitruvius Pollio in Book III, Chapter 1 of his treatise *De Architectura*.

> Similarly, in the members of a temple there ought to be the greatest harmony in the symmetrical relations of the different parts to the general magnitude of the whole. Then again, in the human body the central point is naturally the navel. For if a man be placed flat on his back, with his hands and feet extended, and a pair of compasses centered at his naval, the fingers and toes of his two hands and feet will touch the circumference of a circle described therefrom. And just as the human body yields a circular outline, so too a square figure may be found from it. For if we measure the distance from the soles of the feet to the top of the head, and then apply that measure to the outstretched arms, the breadth will be found to be the same as the height, as in the case of plane surfaces which are perfectly square.

Vitruvius Pillio. 1941. *De Architectura*. Translated by Morris Morgan. Cambridge, MA: Harvard University Press. (Orig. pub. C. 30-20 BCE.).

The Vitruvian Man

Vitruvius wrote *De Architectura* in the first decade of Pax Augustus, c. 30-20 BCE. It is the only major work on architecture or engineering to survive from classical antiquity.

Yet, Vitruvius remains a mystery. Other than what he reveals about himself in *De Architectura,* we know almost nothing about him. Even his name, aside from his family name, Vitruvius, is debated among scholars.

Vitruvius lived during Rome's most decisive years: the desolation of the Republic, the rise and murder of Julius Caesar, and the ascent of the Empire and Pax Augustus.

We also know that Vitruvius was not wellborn. His name is featured in lists of *apparitores,* public servants assisting magistrates. The apparitores occupied a position within the Roman social hierarchy between the equestrian order and the plebeians. We further know Vitruvius was exceptionally well educated and held the position of military engineer under Julius Caesar. He took part in many of Caesar's campaigns, and he counted Octavian (Augustus) as his patron, from whom he received a *commode* (stipend) when he wrote *De Architectura* later in life.

This novel imagines the life of Marcus Vitruvius Pollio as an aged Vitruvius might have told it in his memoirs and as he might have lived it in the shadow of monumental events. I have endeavored to be historically accurate with respect to events, culture, and Vitruvius's own words as he relates them in *De Architectura.*

As many Latin words and Roman names are not familiar to our modern ear, I have included both a glossary and a list of characters at the end of the book.

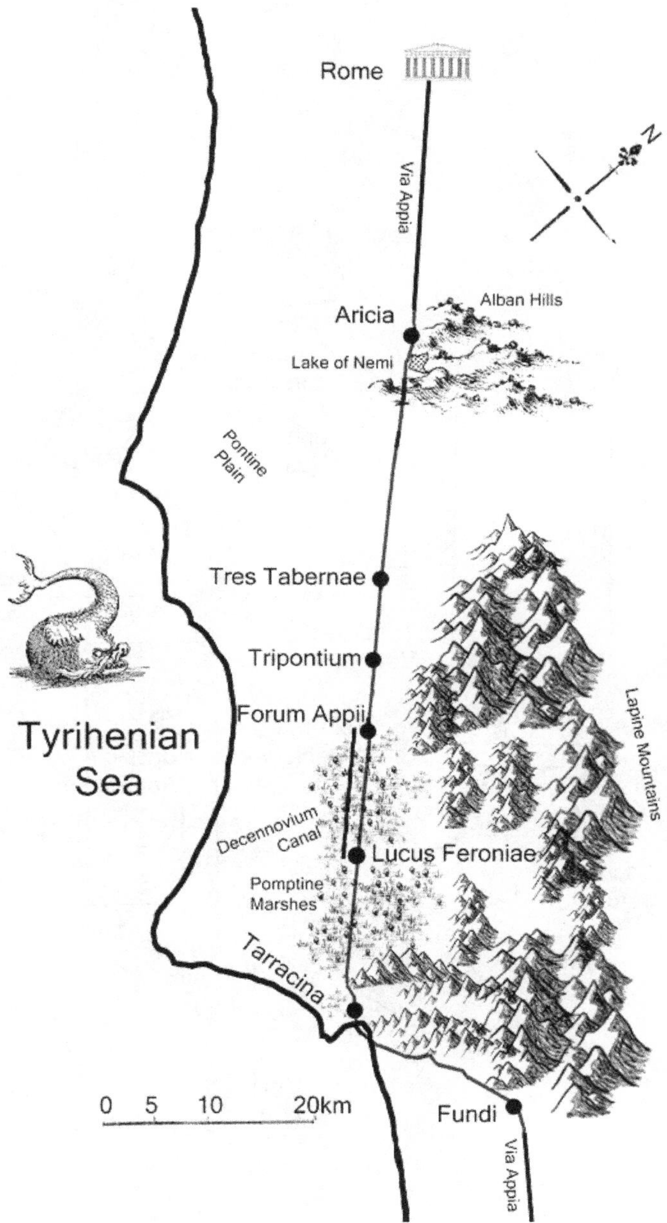

Figure 1: Via Appia c. 63 BCE

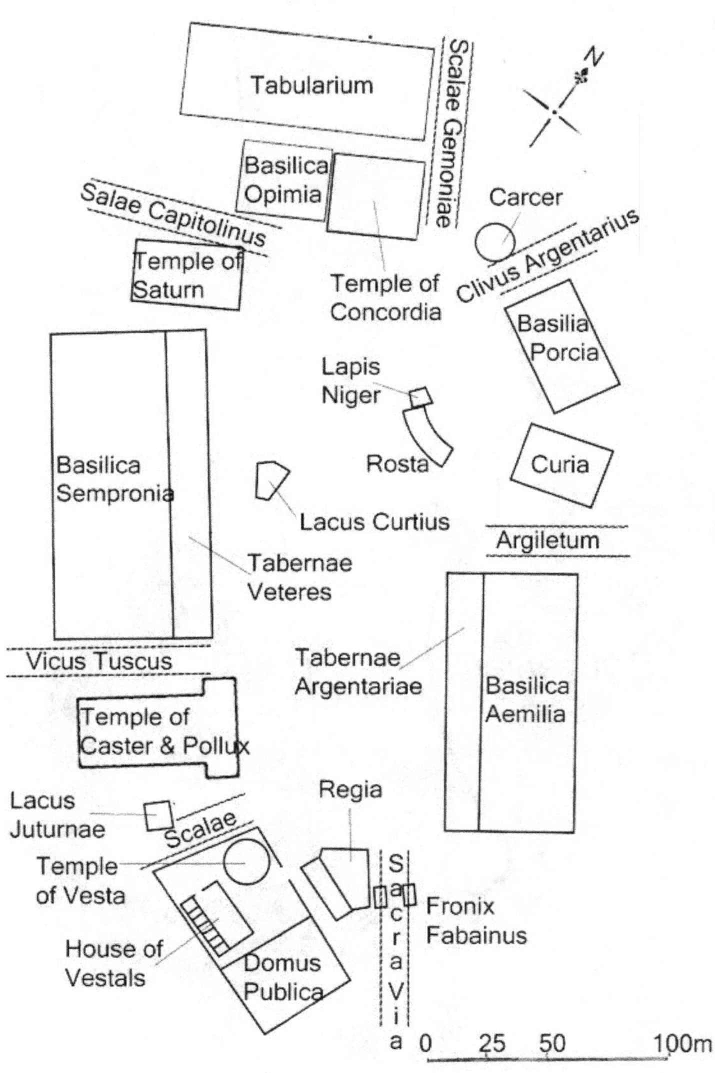

Figure 2: Roman Forum c. 63 BCE

CHAPTER ONE

SIC INFIT
So it begins.

I am a learned man, but this has brought me neither fortune nor fame. I long labored in the shadows of great men, Imperator Caesar among them, but I never desired such a singular light. The gods set for me a different path. I have not sought to amass wealth through the practice of my art; rather, I have been contented with modest means and a good reputation. But that is not all to the detail of my days, for much of my story now lies buried in the grave or kept beneath the rose. To tell my tale will, in fact, forfeit my life, but I am old now, and my years have run their course. The gods would want an accounting before I pass, so I write this memoir.

In the span of my life, I have witnessed the death throes of the Roman Republic and the violent birth of the Empire. The Republic stood for 675 years, the strongest power the world had ever known. But its very success brought about its downfall. The stage was set, and I, the Republic's staunch defender, compromised my values and helped seat a dictator.

But I get ahead of myself, for I must give you the beginning of my story before I can give you the end. My name is Marcus Vitruvius Pollio. If you know of me, you know me as an architect and engineer. My family is from Fundi, a city nestled in a fertile valley astride the Via Appia, midway between Rome and Neapolis. We were neither wealthy, nor were we poor. My father farmed the family land where olives were plentiful.

I will tell you first of my life in Fundi, and the events that led me to leave, for this is where my story rightly starts.

***

It begins in late autumn of my eighteenth year, when my father called to me from outside my room. "Marcus, where are you?"

I knew that tone of voice all too well, a mixture of irritation and resignation. I sighed and put down the scroll that occupied my attention. I had hoped he wouldn't want my help counting and grading the olives before we shipped them. Farming didn't much interest me, and as a young man studying for a profession, I would rather have gone on reading.

"In a minute," I replied.

"Now," he stated with finality.

When I joined him outside the house at the edge of the grove, his weathered face held none of the roughness I had heard in his voice. He smiled at me, and with calloused hands, offered me a waxed wooden tablet and stylus. Over the next hour, he sorted through the baskets of olives, calling out their number and condition as I wrote these down. This year had been the second consecutive year of wretched weather, and the harvest, of what should have been the bountiful year, was but a meager one.

I read back over my ledger, noting the small numbers. "The harvest won't be enough, will it, Father?" I knew from the past that the amount earned was far short of what we needed to maintain the family and the farm.

My father, a smudge of dirt on his forehead where he had brushed away an insect, sighed heavily. "No, it won't be enough. Pomona has abandoned us this year. Even with what we may make from livestock, the income won't be sufficient."

A thrill of unmitigated despair ran through my young body. "What will you do?"

"I'll do what I must. What choice do we have? I'll talk to Gaius Gargonius about another loan."

Father would always say, "*We do what we must.*" He was a dedicated Stoic, a loyal follower of Zeno of Citium. At every opportunity, he would tell me that happiness was found by accepting the moment and not allowing the desire for pleasure or fear of pain to control oneself. Such was a state of mind I could never master.

"Will he give us another loan?" I asked. "The Gargonii want our land. If they call in our debts, we will lose everything."

Though Father's jaw was set, he gave me a kind smile. "That won't happen. I'm going to Rome next week to meet with Quintus Annius Chilo. I've done a small favor for him, and he's agreed to give us money to pay off the Gargonii at the end of the year."

This surprised me, but I felt a great sense of relief. I had not been aware that my father had ever done Annius a service to warrant such a reward. More than that, Father was going to Rome. Visiting Rome with my father was the one thing I looked forward to above all others. When I was young, Rome loomed large in my imagination as a delight for the senses, a feast for the soul… and, oh, the buildings. Rome boasted some of man's greatest achievements. I would spend hours sketching them every time I went.

"Can I—"

"No, you cannot. Not this time. I have to do this by myself." He picked up the tablet upon which I had been writing.

"But—"

My father turned and looked me directly in the eye. "No."

He said this with no hint of emotion, something he only did when completely intransigent. On this particular point, I then knew I couldn't move him.

"Very well," I said, letting my face show as much disappointment as I judged I could safely get away with.

He looked down for a moment and then raised his gaze to me. "Don't tell your mother. Let me do that."

Though curious, I simply nodded my assent.

When we entered the house, we found Mother sitting on a small stool in the open courtyard of the peristyle garden, surrounded by colonnades and the fragrance of herbs. She rose and kissed my father before turning a warm smile on me.

I can still see her, as the late-afternoon sun lit her face, the very vision of the stately statue of Athena I had seen the year I spent studying under the great architects in Athens. As with the crafting of that statue's features, my mother's face was rather more oval than actually round. Her hair was rich in luster and abundance, combed rearward over her temples, and floated freely down her back. With intelligent gray eyes, the corners of which would crinkle when she smiled, she always seemed on the edge of laughter.

Yes, my mother was the rarest of flowers, exceedingly kind and extraordinarily educated. She was also Greek and my first teacher. From her, I learned art, music, and literature. Above all, my mother taught me that the gifts bestowed by fortune can easily be taken away, whereas education, when combined with intelligence, never fails, but abides steadily to the very end of life.

"Did you finish the play Epiphanes gave you?" she asked me in Greek.

"No, I didn't," I replied, also in Greek, and cast a glance at my father, who was pouring a goblet of wine. My mother read the glance and her eyebrows rose slightly.

"Well, I'm sure you'll have time tomorrow. Epiphanes will not be back for two days, anyway. But do come and talk to me about the play when you have read it."

After finishing the evening meal, I went to my room, lit the little brass lamp I kept next to my bed, and finally returned to my reading. The time was late when I heard Mother and Father arguing in low but angry voices. Though I could understand little of the discussion, I could clearly tell that the disagreement concerned my father's trip to Rome. I wasn't entirely sure, but I thought I detected a note of fear in Mother's voice.

***

The next morning dawned calmly, with no trace of the prior night's tempest. My parents were eating a breakfast of porridge, sausages, and figs when I joined them. They smiled and greeted me and then continued their amiable conversation. I ached to know the substance of their earlier argument, but they hid it as one would conceal a secret and ugly wound.

I had nearly finished eating when my sister, Vitruvia, entered and took her seat opposite me. She was a year younger than I, and, though she would bristle at the comparison, she looked so much like our mother that, except for their ages, the two could have been twins. My sister's resemblance to Mother was, in fact, more than mere form. She had Mother's kindness and intellect, but the gods had played a cruel joke on her and made her life hard by way of a lame foot. Most men do not seek a learned wife, fewer still a lame one. I always thought that she would one day be my responsibility, for she was family.

"Good morning," I said, and she smiled back at me.

She looked me in the eye and then tilted her head slightly toward Mother and Father, as she raised an eyebrow. I knew the question she was asking. She, too, had heard them arguing the night before.

"Epiphanes gave me a play. Would you care to see it after breakfast?" I asked.

"Thank you, Marcus. Yes, that would be nice," she replied in a voice that was just a little too formal.

After breakfast, I walked with her out to the olive grove. The weather was cool in the aftermost days of autumn, almost cold. Lazy clouds drifted aimlessly across the azure sky, and the olive leaves shimmered silver in the sun like so much broken glass. We walked slowly, the best speed Vitruvia could manage, and arrived at the small covered area we used for storing olives after harvest. The emptiness of the space there now was a painful reminder of how slender the last harvest of the season had been. For many years, we had gone there to talk.

The old three-legged stool squeaked as she sat down. "Well?" she asked.

I recounted my conversation with Father, and what I had overheard that night.

She was quiet for a moment as she looked off into the distance. Then she took a deep breath and peered up at me. "What Father said scared Mother—that much, I could tell in her voice. Something more is at risk in Father's trip to Rome."

"Maybe, but Mother fears for our finances," I disputed.

"No, no, whatever is at issue amounts to more than that," my sister put in. "Mother and I have talked. She can read a harvest as well as any farmer, better than most. No. The trip to Rome frightens her. She fears for him." Vitruvia was quiet for a moment. "Can you go with him?"

"No. I asked. He was adamant, and you know how stubborn he can be." I sighed.

She thought for a moment. "Well, Syphāx, Caster, and Lepidus are going with him. That should be enough."

"If Caster and Lepidus don't kill each other first." I laughed. "Father will have to listen to the two of them insult each other all the way there and back." The image of the two slaves faded from my mind, and I saw my father's face again. "We don't really know what Mother fears. Perhaps you might pour a little honey in her ear?"

Vitruvia laughed and shook her head slightly. "I'll see what I can do, but Mother can be even more obstinate than Father."

As my sister headed back to the house, I walked without purpose or direction through the quiet olive trees, now deserted of pickers and planters. The morning was so peaceful, so silent. The cool breeze and warm sun on my face were a sharp contrast to how I felt. I had a deep and nagging sense of unease. My father would tell me to accept the things I could not change and my mother would tell me I didn't know what I could change until I tried. I didn't even know what to try.

***

Epiphanes, my tutor and taskmaster, came to our house every three or four days. He was a tall, thin, white-haired Greek scholar with a long nose and a walking stick. With him, I studied geometry, history, and philosophy and acquired more than a passing knowledge of music, medicine, and the opinions of the jurists. I also learned the arts of engineering and architecture.

He arrived early that day, as was his practice. "Good morning, teacher," I said formally when he entered the vestibule. We always spoke in Greek unless we spoke of Roman law, for words have a power all their own.

"Good morning, Marcus. And what do we need to know to find the volume of a dome?"

This was his custom and a little game we played every time we came together. "We need the radius of the base of the dome and the height," I answered as we walked across the black and white tiled floor of the atrium, passed the *lararium* housing our family's gods, and went into the *tablinum*, my father's office where the household archives were kept.

The tablinum was decorated with rich frescoes depicting scenes of Pomona, the goddess of our orchard, and these glistened in the morning sunlight that streamed in from the peristyle beyond. Here was the study where my father worked, but he gave it over to Epiphanes when my mentor tutored. On this day, we studied the qualities of sand used to make concrete when pozzolana, the special sand from the towns round about Mount Vesuvius, was not available.

Epiphanes began by reviewing how we fashion concrete, but I found concentration difficult as my mind meandered. The ominous image of the empty storage area kept playing in my thoughts.

After some time, my instructor hit me on the head with his walking stick. "Marcus, pay attention."

"Ouch. Sorry, teacher." I rubbed my head and turned my attention back to the four little piles of sand he had poured onto the table. I had been thinking about the fear in my mother's voice.

He looked at me for a moment. "What is it, Marcus? This is not like you."

"Nothing, teacher. I'm just tired. I didn't sleep well." That was the truth, but not the whole truth. Epiphanes was like family, but he was not family.

"Was there a… problem?"

He had misread my reluctance. When I was young, I was much more comfortable with written documents than people. I would withdraw from crowds and was loath to talk about the issue, so perhaps he thought some incident had occurred. "No, teacher. I'm just tired."

"Then let us talk about how the sharpness of sand determines the strength of concrete, and this time you pay attention."

"Yes, teacher."

"We have four kinds of pitsand," he said, "black, gray, red, and carbuncular. Of these, the best is that which crackles when rubbed in the hand. That which has much dirt in it will not be sharp enough. Throw some sand upon a white garment and shake it out. If the garment is not soiled and no dirt adheres to it, the sand is suitable."

As the sun set, Epiphanes bid me farewell with a final instruction, and departed. The land had that late golden glow that I now appreciate to be unique to the country south of Rome. Later, during dinner, my father asked what I had learned that day, and I told him more than he ever cared to know about sand and concrete. Everyone smiled and feigned some interest. Sand was not really of such great importance to the others in my family.

I went to bed that evening much troubled, and sleep proved as elusive as remembering a dream. What I didn't yet realize on this day in the late autumn of my eighteenth year was that my comfortable, small world had already started to fall and would soon shatter apart.

CHAPTER TWO

QUALIS PATER TALIS FILIUS
As is the father, so is the son.

I must pause my tale for a moment to say more of me you must know. I was never an athletic youth, being short of stature and thin of frame. Though I did work hard in the orchard with my father, I preferred to remain inside and read rather than join in the games other young men played. The reason was not that I didn't desire to be social—I simply had no understanding of *how* to be social. My mother would always say I was shy, but my problem was far more complicated than that. Shyness infers a choice to not take part, but I simply couldn't at all do what others did effortlessly.

Nor was that the entire explanation for my lack of grace in this area. I had learned long before that I don't think the way most do. I see things in my head in vivid, detailed images—music, numbers, even words, Latin or Greek. If you show me something, I will never forget it. If you tell me something, I must first think about it and put it into pictures so I can remember it. For most of my life, I have understood that my memory is a gift from the gods, but for the gifts they grant, they demand a great price. They foredoomed me to be always different.

But on that day, I had to overcome my reluctance and support my father and family. Father was taking three slaves with him to lead the two wagons. Among the slaves was Syphāx from Crete, a massive, muscled man who had lost his freedom in Pompey's wars against the

Cilician pirates. He was our chief slave and a bodyguard of sorts. He was a good man, and I accompanied him to buy supplies for father's trip.

This was not a day in the nine-day market cycle, so the *nundina* was not being held in the forum. Syphāx and I had to shop in the *macellum*, the open arched stone market near the basilica. As I have said, our town was not large, but one would not have known that from the macellum's central courtyard. The paved area was surrounded on all sides by *tabernae*, small enclosed shops, all the same size with counters facing out. Fully half of Fundi's inhabitants were there that day, kitchen servants, maidservants, house mistresses, and even a salting of wives and grandmothers. I was the only free-born male I saw among the throng of shoppers.

At the first stall, we bought beans. I knew that should have been easy, but on meeting the stall holder I had difficulty looking her in the eyes when I spoke to her. I realized I should, but I couldn't lift my gaze, no matter how hard I tried. I had dealt with the woman before, and she was familiar with my odd ways. She said nothing as she took my money.

We continued traveling the path along the shop fronts, purchasing necessities—wine, flour, figs, and other items—until we arrived at a stall selling medicinal herbs. As I approached the stall, I noticed a young woman, free-born by her dress, whom I had never seen before. She was rather pretty, and I was drawn to her smile, which lifted every part of her face as she spoke. I watched her for a moment until she glanced up at me, then I quickly looked down. I spotted the herbs we wanted, datura, to calm one of our horses, and told the young woman. I cast my gaze away from her eyes.

"Hey. Hi there," she said and waved her hand in front of my face, catching me by surprise.

I stepped back and looked up, meeting her eyes. They were large, dark, and kind. But I glanced down quickly as I flushed.

"You know what to do with datura, don't you?"

"Yes," I replied while still looking down.

She gathered up the herbs and then paused. "Hi there." She waved her hand again, and once more, I glanced up before I could think about it. "Thank you," she said. And before I could look away, she smiled.

As I hurried off, Syphāx jogged to catch up.

We didn't speak, Syphāx and I, as we walked back home. I knew he wanted to, but I didn't. I was sick with embarrassment. After some time, he said as if to no one in particular, "I wonder if a person might simply pretend other people are invisible and not see them?"

I was instantly angry with him. He had no right to tell me what to do, but I said nothing because, as I thought about his words, suggesting I see others as invisible, I realized it might work. Though we continued to walk on in silence, I smiled.

***

The next morning was when Father was to leave for Rome. We had lived these last few days in an agony of anticipation, searching for omens that might portend the outcome of his journey. All we observed was a flock of birds passing overhead as he stepped outside, and we didn't know what to make of it. The day before, we had sacrificed a goat to Abeona, the goddess of outward journeys, for Father's safe trip and had roasted it overnight for a meal this morning.

After eating, we were all present in the atrium to see him off. He smiled, but the expression was shallow and didn't fully reach his eyes. My mother and sister wore the facades of well-wishers, and I couldn't myself judge the success of my own mask.

"All this? I will be gone only a little over a week," he said, his voice unnaturally light. "Syphāx will be with me. Look at his muscles. What could happen to me?"

My mother reached out and embraced him. She pulled him in, her arms drawing taut as bowstrings. My father had to pry himself free. She pressed an amulet into his hand to protect him on his trip. As tears welled up in her eyes, she turned away.

He looked to me. "Take care of everything, Marcus. I'm depending on you. You are family Vitruvius."

"I will watch over all, Father," I said. "Please be careful." I resisted the urge to hold him as my mother had. He would not have approved.

With that, he left. Syphāx followed at his heels as they joined the two other slaves and the wagons on the road.

My sister, who had remained silent and unmoving throughout, quickly withdrew to the privacy of her room. After a moment, my mother looked at me and nodded toward my sister's area of the house.

Vitruvia's curtain was drawn, and she was quietly sobbing. We had long ago adopted an unvoiced agreement to not enter the other's room when the curtain was drawn, but I discarded that custom and pulled it back. She was lying on her bed, so I sat beside her.

"We really don't know if we have anything to fear. I can't believe the gods wish us harm."

Her crying subsided. I didn't credit my words for this; rather, my presence by her side was no doubt a comfort. She had always taken solace in the simple company of family.

At last, she spoke. "That doesn't make me feel any better. The harvests of the last two years have placed us in a precarious position."

I tried to reassure her. "If the worst happens, we can still manage," I said. "We could find other loans to cover our debt. We have friends."

She sat up. A small smile touched the corners of her mouth, and she placed her hand on my arm. "You're a remarkable person with remarkable gifts, but I don't think you have the skills or inclination to haggle for money. Such is not a part of your *anima*."

The candor of her judgment wounded me, but I recognized she was likely correct. "Mother knows—" I began.

"Mother!" She rolled her eyes. "Mother is smart, very smart, but she is a woman. A woman, Marcus. No one will lend money to a woman, especially to run a farm that is in debt. If something happens to Father, Mother and I have no future. We are done." Her eyes pooled with tears. "I am seventeen and should have already married. No man will ever take me as a wife on suitable terms without a sizable dowry. My future is bound to the fortunes of this family. As it goes, I go." She said the last as a parody of the wedding vow: *Where he goes, I go.*

"I will always take care of you and Mother. You must believe that."

She smiled then, a real, full smile, and hugged me. "You have a good heart. I hope you never change."

Later that evening, I sat alone in my room. The sky was dark outside, as we were well into the first watch and this would be another late night for me. The lamp I had lit for reading was guttering. I used that as an excuse to set aside the scrolls and seek sleep, but sleep proved elusive.

My sister's voice came into my head. I had never really appreciated my father's importance to them until then. I had always expected I would someday run the family, but I had thought that would be at some distant point in the future. And as with all futures when you are young, I thought I would have sufficient time to prepare.

Again, I heard my sister's voice in my mind and knew she was correct. I could not fulfill the role Father held in our family even if given a lifetime to prepare. I vowed to make an offering to the goddess Adiona for his safe return and hoped all our apprehensions were ill-founded.

***

My father had been gone for three days, and life in our family went on. I roamed the town. Again, not something I sought, but Epiphanes had given me the task of noting the type, composition, age, and state of concrete used in the construction of buildings and fountains. I was to report back to him with a tract on why some concrete aged well and some did not. Based on the last set of lessons, and recognizing his didactic inclination, I speculated the answer lay in the quality of the sand used. I had sketched many of the buildings and walls before, but had paid little notice to the concrete used.

As I wandered down the cobblestone street, taking in and remembering every detail of every building, a voice startled me.

"If it isn't little Vitruvius. What brought you out of the library? Perhaps you lost your way."

The voice belonged to Gaius Gargonius the Younger. He was two years older than I, and far bigger. He was also a prick—a crude, rich, privileged prick. And he was his father's son—only without his father's intellect or cunning. The other two men with him were much like flies on feces. I didn't know who they were, but I was sure of what they were, and I despised them.

Gargonius the Younger and I had shared a tutor when I was ten. I always got the answers right; he never did, and the Greek tutor would praise me and strike him. Gargonius the Younger had resented me ever since and would beat me up when no one was watching. The violence had reached such a point that my mother had found me a private tutor, Epiphanes.

"So, what are you doing, Vitruvius, counting the people who don't like you? You'll need a bigger writing tablet."

I said nothing and tried to move around them. One of them, the tall one with rotten teeth, stuck out his leg and tripped me. I fell sprawling on the road. My writing tablet landed with such a clatter that people looked over to see what had happened. Some even came out of their shops, but none came to my aid. They all knew who he was. More importantly, they knew who his father was, and many owed him money.

I lay on the paving stones, tunic disheveled, knees scraped and bleeding.

"A pity that it wasn't his sister. The view would have been better," Gargonius the Younger said.

"Yes, but you don't have to trip her. She falls down by herself," the other sycophant said. They howled at his clever joke and moved off down the street, having grown bored with their game.

Now that the prick had gone, two people from the leather goods shop came to assist. I stood up, retrieved my writing tablet and resumed my study of concrete. Focusing on the task helped ease my mind.

Dinner that evening was a melancholy affair. We gave up even the pretense of indifference, with little conversation and no smiles. Vitruvia looked at me, but I avoided her gaze. She continued to peer at me until our eyes connected, and then she raised an eyebrow. I shrugged slightly and she let it pass.

As I lay in bed later that evening, I reflected on the events of the day, and I was ashamed. Not for what happened to me but for not responding when they had said those words about Vitruvia. She didn't deserve such discourtesy. She was worth a hundred Gargonii. This made me think back on her earlier appraisal. She was right. I didn't have the skills to be the head of the family.

***

Four days later the skin of my knees was healing nicely. The sense of dread that had lingered in the house like the smell of old fish had faded. My mother and sister now wore genuine smiles. Even I felt lighter. We had heard nothing of father's journey and accepted the lack of any word as a good sign. But Epiphanes's voice reached into my head. As he was fond of telling me, a great fallacy was to assume that because you have received no news, no news is to be had. But this is what we mortals do.

Epiphanes had come the day before to discuss medical herbs. The lesson had ended with the table covered by small piles of plants. I was to identify each one and describe its uses according to Hippocrates. I understood I must learn about medicine, but the art of healing was never my passion. It was too subjective. I preferred mathematics and natural philosophy. They were exact and unyielding. Every problem in these has a solution if one persists.

I was sitting on a stool in the peristyle's colonnade, reading about Cicero's successful prosecution of Sicily's former governor, Gaius Verres, for corruption—an event that had occurred about seven years earlier—when my mother entered the garden.

"Are you busy?"

Normally, I would have been sharp with her for breaking my concentration, but I had tired of Roman law. "No," I said simply and set down the scrolls.

"As you are aware, our finances are not what we hoped," she said in Greek. "We'll have to make some adjustments."

"I thought as much."

"Well." She hesitated, apparently apprehensive. "I think we must reduce the amount of time Epiphanes tutors you. He's a sizable expense."

"No! Mother, no! I need him. I have still so much I need to learn."

"Marcus, you—"

"No, Mother. I—"

"Marcus!" she said in a tone she seldom used with me. "We cannot afford it anymore." She balled her hands into fists and then slowly relaxed them.

"I'll cut something else," I said. "Surely, we have other places in which we can save."

"We do, and I am already assuming we'll do each of those. That still leaves us short."

Her last statement chastened me. I should have seen this coming. "What can we afford?"

"I spoke with Epiphanes yesterday. He is willing to come once a week. We could still afford that. He also says he doesn't have much else he can teach you. You know more than any student he has ever taught."

"But what will become of me?" I asked anxiously.

"Epiphanes says you've learned all that is necessary to be an architect and engineer. He would have had you seek a position of that kind within the year, anyway."

Mother kissed me on the cheek, and left.

I hadn't considered that they would expect me to find a position so soon. I wasn't prepared.

A commotion in the vestibule interrupted my thoughts. As I entered, I saw Syphāx, supported by two men. He was dirty, his chest heaved from exertion, and his eyes looked deeply troubled. My mother and sister came running from the other side of the house.

"Syphāx?" I asked. His name was all I could utter. My chest was so tight I could scarcely draw a breath.

"I am sorry, so sorry. He would not allow me to accompany him. There was nothing I could have done." He paused as if gathering the last of his strength. "An accident occurred. Your father…" he almost whispered "was killed."

CHAPTER THREE

VIVA ENIM MORTUORUM IN MEMORIA VIVORUM EST POSITA
The life of the dead is retained in the memory of the living.

A ripple of icy silence passed through the vestibule. Only Syphāx's deep, raspy breathing could be heard, somehow emphasizing the naked brutality of his words. My mother sagged, and my sister caught her.

"Bring him into the atrium and sit him down," I said to the men supporting Syphāx. "Cinna, bring some wine and water."

I helped my sister sit Mother on a couch in the atrium while the men supporting Syphāx sat him on a chair opposite her. Cinna returned with a generous cup of watered wine, which Syphāx drank in great gulps between breaths. Everyone was tense, poised for his next words.

"What happened?" I asked.

He waited a moment to catch his breath and then answered. "Four days ago, we had already sold the olives to one of the warehouses outside of town and had taken rooms in an apartment on the Quirinal Hill. Your father told us to stay in the apartment and meet him at the Latiaris stairs at the beginning of the sixth hour. He said that he was going alone to visit Annius. I asked him to take me with him, but he said Annius would only see him if he came alone."

Syphāx took another drink from the cup and continued. "We arrived at the bottom of the stairs just before the sun was at its zenith, as your father ordered. A crowd had gathered. We pushed through and found your father lying face up at the bottom of the steps. People in the crowd said he had tumbled down the stairs just before we arrived. They said he was dead when they reached him."

"The Latiaris stairs?" I closed my eyes. I had been there before with Father, and I remembered those stairs well. I could see them in my mind as clearly as if I were standing before them. They were the shortcut down from the Quirinal Hill, eighty-six flat stone steps about a span wide, cut through the hillside. "Did anyone see how he fell?"

"No. I asked everyone. No one actually saw him fall. They all heard the commotion and then saw him tumbling."

"You looked him over?"

"Yes. He had…" He looked toward my mother and grimaced. "The back of his skull had been knocked in, and his neck was broken. That was clearly what killed him. All of his other injuries were just cuts and bruises."

He looked down, his breathing still ragged. When he looked up again, his eyes were wet with tears. "We went through his clothes and retrieved his belongings." He reached into his tunic and handed me several scrolls and a purse. Then, with deliberate reverence he handed me father's *pugio,* the family dagger, the mark of the Vitruvius household.

I took it, but it felt far heavier than its weight alone.

"And his body?" my mother asked in a flat tone from the couch behind me.

"We had him taken and wrapped up. I took some money from his purse and arranged to have him brought here for a funeral. His body will be here in two days. Caster and Lepidus are bringing him back with the wagons and the baggage." He looked over at me. "That was all right, Master?"

"Yes. Thank you." I realized with a start that he was asking me because I was now the head of the Vitruvius family. I put my hand on his shoulder and squeezed it gently.

Later, after Syphāx had gone to the baths, we gathered in the triclinium. As we sat amongst the smiling faces decorating the mosaic floor of the dining area, none of us spoke for some time.

"Mother, why were you so worried about father going to Rome?" I finally asked. I nodded to Vitruvia. "We heard you and Father arguing."

She just sat, not moving, not speaking. She didn't even look at me.

"Mother?"

She shook her head as if to clear it. "Quintus Annius Chilo, I don't trust him. I told your father that. The things people say about him. I only met him once, but I could see he was an evil man, that scar at the edge of his mouth." She shuddered. "Annius told your father that if he did a small service, he would give him enough money for us to repay all our loans from the Gargonii."

"What kind of service?"

"Delivering messages for Annius. Your father was to put the messages into jars and bury them among the last of the olives that we would be sending. That was all."

"That was all? That isn't much, yet still you were scared?"

"Yes. A fish only smells if it is rotten. What message would be worth that much money to hide?"

"One that could kill you," my sister answered solemnly.

***

Two days had passed since Syphāx's news, and we were all still in a state of shock. My sister had mostly stayed in her room, unlike her usual behavior. We in the family as well as the servants moved on unsteady ground, having had our foundation ripped from beneath us.

The previous night, before bed, I had finally looked at the scrolls that Syphāx had retrieved from my father's body after the accident. Among those otherwise unremarkable documents was one covered with random letters, a very odd thing, indeed. The papyrus was of fine quality and expensive. The seemingly random letters were drawn in a practiced hand, so I could only assume they were important and meaningful. The sole conclusion I could come to was that the papyrus was written in some cipher and was likely the message my father had been asked to hide in the olive shipments.

My father's body arrived in the afternoon. He was in one of the wagons and wrapped in white linen. The family came out of the house and gathered around the wagon, compelled yet frightened to view him in death. Despite the fetor, my mother unwrapped his head to kiss his cheek. Someone had undertaken to wash his body, and his bone white face showed no sign of damage. Mother, her hands covering her face, sobbed uncontrollably, and my sister helped her back into the house.

I stepped close to my father's body and gazed down at his face. A torrent of memories rushed through me, but what surfaced most strongly was an image of my father smiling with that glint he had in his eyes. He was a wise and caring father, and I loved him immensely. I couldn't reckon with his death just yet.

Syphāx approached deferentially. "You can see where he was injured." He turned Father's head to show me the broken neck and skull fracture.

I looked down at my father's head, the head I had known for eighteen years, the head whose form was fixed in my memory. "Wait," I said, for what I saw of the skull fracture made little sense. I grimaced as I ran both hands over the injury. My inspection revealed a square indentation on the back of my father's head. The wound was about one and a half inches across, perfectly square and uniformly pressed in about an inch. I thought back to the image of the Latiaris stairs stored in my mind. They were bland, undecorated stone stairs. No part of them was square or of that size. "This injury was not caused by the stairs, Syphāx. In fact, it would seem to be a perfect match for the head of a carpenter's hammer."

"Sir?"

"Syphāx, look here." I stretched the skin on the back of my father's head to show Syphāx the wound. "He must have been hit on the back of the head, probably with a hammer, which likely caused him to fall down the stairs. That means he would have been dead when he started his fall. He was murdered, Syphāx."

"Are you sure?"

"No, I cannot be certain, but it seems likely. Nothing else explains the type of injury I see. Thieves and murderers often use hammers in the night. No one would give a thought to a tradesman with a hammer."

"But why, sir? Why? They didn't rob him."

Could it be? It must have been. Nothing else made sense. I said nothing, but I thought the answer might lie on a sheet of papyrus covered with what appeared to be random letters.

We held Father's funeral the next day. We hired mourners to sing lamentations, only a few, as Fundi was not a large city. The procession snaked through the town at midday, made of family and friends, of which many joined in, for my father was well respected. Our slaves carried Father on a bier. My mother, sister, and I came next in a ceremonial chariot, wearing our family's ancestral masks, followed by everyone else. The masks bore the likeness of my father's father and mother and of their fathers and mothers. The procession continued out to the city's cremation site, where we moved my father's body to the funeral pyre and set it alight.

Later, while the rest of the family retired, Syphāx and I watched the flames guide my father to Elysium. I was left to wish that he had told me more of his affairs, for they now seemed to be my affairs, too, and I was weighed down by their gravity.

***

Over the next two days, my mother, sister, and I discussed my observations. While didn't disagree about my conclusions, we did engage in considerable controversy about what we should do next. With three of us talking this over, unsurprisingly, we offered up three differing opinions. My mother would have us try to renegotiate our loans with the Gargonii. I wanted to find who murdered my father, and my sister believed we should appeal to Quintus Fabius Sanga, my mother's family's patron of old, for a new loan.

We sat in the evening to again go over our options. They looked to me for resolution as I was now, by law, and by custom, the head of the house. In my new role as decision maker and final arbitrator, I chose the safe answer. "We'll do all three."

"Marcus, that's not a decision," my mother said with some irritation in her voice.

"No, no, it is," my sister said as she looked at Mother. "To choose not to decide is a decision, just not a very good one."

"Why *not* do all three?" I replied defensively. "First, I will seek to renegotiate our loans with the Gargonii. Whether or not that is successful, I will travel to Rome and try to learn more about Father's murder. If I am unsuccessful with the Gargonii, I'll call on Quintus Fabius Sanga while I'm there and see if he can help us."

They just stared at me.

"Well, that makes some sense," my sister finally said, "but it could be dangerous. We don't know why this happened to Father."

My mother frowned and remained silent for a moment. "Quintus Fabius Sanga is a respectable man. He does not like bullies such as the Gargonii."

We continued to consider the course we should follow. In the end, they agreed with me, and I realized, for good or ill, the sole responsibility rested on me.

***

The day was still young, and I strolled through town. I had to file official documents. We Romans observe every event in life with documents. The greater the event, the more numerous the documents. My father's death had been the genesis of a vast quantity of documents. If I ever wished to bring the Roman Republic to its knees, I would first destroy all its papyrus.

My walk took me past the town's small forum, where I heard a haughty voice from one of the upper balconies.

"Oh, it's Marcus. Come see. He must be looking for a house to rent."

The speaker was Gargonius the Younger, the prick, and I didn't answer.

"We like your house," he shouted. "My father says he'll give it to me once our family takes it over. I'll have to remodel it a little, of course. It'll have to be thoroughly cleaned."

I continued walking, pretending that he didn't exist.

"You know, Marcus," came the voice from above, "I could let your family stay in the house. I mean, once we own it. I could let your sister pay the rent in trade. Nothing about her foot would keep her from spreading her legs for the family."

The laughter of the prick and his friends tumbled down from the window. Rage boiled within me, but I knew that was what they wanted. My heart raced, and my muscles tensed. I breathed deeply and forced myself to ignore them. I made an oath to all the gods who were listening that I would have my vengeance on that prick one day.

Fundi was but a small town. We had a magistrate appointed by Rome whose job was to keep the peace and supervise official business. As for keeping the peace, not a single unpeaceful act had taken place in our town in my lifetime. As for official business, the magistrate had an *apparitor*, a *scribae*, who performed all the work. Few in the town ever interacted with the magistrate himself. However, we all knew the apparitor and we didn't like him. The apparitor occupied a social position above the rest of the town's citizens, and he made sure we all knew it.

After signing the necessary documents, I took a different route home to avoid the prick. The course took me near the macellum. Surreptitiously, I looked for the girl from the herb stall, the one with the marvelous smile, but the stall was closed, and the girl was nowhere to be seen. My already foul mood deteriorated further as I walked on for half a block.

"Hi, there," I heard from right behind me. I spun around to find the herb girl standing there, her arms full of herbs that she had been gathering. I was so surprised that I stared straight at her.

She smiled at me. "Hi. Are you searching for someone?" she asked.

Her presence, her nearness, befuddled me. I was speechless, but I continued to gaze at her.

"If you are looking for someone, I know most of the people here. I could maybe help. I'm Aemilia."

I finally shook my voice free. "I'm Marcus—Vitruvius." I looked down.

"I know. I am sorry about your father. I would sometimes see him in the market. You sound like him, you know. He was Marcus too, wasn't he? My uncle said he was an honorable man."

"Your uncle?"

"Epiphanes."

I jerked my head up. I was surprised enough to peer back up at her. "Epiphanes is your uncle? I was aware he had family here. I just thought they would be… well, older."

She grinned. "No, just me. I help take care of him. He's not so young anymore." She paused. "He talks about you sometimes. Says you are the best student he's ever had."

She smiled at me, and her whole face lit up with the smile I remembered from a few days before. I realized I was staring at her and quickly looked down.

Her voice was soft. "You remind me of my brother. He was… quiet, like you."

"Was?" I asked, but I didn't look up.

"He died two years back."

"I'm sorry."

This time, she didn't continue so I looked up at her. She was staring off into the distance, but the stare was vacant, and I didn't think she was really looking at anything. Finally, she turned her gaze back to me.

"Anyway, can I help you find someone? As I said, I know most of the people in the macellum."

"No, thank you. I was looking to see what was open." Even to my ear the excuse sounded thin, but I couldn't move past the fact she was

Epiphanes's niece. I'd had no idea. A surge of questions rushed through my mind. What had Epiphanes told her about me? I had always assumed that my discussions with him stayed between us. I was embarrassed, though I didn't know why.

Another thought occurred to me. "Does Epiphanes teach you?"

"When he has the time, which is rarely. Mostly, he has taught me about medicine. That's my interest."

"Medicine, yes, of course, the herbs."

"That is part of it. I hope to find a position as a *medica*. I studied under Surius Publicius, a *medicus* who lives on the north side of town. He was once the physician to an important patrician family."

"What kind of medicus is he?" Epiphanes had told me that there were different schools of medical thought.

"He's a methodist."

"I've never heard of that."

"Well, the rationalists insist on obtaining knowledge of the hidden cause of the disease before they treat it," she began, clearly enjoying the opportunity to discuss the topic, "And then the empiricists rely on their own experience and the experience of the past to treat disease. I'm a methodist. We do both. We treat disease based on our experience but change our methods according to what we can learn about the cause of the disease."

I found we were walking along the street together, though I couldn't recall how we had started. I suddenly realized I was speaking to Aemilia, looking at her, walking with her, at a level of comfort I hadn't known with any young woman except my sister. And she was fascinating.

She glanced at me and smiled again. The air between us seemed to have grown warm.

"Where are you looking for a position?" I asked.

"Anywhere. Everywhere." She let out that wonderful laugh again. "But likely in Rome. That is the best place for opportunities. I will have to go there soon, but I don't want to leave my uncle by himself."

We came to an intersection, and she stopped. "Well, I have to go this way. I'll see you." She turned and walked off, her arms full of herbs.

I watched her go. Then I remembered I had said nothing in response. "Yes, I will see you," I said in a raised voice and instantly realized how stupid it sounded, my wit having totally failed me.

She turned and smiled before continuing, and I watched her until she walked around a corner and was lost from view. She was going to Rome. I had planned to speak with Epiphanes about Father's death, but now I needed to talk about other things as well.

CHAPTER FOUR

ALIENUM AES HOMINI INGENO EST SERVITUS
For a free-born man, debt is a form of slavery.

By the end of the week, we could feel a chill to the dawn. Aquilo, the north wind, breathed across the countryside in fits and starts, driving the dead leaves about the fields. This was the first morning of the year where I sensed the change of season moving toward winter. I sat upon the three-legged stool in the small covered area, waiting for Epiphanes. I had asked him to come over that morning, and he was late. That was the first time I had ever known him to be so.

"Good morning, Marcus," he said as he approached. "Tell me of Aquilo. I feel it this morning. What is its form?"

I knew the answer to that one. "It is a breeze from the mountains far to the north and, like all wind, is a floating wave of air whose undulation continually varies."

He smiled. "Very good, Marcus. But I'm not here to talk of the winds, am I?"

"No, I would speak of my father's death," I said solemnly.

I told him of my observations, of Father's injuries, the writing on the scroll, and my suspicions.

He sat deep in thought for some time. Finally, he said, "I think your conclusions have merit, though we cannot prove them. Absent any other evidence, the best line of inquiry is likely the cipher. May I see it?"

I took the scroll I had brought out of my tunic and showed him the apparently random letters. He studied it for some minutes and then handed it back.

"Marcus, the letters here are not random. Some appear more than others. They are of a pattern, though I cannot see what it signifies. You have a sharp mind. You should try to determine its meaning."

I was doubtful I could solve it, but I did not tell him so. Instead, I spoke of my plans to meet with Gargonius and go to Rome.

Again, he was thoughtful. "That may be the best course, but I think a meeting with Gargonius will not end well. He is not a dishonest man, you see, but he is a ruthless man and would want you to fail. Your land would be too valuable to him. And the trip to Rome will be dangerous. If what you suspect is true, you tread perilous ground, indeed. It has already taken your father's life, and you will be at greater risk than he, for you know less of his intrigues."

"Are you suggesting I shouldn't go?" I asked, surprised.

He shook his head. "No. No, you *must* go. You are in peril whether or not you go, if not from Gargonius, then from your father's enemies. Facing them on your own terms rather than waiting for them to come to you at a time and place of their choosing would be prudent."

He paused for a moment. "Marcus, I cannot teach you anything more. The time has arrived for you to chart your own course. This is as good a place to start as any. You may be surprised how much you know of the world, though you have seen so little of it. You're the best student I have ever had, or have ever heard of."

That reminded me of my conversation with Aemilia. I smiled at Epiphanes as a conspirator might share a knowing moment. "Aemilia said you told her I was your best student. I met her yesterday."

He returned my grin. "Yes, she told me you did." He looked me in the eye. "I didn't tell you about her because I keep my own affairs private, but I'll tell you now." He paused and took a deep breath. "She is my sister's daughter. They lived in Brindisi. Two years ago, a fever swept through the town and killed all the family but Aemilia. I'm her only relative. She came to stay with me and now I'm responsible for her, *patria potestas* the head of my family.

"But she, like you, must now find her own way in the world. Since the fever, she has had a keen interest in medicine, so I taught her what I could, and she has apprenticed with Surius Publicius. Though not a particularly respectable trade, medicine is one of the few paths open to a learned woman. I hope she will find a position with a medicus or a good family."

I paused. "She said you told her of me."

He shook his head. "No, nothing of you, only that you were my best student, but I think you captured her eye." He paused for a moment and then smiled again. "I am not unhappy you two have met."

***

I spent two days sitting at Father's desk, going over his ledgers, preparing to meet Gaius Gargonius. I believed the confrontation would be more difficult than any narrow mountain pass I had ever crossed, and far more treacherous. Given my fear of heights, that was saying much. I would not grovel before that man, but he held the future of our family in his hands. He deserved deference. I only hoped that his son would not be in attendance.

I arrived at Gaius Gargonius's house at the fourth hour, late morning, as he had instructed, and his servant led me into the vestibule where I was told to wait until he could receive me.

I was left to stand there, not invited into the atrium, as was the normal, courteous custom. Though I had arrived at the appointed hour, I was kept waiting. I waited until close to midday. This power play of a low sort was a game, part of the drama to emphasize that my family was at his total mercy. I knew this. Whether farce or tragedy, I had to play the role in which I had been cast. I silently prayed to Minerva, whom I had adopted as my own private deity. She was the goddess of both wisdom and war, and I needed help with both, if I was to survive the weeks ahead.

Midday passed, and I was finally invited into the tablinum to meet with Gaius Gargonius. He was a short, corpulent man sitting on a tall stool to give him added statue. His eyes were small, black, and deeply recessed in a ruddy face. He waved me to a stool opposite him, a short stool.

"I am sorry about your father, Vitruvius. He was a good man. What can I do for you?"

I required all of my effort to bring my eyes up to meet his. "I have been going over my family's accounts. My father borrowed money from you."

"Yes, a large sum, and it is due soon. He said he would pay before the year's end. Are you here to pay it back now?"

"No, I am not, as I am sure you are aware. I have come to ask for an extension until the next harvest. My father's death has upset our finances, and we need some time to adjust."

He was quiet for a moment. I could perceive the cogs of his mind turning, calculating. "I would like to help you, Vitruvius, I really would, but the weather was bad for us as well, and I don't have the money at hand that I think prudent for these times. No, I cannot offer you an extension. You must find another way."

He didn't smile. He didn't gloat. If not for his reputation, I could almost have believed his sincerity.

I gritted my teeth and forced down the bile in my stomach. "Then would you be willing to renegotiate the current loans for more interest but a later due date?"

He looked me in the eye, and I used all the strength I possessed to not break contact.

His face was almost sad, though I suspected he displayed a well-rehearsed mask. "No, I'm sorry, Vitruvius. I can't do that. It is time that I clear up all your family's debts."

"Then I will leave. I thank you for your time, Gargonius." Without being dismissed, I rose.

"Tell your mother that I mourn her loss," he said as I walked out.

I returned home, feeling oddly relieved and totally exhausted. The outcome was what we had expected. Though we were in serious trouble, the immediate ordeal was over, and it had weighed heavily on my mind. My sister was right. I didn't have the inclination to haggle, and I didn't like conflict, but I thought I had done rather well all considered. I used the trick Syphāx had suggested. I looked Gaius Gargonius straight in his small, beady eyes and pretended he was invisible.

***

The family sat for breakfast later that week under a dark cloud. My sister fidgeted, my mother was distracted and withdrawn, and my confidence had vanished as thoroughly as a flame from an extinguished lamp. True, we had not expected Gaius Gargonius to be helpful, but we hadn't expected his deviousness, either. Since my meeting with him four days past, we had found conducting the household business more and more difficult. Deliveries were late, sales had been canceled, and workers hadn't shown up.

"I don't know if I can go to Rome," I said. "Gargonius is actively plotting our failure. I'm needed here to keep the fragments together that Gargonius is ripping apart."

"If we don't piece together money from somewhere, we are done, and we only have a little over two months," my sister said.

Though she had stated the obvious, I didn't point that out. While I put my thoughts into pictures, she puts hers into words. I kept quiet.

"If we cannot find money here," my sister continued, "then we have to find it somewhere else. Two months does not give us enough time to exchange correspondence, so we must appeal in person. That means you going to Rome no matter what is happening here."

"Your father was killed because he went to Rome," my mother countered, her voice raising with a note of desperation, "and we don't even know why."

"Mother, he has only two choices, stay here or go to Rome, and he cannot stay here," my sister said.

"Wait. Wait," I countered. "I'm not worried about going to Rome. I'm worried about leaving here. If I leave, how will you survive?"

"Well, I'm worried about you going to Rome," my mother answered. "You—"

"Mother, we have no choice," my sister interrupted, gesturing with her palms up. She turned to me. "We are not helpless. We can survive for two months if you go, but we cannot survive at all if you don't."

"I don't trust Gaius Gargonius," I said. I thought about my sister and the things that Gaius Gargonius's son had said about her.

"I don't trust Gargonius either," my sister said, "but I do trust that he will try to ruin us, and to do that, he wouldn't jeopardize his plan with something so public as physical harm."

"I'm not sure about that. And I'm worried about the son, not the father."

My sister shook her head. "I've heard what he has said about me. He is all full of bluster and talk and a weak excuse for a man. I am not afraid of him." She put her hand on my arm. "Go. I can take care of myself."

But I didn't think she could. I could easily see her overwhelmed in an assault by Gargonius, and he would do it. I was sure of it.

***

The next morning, I woke early and walked out into the orchard. The sun hadn't yet breached the horizon, and a red hue lay over the mountains, to announce the hour was no longer night but not yet day. The air was still and cold. The colors shed by autumn lay strewn across the landscape, announcing the flight of autumn but not yet embracing the arrival of winter, a time somewhere in between. My life, too, was in between where I had been and where I needed to be, neither this nor that. The sun would bring clarity to the day, and the icy wind transparency to the change of seasons. What would bring me clarity of purpose? For what did I wait? I walked back into the house.

My sister and I ate breakfast, but Mother hadn't risen yet. She who had always been up to greet the sun now spent more and more time in bed, communing with Miseria.

Vitruvia turned her head toward my mother's room as if she could see through the intervening walls. "What are we to do?"

"We wait."

"For what?"

"I don't know. But I know we will know when we know."

"What?" Vitruvia looked as if I had spoken in some barbarian tongue.

I had to gather my thoughts into words she could understand. "We stand at an open door. Once we step out, we are on a path and must follow it, leaving all else behind. The path we need to take is known. What is unknown is what happens to everything we leave behind. I do not want to step over the threshold until I know the consequences."

"But—"

"I don't know what I need to know, but I do know I will know when it happens."

She paused for a moment, frowning. "I have no idea what you just said. Your words sound like prevarication, or at best, procrastination. We don't have the luxury of either."

Before I could form a suitably cutting retort, Cinna, her green eyes wide, entered, carrying a scroll. "Two men delivered this for you, Master. I think they work for Gaius Gargonius."

The seal on the scroll was indeed that of Gaius Gargonius. Vitruvia sat beside me to read the scroll with me. The document was a legal notice of his intent to take possession of our property and lands if we did not pay our total loans to him, with interest, by the first day of the coming year, two months hence.

The blood drained from Vitruvia's face.

"Well. Now we do know," I declared. "Fortuna has spoken."

CHAPTER FIVE

INGENIUM MALA SAEPE MOVENT
Misfortunes often stir up genius.

Every time I thought of my father's murder, anger and sadness coursed through me in equal measure. But this latest development, that we were to lose everything my father and his fathers before him had built, and to the likes of Gaius Gargonius, threatened to drown me in despair. My mother, sister, and I sat at a table in the atrium's corner after a dismal dinner, discussing what needed to be done now that going to Rome to find a loan was our sole option.

As Mother peered off into the distance, the sadness in her eyes was easy to see. I wondered if she blamed me in some small way for Father's death. Perhaps, if I had insisted on going with him, he might still be alive.

"Mother?" I began.

"Yes," she said, shaking her head. "Yes, I'll write a letter of introduction for you to take to Quintus Fabius Sanga. I don't know how receptive he'll be. I haven't met with him in a long time, but the letter should at least earn you an audience."

"His willingness to help us doesn't sound likely to me. Your family was his client. We aren't. We haven't delivered him a single vote or done him a single service."

Mother took a deep breath, so deep I could hear its intake across the table. "We, you, will have to persuade him we can be useful to him at some time in the future. He is a good man, and he was fond of my family. I believe we have a chance he will help."

"That's a start, I suppose. All we have."

She hesitated, her eyes haunted. "Swear you will not seek Annius. He is a ruthless man and far too dangerous." Her gaze pierced me. "Stay away from him and his men. Promise me, Marcus. Promise me. I won't lose you the way I did your father. I couldn't stand it."

I searched my mother's pleading eyes, but I couldn't find it in myself to make that promise. The anger in me wouldn't allow it. If Annius had a hand in Father's death, I would have my vengeance, though I didn't know how to go about it.

"Marcus, you must find another way, any way. Leave Annius alone!"

"That only leaves me the cipher."

"Then you must make of it what you can."

Later that evening, I sat in the tablinum, studying the cryptic document. The writing made no sense, but Epiphanes was right. The written letters were not random. The letters *H* and *M* were used more than the others. If a message was hidden there, the letters had been changed according to some scheme. But how? There must be a pattern. How might I see it?

Then I had an idea. If one wanted to see a pattern, one needed to draw it. Excited, I grabbed a blank scroll and some ink and wrote the alphabet across the bottom. Then I took the cipher and counted the number of *A*s. For each one, I wrote an *A* above the letter *A* on the blank scroll. Now I had a stack of *A*s where the height of the stack was the number of *A*s in the cipher. I did this for each letter.

When I finished, I had a picture of how the letters were used in the cipher. The results looked like a mountain range with two peaks, one at *H* and one at *M*. Before, between, and after the peaks, were valleys of roughly three different heights.

I sat back and stared at my drawing: low valley, peak, low valley, peak, medium valley, high valley, low valley, high valley. Here was certainly a pattern, but I didn't know what it meant. I knew something was hidden there; I could feel it, but the answer lay just out of my grasp, the indistinct whisper of something trying to grab my attention.

The hour was late, so I snuffed out the lamp and went to bed, praying that Mercury, the divine messenger and god of puzzles, would bring an answer to me while I slept. In the stories, the gods did such things, if you were deserving. My cause was just, and my need urgent. Why should Mercury not aid me?

***

When I awoke the next morning, I found that the gods hadn't answered me. This was not the first nor the last time I wondered of what use the gods were.

Vitruvia was already eating when I sat down for breakfast. I explained the work I had done on the cipher and she asked to see my drawing.

She studied it for a while, turning it one way and then the other. "This is truly interesting," she told me. "But I don't understand what it means, either. I can't relate hills and valleys to words. I don't see many vowels. Wouldn't there be more vowels? What kind of picture do actual words make?"

The hoped-for answer arrived, not from the gods in a dream, but from my sister while she was eating breakfast. I stood, kissed her on the top of her head, and then ran back to the tablinum.

"Marcus? Marcus, what's wrong?" she called, but I didn't answer. I didn't want to lose the ghost of a thought that lingered in my mind's eye. I knew what the puzzle meant this time. I saw it.

I unrolled another blank scroll on the table and retrieved the scroll I had been reading of Cicero's successful prosecution of Sicily's former governor, Gaius Verres. This was normal Latin that I could read. What did normal Latin look like? I wrote out the alphabet along the bottom of the new scroll and repeated the previous night's work of counting letters with the scroll of Cicero's speech.

When I finished, I looked at the drawing. It had a pattern too: high valley, low valley, peak, low valley, peak, medium valley, high valley, low valley. My heart fluttered.

I took the drawing I had made of the cipher and placed it beside the one I had just finished. Their shapes looked almost identical, except the peaks of the new drawing were at *E* and *I,* vowels, rather than *H* and *M,* consonants, as in the cipher's drawing. What did that mean? Did all writing have the same shape?

I walked over to our library shelves and took out a scroll at random. This was of some writings of Plautus. I made the same diagram, counting its letters. Now I had three drawings. As the table had no more space, I unrolled them on the floor, one drawing beside the other, three in a row. Then I stood back and stared at them.

All three drawings had the same general shape, but the drawings of the Plautus and Cicero documents both showed peaks at *E* and *I,* whereas the cipher drawing had peaks at *H* and *M.* Its peaks were three letters over from the other two documents. That was it! The same shape but shifted over by three letters.

```
DEFGHIKLMNOPQRSTVXYZABC
ABCDEFGHIKLMNOPQRSTVXYZ
```

Now that I understood the method, I needed less than an hour to decipher the message on the scroll. I could hardly contain my excitement as the words took form beneath my pen. What I now had was readable, though not completely comprehensible. It was a message, neither signed nor addressed, commanding the persons receiving it to seize Praeneste, a city between Rome and Fundi, about twenty miles southeast of Rome. The receiver was to take Praeneste by force of arms in a night attack on the first, the *kalendas* of November. The letter continued to detail how to access the city and what buildings to destroy. But the most disturbing part came at the end:

All officials and any of the garrison who are not sympathetic to our cause are to be put to the sword. You are to fortify the city and hold it until the rest of our forces can join you. Then we shall march on Rome.

I had been to Praeneste once before with my father. The city was secure and on high ground. It could easily be held against a large force and would be the perfect place to use as a base of operations close to Rome. Today was the third of November, so the first had been two days previous. I remembered that yesterday rumors had reached our town of some problem in Praeneste, but the information had been vague, and I had thought nothing of it at the time.

My father had received this letter at the beginning of October, a month prior to when action was to take place. I didn't know if the actions described in the letter had come to pass. If the letter represented anything more than mere fantasy, then what I held in my hand was nothing less than treason—and of the most terrible kind. I had no idea if my father was aware of the contents of the message he had carried, but he had surely been killed because of it, and whoever had given him the message likely knew why.

***

After lunch, I set out to discover what I could of the events in Praeneste, and perhaps, the role my father had played. Our town, like most along the great roads of Rome, had a transport station where those traveling along the Via Appia might rest, change horses, or buy a ride in the spare wagon space of a merchant. It was also the best place to exchange *lingulaca*. Though I do not understand by what means, gossip travels the Via Appia faster even than the flight of birds. Fortunately, Epiphanes never asked me to write a tract explaining how it happens.

I entered the squat square building and sat on a bench against the wall, joining others already sitting there, waiting for either someone to arrive or their own transportation. Everyone was talking, and an indistinguishable din of voices reverberated off the red-tiled floor and plastered walls. I sat and listened.

After some time, I recognized the words *Praeneste* and *trouble* from one of the recent arrivals from the north. Donning my best impression of disinterested nonchalance, I took a seat closer to the man.

"Trouble in Praeneste, you say? What have you heard? What happened?"

"Nothing. Nothing happened. From what I was told, something was *supposed* to happen on the first but didn't. That morning a number of armed men showed up, about a cohort of legionaries, I'm told, including most of the garrison from Reate. Consul Cicero sent them, and they took up positions all over town, but nothing happened. They say most of them went home the next day."

"That was it? They just left?"

"Most of them, yes. Some men are still stationed there, though. A *centurion* and a couple of *decani* are questioning people."

"Questioning people? About what?"

"About some sort of plot to take over the town. Can you imagine that? Praeneste. Why would anyone want to do that? The men interviewing people say they are searching for anyone who knows anything about it—the conspirators, they called them."

"Conspirators? They're calling them conspirators? Sounds serious."

"Oh, it is. The officials questioned me none too gently just because I was coming through the town. I told them I didn't know a thing, but getting them to let me go on my way took a while. They would arrest a blind man if they thought he had seen anything."

I sat back, hardly able to breathe. A deep hole had formed in my stomach and I came close to vomiting. If they found the letter I had deciphered, I would have a hard time convincing them I knew nothing about the planned attack. They would take me to be a conspirator, or at best, the son of one. And they would confiscate our lands and likely take our lives.

I returned home as quickly as I could without showing the panic I felt. I opened the deciphered scroll with shaking hands and stared at it. It had played some part in grand events, but I couldn't see how. Nothing

I had ever studied had prepared me for this. After some time, I threw all the scrolls into the fire. It would be wise not to keep them for anyone to find.

***

We met after dinner. I had my mother and sister follow me to the storage area in the grove, away from servants or other eyes and ears. I told them about the cipher's contents and of what I had learned at the transport station. In the noticeable silence that followed, we realized the contents of my father's message had increased the gravity of our position. Against our will, we had become players—granted small ones—in the game of Republic politics. That was a game where the opening wager was always your life. A chill ran down my back. My mother and sister were both pale.

After some time, my mother slowly exhaled and peered up at me. "Marcus, you cannot go to Rome. The trip is far too dangerous now. It killed your father."

"We've been over this before," I said. "We have no other choice. If I stay, we will fail. If I go, we may succeed and perhaps attention will follow me and leave you alone."

"You are plunging into dark waters, Marcus. You don't know how to swim in that water, nor do you know what lies beneath the surface. I don't want to lose you. I couldn't bear it." Tears flowed down her cheeks.

"Mother—"

"No, you don't understand." She turned, an anguished expression on her face. "Just to be associated with this… this… Rome will bend all effort to discover those who know anything about this, anything at all, and will not bother to sort the guilty from the innocent. It is not their way with such things. They leave that detail to the gods."

She burst into sobs and left the grove.

I looked at my sister and was surprised to see tears pooling in her eyes as well.

"Vitruvia?"

"Yes, yes, you must go. We have no other way. I wish we did." She rose and left, too, leaving me alone with my thoughts in the gathering gloom.

That night, I lay awake, unable to sleep. I was terrified about leaving but equally terrified about staying and even more terrified that I wouldn't be able to decide. For my whole life, I had been told I was a smart person. Why was it, then, that I couldn't think of some clever solution? Our situation was but a problem, after all, and all problems have solutions. I had to find the solution. I had to!

CHAPTER SIX

OMNE INITIUM EST DIFFICILE
Every beginning is difficult.

I awoke the next morning wrapped in a quiet sense of calm. Our family's fate was balanced on a knife's edge with but two months until the end of the year and our loans due, and now we were associated with high treason, a crime that could surely bring about our deaths. But in the maelstrom's midst, I was at peace. My father's Stoicism had taught me focus. Fear of failure did not rule me. We would succeed, or we would go down fighting, knowing we had done our best.

I hoped I really believed it.

The shroud of tranquility settled over me as I headed for breakfast. My sister was already there. Mother, as had been her habit of late, was still in bed.

Vitruvia looked up at me as I sat. "You look different," she said as Cinna put a plate on the table for me.

"How so?" I replied and took a bite of a date.

"I don't quite know. More at ease, I suppose."

"That is how I feel. I think the shock has gone, and I can remember father's teachings—and I have a plan."

"A plan?"

"Yes. I understand what needs to be done. I've figured out how I'm going to travel to Rome, and I have an idea for what I'm going to do when I'm there."

"All figured out then?" she said, but her words sounded more like a question than a statement.

"All except how to protect you here while I'm gone."

"Marcus, I told you we are *not* helpless." She said with a touch of defiance in her voice. "We can find a way to take care of ourselves for two months."

"I don't think so. You are capable, yes, but the wolves are wearing togas and drawing near. I won't wager your life on either their friendly behavior or your prowess."

"But—"

"No buts. I'll have people staying here to protect you and mother. That is not negotiable." I assumed the best "I am in charge," expression I could muster.

She clenched her jaw and ground her teeth. It was something she used to do with Father. The action made her seem as though she was forcibly keeping words from coming out. Perhaps she was.

"I plan to leave Syphāx and everyone else here with you."

"No! Father was killed going to Rome. You realize what's at stake, don't you? Given the contents of that message, you will be in grave danger."

"And Syphāx didn't prevent Father's death. If, as you say, we are dealing with powerful people, his being with me won't make an iota of difference but he could make a great deal of difference to you here."

"Then what are you doing to protect yourself? You must do something," she objected.

"I don't know yet, but I have some ideas."

She wasn't satisfied with my answer.

"Marcus, I need to know what you're thinking."

"I'll tell you when I have it all figured out."

She slammed down her mug and walked back to her room. I watched her go. She was right, for I had no idea whatsoever. This was clearly a question left to divine intervention.

***

"Sorry," I said after I collided with a woman carrying a basket of flowers. I had been looking down, and my mind was elsewhere as Syphāx and I walked through the passageway into the macellum. In truth, I was thinking of Aemilia, wondering if she would be there. I had seen nothing of her since our chance encounter almost a month before, and I very much wanted to see her again.

I had to pick up stores for my trip to Rome. An intense sense of having done this before came over me. When we visited the stall selling apples, I made use of Syphāx's trick of pretending the woman there was invisible. I met her eyes for a moment, and she smiled in surprise.

We moved on from stall to stall until we arrived at the one selling medicinal herbs. I looked up hoping to see Aemilia, but she wasn't there, nor were the medicinal herbs. Instead, the stall now sold lamp oil and was presided over by a woman wearing such a severe expression that I involuntarily shivered. My first impression was that if she were to smile, her face would likely fracture beyond repair. She left me wondering who had let her out of the underworld.

"What happened to the herbs?" I asked.

"Oh, she left, the one with the herbs."

"When?"

"Don't know. Not long ago."

"Where did she go?"

The crone looked annoyed, even more so than she had when I arrived. "I don't know that, either. She left. That's all I know."

She stopped moving and stared in my eyes. A sudden chill came over me.

"I will not sell you anything. You have blood on your hands."

I was stunned. "What?"

"You'll see. Oh, yes, you'll see."

I didn't reply, but moved on. I needed to escape from her range lest she transform into a Fury.

Aemilia's absence deeply disappointed me. Had she already left for Rome? Why had Epiphanes not told me? I needed to talk with him, and soon.

Syphāx gathered up our purchases as I strolled out of the macellum and down the little passageway where I collided with someone for the second time that day. I staggered back a few steps to keep my balance and glanced over to see that I had just knocked Gargonius the Younger on his ass. I required all of the self-control I possessed to suppress the laughter that threatened to break free.

Needless to say, that was not the emotion showing on the prick's face, which was contorted in pure rage. He bolted up and strode towards me just as Syphāx came up behind me. Syphāx could intimidate an enraged bull in full charge, and his effect on the pompous prick was almost comical. Gargonius the Younger slid to a full stop in mid-stride. His hands were still balled into fists, and his mouth moved without forming words. Obviously, the situation exceeded his intellectual grasp. He was without his sycophants. Onlookers had quickly surrounded us, as we were blocking the passageway, and Syphāx loomed behind me.

The prick looked at Syphāx and the bundle of goods from our shopping. "Going someplace, Vitruvius? Ah, yes, off to Rome to beg for money. It won't do you any good. No one will lend to you anymore. You're finished." He narrowed his eyes. "I think I'll call on your sister while you're gone. Keep her company. Check her out. Maybe tutor her in a few things." He made a crude gesture.

Syphāx stepped forward. The grin slipped from Gargonius's face as he reflexively took a step back. I held out my arm to stop Syphāx. Gargonius the Younger looked at us with pure hate. Then he spun around and walked off, and the crowd parted to let him pass.

As Syphāx and I walked home, a chilly wind ruffled our hair and stung our cheeks.

"You should have let me hit him," Syphāx said after a few minutes.

"They would have had you whipped."

"They have whipped me before. It would have been worth it."

"No, Syphāx, it would not have been. You are far too good to involve yourself with that prick," I said, but it embarrassed me that I had been fantasizing about Syphāx doing precisely that.

***

When Syphāx and I returned shortly after midday, I asked him to relate the encounter with Gargonius the Younger to my mother and sister. I needed them to understand why I would leave him at home to help protect them and the property. Gaius Gargonius the Younger was all bluster and bravado, a coward at heart, but I felt uneasy nevertheless.

As the afternoon came on, I sat on the table in the covered area we use for storing olives. The azure sky was crisp and clear, the groves were quiet, and the leaves shimmered silver and whispered in the light wind. I knew the sights, smells, and feel of the place well and loved it so. I did not want Gaius Gargonius to have it. He would not appreciate its little ways and all that made it special. I would rather burn it to ashes first.

I waited for Vitruvia to join me, but some time passed before she came out. When she finally sat opposite me, her eyes were deeply troubled.

"I'm sorry you had to hear Syphāx's story, but you need to appreciate what is at stake for you and Mother and why I'm leaving Syphāx here," I said.

She was silent for some time. "Yes, I understand, but Syphāx is a slave. He cannot command Gaius Gargonius or his son. And Mother and I are women. I doubt he will listen to us, either."

"I agree. That is why I plan to ask Epiphanes and his slave to stay here while I am away. His niece, too, if she is still in town. Epiphanes has tutored many of the city's best families and is esteemed by everyone. Gargonius would have to listen to him."

She smiled and let out a long breath. "That may well work, but you will still be in danger. The people behind that message are far, far more dangerous than Gaius Gargonius, the father or the son. How will you be safe?"

"I have some ideas."

"That's what you said yesterday. I would like to know what they are."

I had hoped she wouldn't ask, for I had yet to receive the wished-for divine inspiration. "Well, I plan to leave quietly and travel under a different name. None of Father's contacts would recognize me by sight. I should be safe on the road."

She considered what I had said and furrowed her brow the way she sometimes did when she concentrated on writing poetry. "Yes, that should get you to Rome. What then?"

"I won't use my actual name until I must. I will hire people to ask questions, and I will stay out of sight as much as I can."

"I dislike it, but I can't think of anything better, and you need to go. We have no choice."

Vitruvia returned to the house, but I lingered outside. I couldn't guess how matters would unfold in Rome and could only hope that I would be wise and quick enough to spy any danger and respond.

***

I had seldom visited Epiphanes at his home. His slave, Hanno, a lean Phoenician boy of my height, was waiting for me and escorted me inside to the atrium, where Epiphanes was reading. He glanced up as I arrived.

"Marcus, water pipes of clay or lead?"

"Water from clay pipes is much more wholesome than that which is conducted through lead pipes. Lead pipes become covered in white lead, and this is said to be hurtful to the human system."

"Correct, of course. To what do I owe the honor?"

I told Epiphanes all that had occurred: the cipher and the attack on Praeneste, my meeting with Gaius Gargonius, his intention to take our property, and the confrontation with Gargonius the Younger at the macellum.

Epiphanes was quiet for so long that I realized I hadn't given him a chance to speak.

"I'm sorry. Epiphanes?"

"Marcus, this matter of the cipher and the trouble in Praeneste has placed you in mortal peril. You are now part of events far beyond your station. These people are among the most powerful in the Republic. They would sacrifice you in an instant." He sat back. "'The strong do as they will, and the weak suffer what they must.'"

"Thucydides."

"Yes, from the Athenian siege of Melos. Thucydides was speaking of the powerful states having their will over the weaker states. In Rome, we speak of the patricians, the powerful, having their will over the plebeians, like us. The Republic has changed, Marcus. The senators are above all law but their own now. They need only ask for a special decree. You know this. You've read about it."

I understood what had become of Rome. "But I still believe in the Republic and the rule of law, Epiphanes. We still have good men in the Senate, though. Cicero, for one."

My mentor smiled, but not with humor. "Yes, but Cicero is a *novus homo*, a new man, and extremely few have made it up from the plebeian class. If you honestly believed that the law was fair, you would have taken that scroll to the nearest magistrate as soon as you had deciphered it."

He was correct, of course. I knew then, as I know now, they would assume my guilt regardless of the law because of my station.

"What are your plans?" he asked.

I told him of my plans for Rome.

"That may work, but you still must be most careful."

"I have a proposition for you."

"A proposition?" He furrowed his brow, and cocked his head a little to the side.

"Yes. Based on my interactions with Gargonius and his son, I fear being away from home. I suspect they are behaving the way they are to prevent my departure. They do not wish me to be successful in Rome. I need to be sure my mother and sister are protected before I can leave. I am leaving Syphāx with them, but they need to have someone there the

Gargonii will respect. The proposition, then, is to ask you and Hanno to stay at our home while I'm away. Aemilia, too, of course."

He hesitated before responding. "That is a good idea. I agree, but I, then, in turn have a proposition for you."

"For me?"

"Aemilia is not here now. I am by myself, well, except for Hanno. So, I would welcome staying with your mother and sister. I would relish the company… and the chance to speak Greek."

Epiphanes glanced back toward another part of the house, his eyes unfocused. Then he looked at me. "Aemilia is at the house of Surius Publicius, just north of town, for a few days before proceeding on her journey. She is there to receive information and references for those she wishes to meet in Rome. She also hoped to secure transportation. My proposition for you is that you meet her there on your way north and escort her to Rome. You can look after her during the trip and…" He looked at me with the same lopsided smile he had given me the last time we met. "If you two traveled to Rome using different names and as a married couple, no one would suspect you."

My face burned. "Epiphanes—"

"I only suggest you *pretend* to be married, not literally be so." He gave me a knowing grin. "Though I wouldn't complain if you actually were. You wouldn't be suspected of being who you are, and married women traveling with their husbands are less likely to be accosted. It seems a fair bargain."

I couldn't argue with his logic, and I had to admit that traveling to Rome with Aemilia would be no great hardship.

CHAPTER SEVEN

VESTIS VIRUM REDDIT
The clothes define the man.

An autumnal chill stung my nose as I stood outside in first light. The air was whisper still, and the olive trees silent silver sentinels on vigil for the dawn. The day seemed to hold its breath, as it waited for the rain that would soon fall from the pregnant clouds piling up in the north. The next day, I would leave for Rome, and this might be the last time I would walk in the grove. Nostalgia had sprung deep from within me. When I was younger, all I could think about was getting away from here. Now that I was leaving, all I could think about was staying.

As I looked over the covered area, I soaked up every detail. I shifted my gaze out to the farm beyond and into the distant hills to the north and east, grabbing at memories as a man might clutch at something to keep him afloat and alive when treading water. I burned the images of the morning in my mind. I would not forget this day.

With the sun up just above the horizon and casting long shadows, I walked back inside for breakfast and entered the triclinium just in time to catch Cinna stifling an enormous yawn. She was up early for me and putting food on the table. She glanced over at me with her bright green eyes and gave me a small, embarrassed smile.

"Thank you, Cinna." I smiled at her to make sure she knew I appreciated her efforts.

Neither Vitruvia nor Mother were present—both likely still asleep—so I ate alone.

I then took a walk into town. As I headed out, I thought back on the little village that I loved. Fundi was an agricultural town. Its heart beat to the pulse of the seasons, the plantings and harvests. It was unremarkable among the countless farming towns in the Republic as grains of sand are on a beach, though perhaps prettier than most. It was certainly closer to my heart than any other. I would miss its regular rhythmic monotony.

As I strolled along the cobblestone street, I tried to absorb everything. The little city, just waking, was full of people starting their day. The bakers were taking their bread out of the ovens and the aroma, a gift from the gods, filled the lane. The last of the delivery men moved their carts and wagons out of the streets. Day workers ate quick breakfasts, and shopkeepers raised their awnings.

I kept one eye out for the prick. I didn't want a chance meeting with him to mar what might be my last images of the town. As I turned the corner, I paused and ran my gaze along the length of the road, searching to ensure he wasn't there. I had lived in Fundi my entire life, and it was small enough that I knew or recognized almost everyone I saw. Only a few faces were new to me, and the prick was not among the people I saw.

I made a point of walking by the macellum. I knew Aemilia wasn't there, but while I was indulging in nostalgia, I was drawn there to relive the memory of meeting her. I saw her stall, now occupied by the creature from the underworld who sold lamp oil, and I quickened my pace so as not to make eye contact with the crone.

As I turned my head, I glanced back the way I had come and noticed two men who looked out of place. They weren't dressed as village folk and were walking at a quick pace, jostling the macellum's shoppers. One was sandy-haired, rather tall, and hard to miss. The other was of average build, bald, and bore a legionnaire's helmet-strap scar under his chin. They both had the look of hard men. I didn't know them, yet I sensed a familiarity as I watched them. Yes! I remembered them clearly. They had been in the street that ran by my house, and I had seen them again when I entered the main part of town. They were the ones I hadn't recognized.

A chill washed over my skin, raising bumps as I realized they must be following me. I continued to walk along the street with a quick but reasonable stride. They kept pace. At the first intersection, I randomly chose the street to the right. They, too, turned right and continued following me. I made a few more random turns at street corners. They stayed behind me, not coming any closer. When I stopped by the town's leather goods shop to look at their wares, the two men stopped at the wine shop in front of them and examined the wine selection. The tall one cast a quick sidelong glance in my direction.

All feelings of nostalgic rumination vanished and were replaced by anxiety and fear. The two followed me all the way back home, keeping their distance no closer than thirty paces, no further away than forty. When I entered the street to my house, they resumed their positions, leaning against a wall up the street where I had first seen them this morning. One thing I was sure of was that they were not Gaius Gargonius's men. This was not his style. These men were professionals, with hard eyes and blank faces. Gargonius would never pay the fees such men would command.

***

By the time we sat down to dinner, I had still not told the family about the day's events. I didn't wish to alarm them or for them to realize how worried I was, but I had never been good at hiding my feelings.

My mother was the first to notice. "You've been quiet, Marcus. You've hardly said a thing. Coming to your senses about the trip? It's about time. You should feel no shame in backing out. You would be a lot safer staying here."

"He has to go, Mother," Vitruvia replied in an exasperated tone. "We've already been over this. *He* might be safer staying here, but *we* would not. Not if we cannot secure another loan."

"I wouldn't be safe if I stayed," I said.

"Of course—"

"What do you mean, you wouldn't be safe?" Vitruvia interrupted. She had understood the implications of my statement.

I told them about the two men following me. Those who knew about my father and the cipher had found me. My life was in danger if I didn't leave.

Silence followed. Finally, Vitruvia broke it. "Why didn't they try to kill you? Surely they could have found a suitable place along your walk."

"I've been thinking about that. They were following me, perhaps to see where I would lead them, or who I'm talking to."

"What will you do?"

"I don't know yet. I'll have to leave town without them knowing it until after I'm gone."

***

I opened my eyes and peered at the ceiling. My head throbbed from too little sleep. Though I didn't remember the night passing, I recalled vague dreams of evil-looking men following me everywhere.

The floor was cold when I finally threw off the covers and put down my feet. Through the high window in my room, I saw the dawn's glow, faint in the east, casting its long rays to illuminate the underside of the low clouds and spotty rain that was falling in dark bands in the distance. The realization that I would be leaving in the rain added to my already gloomy mood. I watched the rain for a moment and was struck with an idea. Perhaps the gods had intervened. I quickly dressed and went into the tablinum, where I grabbed a scroll and pen to write to Epiphanes.

After a short time, Cinna entered.

She must have heard me and started work early. "Do you want breakfast?"

"Yes, and call Syphāx, if you please."

A few minutes later, Syphāx entered. He was still rubbing sleep from his eyes.

I handed the scroll to him. "Take this to Epiphanes. Hand it to him, not Hanno, and wait for a reply. Yes, it's raining, but make sure our new friends see and recognize you. One of them will probably follow you."

He nodded, took the scroll, and left.

"I set your breakfast," Cinna said. "You should eat it while it is hot."

I was done with breakfast when Syphāx returned about an hour later, his clothes drenched.

"You gave Epiphanes the scroll?" I asked as soon as he entered.

"Yes. He said I should tell you it is a good plan and he will do as you ask."

"Are the two men still out there?"

"Yes. The tall one followed me to Epiphanes's and back, just as you said." He paused and looked at me. "I could have dealt with him. In the rain, no one would have noticed."

"I am sure you could have, but that would only have alerted them, and more of them might be about. I have a better plan."

By midday, the rain had increased. Syphāx and I had harnessed two horses to a small, low side wagon and put my four bags in the back. The time had come for me to leave. Mother and Vitruvia were waiting in the vestibule. Their differences were so obvious: Mother had tears in her eyes and seemed suddenly frail, while Vitruvia stood like an iron pole, her eyes hard. I embraced my mother, and she held me tightly, making it hard for me to pull back. This reminded me of how she had hugged Father before he had left.

I embraced Vitruvia. She knew what I was doing was necessary and seemed determined to send me off with no remorse, though her eyes were red. For my part, the calm before action had crept back into me, something that became part of me later in my life as a soldier. I nodded at them and walked out the door.

"Write!" Mother yelled.

The rain was harder now and icy cold. Even so, Syphāx and I left our hoods down. Our new friends had to see us and note our leaving. True to their practice, they followed us as we slowly plodded through the streets. The horses were unhappy with the rain and refused to move any faster.

When we arrived at Epiphanes's house, the two men took positions under an overhang by a shop at the end of the street. We grabbed the bags from the back of the wagon and ran in through the door that Hanno held open.

As soon as we stepped inside and closed the door, Hanno and I quickly exchanged clothes. Epiphanes grabbed my shoulder.

"I've done as you wished," he said. "The cart is at the livery. They should already have it ready. Be safe, Marcus."

"I will. Look after them, Epiphanes. I would not go if you were not there." I looked over at Syphāx. "Listen to Epiphanes. Do what he asks. He is a wise man."

"I will. You can depend on me."

"I know." I reached out and grabbed his arm. "Thank you, Syphāx."

Epiphanes pulled two scrolls out of his tunic. He handed one to me, saying, "This is for Aemilia," and then the other, "and this one is for Surius Publicius when you pick up Aemilia."

"Thank you. May the gods favor you."

"Marcus, you know I don't believe in the will of gods," he said, shaking his head.

"Then may fortune favor you, teacher and friend."

The three men pulled up their hoods to cover their faces, and then stepped through the door and into the rain. Hanno, wearing my tunic, shoes, and cloak, hopped up into the wagon next to Syphāx. In my clothes, he looked just like me. Syphāx flicked the reins, and the wagon moved through the rain.

I closed the door and ran to an upstairs window to watch them move down the street. When the wagon turned the corner on the route back to my house, the two men moved out from underneath the overhang and jogged down the street after them. At the intersection, they stopped, peered around the corner, and turned to follow the wagon.

Epiphanes might not hold with the gods, but I felt much in Abeona's grace.

***

A dark squall swept in with a tremendous roar, and the heavy rain bounced up from the street. I remained just behind the upstairs window, observing the street for another few minutes. No one was on the road. People were waiting for the rain to let up. I went back downstairs, pulled Hanno's hood over my head, hoisted the four bags over my shoulders, and stepped out into the street and the downpour.

I made my way along the street, bent and burdened by my bags and the incessant rain. No doubt, I looked like an idiot out in this weather and carrying such a load. I was fine with that as long as the idiot looked like Hanno.

The livery was not that far away, but the load was heavy and I had to stop twice to resettle it. The second time I stopped, I saw someone else out in the rain. He was a block away, standing underneath a shop's overhang at the end of the street. He leaned his head out and around the corner, peering down the intersection towards my house. He was not someone I recognized from town. Something about him didn't feel right, the way he stood, like a cat watching a mouse hole, ready to pounce. I now understood that more than just the two men were watching my street.

I had no choice but to pass by him to make my way to the livery. Tugging the hood as far down as it would go, I picked up the bags again and started along the street. I couldn't believe I had ever thought my plan was so clever. Not only was I going to be caught and probably killed, but it would be when I was exhausted, soaking wet, and wearing Hanno's smelly tunic. The gods had a dreadful sense of humor.

The roar of the rain on the street was so loud that the man did not even notice me until I was almost beside him. He jerked around and stepped back. Bent over under my load, I kept my face down, the hood covering me, but I could see his feet. He made room for me to pass under the overhang next to him.

I passed so closely that I heard him mumble, "Poor bastard," as I walked by. I could tell from his feet that he had turned back to continue his vigil on the street to my house. The smile on my face was fleeting as the implication of this other watcher sank in. How many more were there? I kept my head down as I walked the last block to the livery.

The livery was a large building with a small office and two rows of stalls, and empty of people now, except for the owner.

"Took you long enough, Hanno," he said as I entered. "The cart is out by the second door, all hitched and ready." He turned his back to me and continued eating from a plate he had set on the shelf against the wall. Thankfully, as a slave, I didn't merit friendly conversation.

I walked through the livery, out the second door, and back into the rain, where I found a small cart hitched to a mule tied to a ring on the wall. The bags fell from my shoulders into the cart. I wasn't sure I would ever stand straight again. Every muscle in my body ached, and I was soaked through, and still the rain fell. I unhitched the mule from the wall and guided it up the Via Appia, toward Aemilia and Rome. I was so cold. I didn't know if I would be able to keep moving. The temptation to stay inside and warm myself was strong, and I had to hurry lest I succumb to it.

***

To my relief, the heavy rain soon passed, leaving a steady drizzle in its place. After the squall's relentless pounding, the easier rain seemed almost nonexistent. Still, the air was cold—freezing, in fact. Now that I was no longer frozen with fear, I was freezing from the elements. Shivers gripped me, making walking difficult.

About an hour had gone by, I thought, since I had left the livery, but I had only made my way just past the edge of town. The mule balked at every opportunity, twice stopping completely. I was normally good with animals, but this one seemed to blame me for taking it out of the warm livery and into the icy rain. I guess, had I been in his place, I would have resented someone making me go out in this weather, too.

Surius Publicius's house couldn't be much further, yet I was so cold I wasn't sure that I could make it. I don't remember falling, but I found myself lying face down on the road. Perversely, the mule and the cart had continued down the road and were now about twenty paces in front of me.

When I made it back to the cart, I realized I had just trudged past the little path that led to Surius Publicius's house. Now I had to convince the mule to turn around. With a fine balance of threats, pleading, pushing, and pulling, the mule, the cart, and I finally arrived at Publicius's door. As I raised my hand to pound on the door, it opened so suddenly that I almost fell into the man who stood in the doorway.

"Be off with you! Whatever you want, we want none of it or of you," he said while closing the door.

"Who is it?" called a voice from inside the house.

"Just a beggar, sir."

"In this weather?"

The door opened further, and an older man stepped forward.

I tried to speak, but my teeth chattered so much I couldn't make a sound. "Epiphanes sent me," I finally said and then actually fell forward and into the man holding the door.

I heard voices. When I opened my eyes, I was lying on cushions in front of a fire and someone was covering me in blankets.

"My, my bags?" I asked, my voice horse and broken due to my chattering teeth.

"Vitruvius?" a woman's voice asked, and Aemilia's face came into view over me.

"We have your bags, in the corner there," the older man said, pointing.

"What are you doing here?" Aemilia asked.

"Bring me the… the smallest bag," I said.

Someone, I think the man who first opened the door, brought the bag to me. It was rough flax, tied with a small strip of leather, and completely soaked. My fingers were cold, stiff, and shaking, and I was barely able to untie the leather cord and pull out the oiled leather case. My hands shook so much that, I needed three tries to unbuckle the document case. I drew out Epiphanes's scrolls and handed one to Publicius and the other to Aemilia. Then I lay back and sank into the warmth.

When I woke sometime later, I changed into a dry set of my own clothes, sat back on a cushion by the fire, and ate the plate of food handed to me. The sun appeared to have set, though, with the low, dark clouds, I could hardly be certain. The rain had almost stopped, however, and promised to be gone by the next morning. The warmth was finally seeping into my bones, but I seemed to have picked up a cough.

Both Publicius and Aemilia had read Epiphanes's scrolls. I didn't know what they said, but I deduced that Epiphanes had given them some idea of my plans and asked that they help me. Publicius had once been a sought after medicus in Rome, but had moved out to Fundi for better air long ago. Clearly, Epiphanes trusted him, so when they came to join me by the fire, I decided I could tell them all that had happened, including the message my father had unwittingly sent to a group of revolutionaries, and what I planned to do.

"So, when do we leave, husband?" Aemilia asked with a broad smile as she shifted her place on the cushion opposite me.

I almost choked on my food and started coughing. I could feel my face growing warm.

"You can't come with me. Didn't you hear what I said about the cipher and the men following me? I'll be lucky if I make it to Rome alive myself. Seeing you with me would put you in danger. No, that plan isn't going to work. I need to travel by myself. You can't go with me now."

"You can't actually stop me, you know. And you will look really silly having your wife walk twenty paces behind you and the cart. What will people think?"

"Aemilia, you—"

"Vitruvius, the plan is a good one. Trust me. I have some ideas, too," she implored, and the reflection of the fire sparkled in her eyes.

CHAPTER EIGHT

CAVEAT VIATOR
Let the traveler beware.

I spent the night on cushions in front of the fire and woke to the drone of muted voices coming from the kitchen, along with the clatter of plates and cups as people set the breakfast table. Otherwise, the house seemed strangely quiet until I realized I heard no patter of raindrops. By the light streaming into the room through the open atrium, I judged that the time must be just after sunrise and the sky mostly clear, thank the gods.

Aemilia entered, and I sat up. My head was swimming, and every joint ached.

"You ready for breakfast?"

"Yes, thank you," I answered, though I was not really hungry.

She smiled and left, giving me the same full-face smile I remembered from the first time I had seen her in the macellum. I couldn't lie there all day, so I rose from bed. The table had been set with what looked to be a feast; olives, porridge, fresh-baked bread, and *garum*.

Aemilia sat, and a servant piled food onto her plate. "No! Not the garum," she said. Too late. The servant had just given her a large spoonful of the fermented fish sauce. Aemilia tore little pieces of her bread and methodically scooped up all the garum. She then pushed the little pieces of bread into a pile on the edge of the plate with a motion that looked part practiced ceremony.

"You don't like garum?" I asked, curious as to her tastes.

"No, I don't. Why would anyone eat rotten fish paste? Do you know what unhealthy airs could be in rotten fish?"

"But it's good. Everyone eats it. Can't be bad for you," I countered.

"Everyone dies, too, but that's not good for you."

Aemilia and I were already eating when Publicius joined us at the table.

He was a big man, taller than most Greeks, with long, gray hair and dark black eyebrows. "How are you feeling, Vitruvius? You were almost frozen when we put you by the fire."

"Fine," I said reflexively and looked away.

He leaned over and looked more closely at me, but I avoided his gaze. He reached out and put his hand under my jaw, turned my face towards him, and stared me in the eyes.

"No, you're not." He released my jaw. "How are you feeling? Let's try the truth this time," he said in a commanding tone.

Dissembling wouldn't work with this man. He would see through any lie. "My head aches and my chest hurts as though that mule is sitting on it. Guess I'm still not over yesterday's weather." I stifled a cough.

"I'm not surprised. You could catch your death in such weather. You should have waited a day."

"I had to leave, and the rain was a gift from the gods. It gave me something to hide in."

"That may be so, but for what the gods give, they—"

"Extract a heavy price. I know, but I had to leave."

"Then you should rest here for a few days, build your strength back."

"I cannot. I don't have time. I have to find help and be back by the end of next month, or we lose our land." Fear knotted my stomach. "Those who watch my house will soon realize I'm not there. I need to be safely in Rome before that happens."

A look passed briefly between Publicius and Aemilia. They must have discussed my situation in an earlier conversation.

"He *will* be all right, Publicius. It's not raining now. He can stay warm. I'll be with him if he should take sick." Aemilia gave me a playful smile. "He can ride in the cart, covered in blankets. That should keep him warm. I'll lead the mule."

Publicius grinned. "Spoken like a proper Roman wife who knows her place." He laughed loudly at the image.

She gave him a vulgar finger gesture. "More like a proper meddica," she said and then looked at me. "If he *were* my husband, he'd never get away with that."

"Wait! Hold on! Didn't you hear *anything* I said last night? You can't come with me. The journey will be too dangerous," I said. The fit of coughing that came over me from my exertion brought a sort of "I told you so" expression to her face.

"You were saying... husband?"

***

I hate to admit it, but I would never have made it had I been forced to walk. While sitting in the cart with our bags and Aemilia's boxes was cramped and uncomfortable, I was also warm and cozy under the blankets. Every time I took a deep breath, I coughed—not a shallow, polite cough, the kind where you can keep your lips closed, but a deep, raspy cough from the lungs.

The Via Appia stretched north through Fundi, but swung west-northwest just out of town to pass along southern side of the mountains. Fundi lay at the east end of a long, fertile valley, flanked on the north and east by the Lepine Mountains. The first town on our journey was Terracina, just fourteen miles west of Fundi, where the green of the fertile valley met the blue of the ocean. Terracina sat on the north side of the mountains where they met the sea in steep, sheer-sided cliffs. The Via Appia passed by the cliffs over a rock dike that Roman engineers had built more than a century earlier and had constantly maintained in the face of the waves and storms that sweep in from the sea. The dike jogged out into the bay and around the cliffs to where Terracina lay.

Terracina was not large, and we passed through it in minutes. From Terracina, the Via Appia turned north, straight as an arrow to Rome, but we first had to travel through the Pomptine Marshes. The great marshes were formed by two rivers that had no easy exit to the sea. The Via Appia crossed them on raised infill and causeways. The road was impressively engineered, but the marshes were unhealthy. Marshes that are stagnant and have no outlets, either by rivers or ditches, like the Pomptine Marshes, merely putrefy as they stand, emitting heavy, unhealthy vapors. Best to move through the marshes quickly, as everyone knew. To dwell in them was to invite disease.

Aemilia led us at a strong pace once we entered the marshes. She said very little, and she scolded me every time I tried to speak, and telling me to save my voice and rest. That left me with nothing to do but watch her nicely swaying hips as she led the mule. The view kept my mind from dwelling on all that had happened over the last month and all I still had to do.

We passed other carts and people walking, seeming to outpace all but the light horse-drawn wagons and the few riders on horseback. Our dress marked us as well-off gentry, so most of our fellow travelers, who were poor farmers and workers, yielded the road.

"The mule will need to rest soon. He is becoming harder to pull ahead," she said through deep breaths and turned her head back to look at me. "Me, too, I guess. I packed some food. We can stop when we make it to Lucus Feroniae. I think that's another mile or so."

"I am amazed you—"

"No need to talk. It'll make you cough."

"But I enjoy talking to you."

"Oh, you do? And here I thought you were only interested in my butt."

My face flushed. How did she know? I thought I was being very discreet. "I, I—"

She laughed. "Oh, so you were watching me. You admit it. Well, in your case that's all right." She turned and continued leading the mule, but she kept on laughing. As my gaze absently drifted back to her hips, I realized that I really knew nothing about this woman. Almost everything she did was so… unexpected.

We had almost reached the town of Lucus Feroniae when I heard horses coming from behind at a canter. No one rode a horse so hard up that road except legionaries, couriers, and thieves. Aemilia heard it, too, and turned to look. We would have to move the cart off the road for legionaries. She looked down the road and then met my eyes and shook her head. I tugged my hood and the blankets down to cover my face and huddled in the cart.

After a few moments, the horses reached us. One of them trotted in front of the cart and stopped next to Aemilia, blocking our way. I could see its legs from underneath my hood.

"Have you seen a young man traveling by himself today? Thin with gray eyes, about five and a half feet tall, brownish hair?"

"No, nobody like that today," Aemilia said. "Sounds kind of cute, though. What's he done?"

The rider ignored her and rode his horse over to the cart and me. He reached out to pull back the blankets covering my face. I didn't know what to do. I didn't even have a knife. I had the pugio blade in one of my bags, but hadn't thought to wear it. I should always keep it with me. What an idiot!

"I'm bringing my husband up to see a medicus in Rome. You see, he caught the fever in Baiae," Aemilia said. "Killed half our family."

The rider quickly drew his hand from my blanket and nudged his horse back a couple of steps. He leaned down to peek under my hood. With little urging, I broke into a long, roiling, deep cough. The rider jerked up and turned his horse away, and both riders cantered on up the road.

Aemilia let out a long breath. "See, aren't you glad you brought your wife along?"

I coughed again, though this time I tried not to. I managed to croak out, "Yes, wife. There is certainly more to you than meets the eye." At once I remembered that she had lost her own family in just such a fever. "Aemilia, I'm sorry about your family."

She was still for a moment, and then turned and started leading our animal, without saying anything.

I didn't know what to say, so I said nothing.

We reached Lucus Feroniae a few minutes later and pulled over at a dry area to eat and let the mule rest and graze. A landing in the town served as the start of the Decennovium canal that ran alongside the Via Appia, from Lucus Feroniae up to Forum Appii. Barges on the canal were pulled by mules and offered travelers a quicker and easier way through the marshes, but a barge ticket cost money—money we didn't have for such things.

The town itself was unremarkable and would have disappeared years earlier had it not been the southern terminus of the canal.

***

The food Aemilia had packed was excellent, but I ate little. My cough was worse, and I had started to shiver. Eating with your teeth chattering is hard. Aemilia quickly pushed me back into the cart and under the blanket.

Two hours after lunch Aemilia stopped the mule and walked back to me. She put her hand on my forehead.

"You're hot. You have a fever. We need to find a place to spend the night. You need to be in bed."

"We can't stop. I have to make it to Rome as quickly as I can."

She rolled her eyes. "Well, I'm stopping, and the mule is stopping, and the cart is stopping. I think you should, too. I doubt if you can walk and carry your bags while shaking like a leaf in a storm."

"All right," I said weakly. She had me. What else could I do?

"The problem will be finding someplace to stay that has a minimum of thieves, and fleas, and bad vapors. I can deal with the thieves, but the fleas and vapors might kill you. We should keep an eye out for a decent inn."

She walked around to the rear of the cart and opened one of her boxes. I couldn't see what she was doing, but after a few moments, she came over with a bottle and a wooden spoon. She poured a thick brown liquid into the spoon.

"Here, take this."

"What is it?"

"Willow bark extract. It'll help with the fever."

"I'm not taking that," I said with absolute conviction. "Not until I know how it was prepared. You could poison me if it was done wrong."

Without warning, she punched me in the stomach and crammed the spoon in my open mouth. She grabbed my jaw and clenched my mouth shut until I swallowed the noxious liquid.

"That was awful! You might have killed me! Don't, don't do that again!"

"Or what? You'll divorce me?"

"Hilarious," I said, and started a long coughing fit.

We continued up the road until we reached a small rest house with a sign outside that said "Room for Let." It appeared to be cleaner than most of the ones we had passed and was the most expensive advertised so far. Aemilia went inside. After a few minutes, she returned.

"Looks all right. They have one room with a bed. Bed looks mostly clean, but I brought blankets we can use." She paused for a moment. "No food, though. We can eat what we've brought."

We unloaded the cart and took all our bags and boxes into the bedroom. While Aemilia unhooked the mule and put it in the house's small stableyard, I brought in the last of the bags, dropped them onto the floor, and looked around. The only thing in the room was the one narrow bed. Then the realization hit me—one narrow bed.

Aemilia entered and shut the door, such as it was. "I fed the mule. That should keep him until tomorrow." She followed my gaze to the bed. "We can both sleep there. You can roll up in one blanket, and I'll roll up in another. Don't worry. Your virtue will remain intact. You're too sick and I'm too tired."

With that, she opened one of her boxes and came at me with her spoon and two bottles.

And that was how we slept, me in my blanket and her in hers. No doubt, she had given me something to make me sleep. If not, I doubt I would have been able to do so, as I could feel every curve and bulge of her body pressing into mine. I kept trying to think of her as my sister, but the effort didn't help. Between her curves, the buzzing mosquitoes, and the constant croaking of frogs, that I actually went to sleep was a miracle.

Late in the night, I started to shiver uncontrollably. I was miserably cold and only half awake when I sensed my blanket being lifted. Aemilia slid in next to me and wrapped her arms around me. Her warmth, her breath, enveloped me and the shivering slowly subsided.

***

I woke to the crowing of a rooster—not very loud, but loud enough. I opened my eyes to the dim light of dawn breaking through the gaps around the shutters. I also realized with a start that Aemilia was asleep under the blanket with me, her head on my shoulder, her arm draped over my chest, a leg entwined with mine, and my arm around her waist. Yes, she and I were both fully clothed, but she was wearing a light tunic that had become somewhat dislodged during the night and no longer covered all that was intended. I also noticed for the first time that she was wearing a gold chain around her neck with a gold pendant that lay between her breasts. The necklace looked like solid gold, worth a small fortune.

She stirred a little and smacked her lips before forcing her eyes open. She looked up at me and then smiled that wonderful smile I had come to know. Then her eyes opened wide. She started and drew back. Sitting up, she stared at me with a quizzical expression before realizing that her clothes weren't covering her very well. She grabbed the blanket and pulled it off me to cover her front.

"I remember," she said after a moment. "You were shivering. I held you to keep you warm. I didn't mean to stay that way. I was just so exhausted." Her face actually had a tint of flush.

I was embarrassed for her and couldn't meet her gaze. "I'm not complaining. It was the best sleep I've had… in months."

She bent forward, still hugging the blanket to her chest, and put her hand on my forehead. "You don't have a fever this morning. How do you feel?"

That was a hard question to answer. I didn't feel sick, and I could take deep breaths without coughing. I also felt alive in a way I never had before from having had her against me, but I doubted that was what she meant. "Much better. Cough seems to be mostly gone."

"Good. I'll wash up and put together some food if you'll hitch the mule."

I staggered up and headed to the stableyard.

Breakfast was meager—dried fruit and gruel followed by watered wine. Two hours later, my stomach was already feeling empty. We both walked today, Aemilia on one side of the animal's head and me on the other. The mule, it seemed, was much happier without my weight in the cart, but he kept eying me with what looked like an accusation. I think he still harbored resentment towards me for the day in the downpour.

The canal continued to parallel the Via Appia to the west as we crossed the Pomptine Marshes. Even in November, the air was heavy with humidity and uncomfortable.

Just after the fifth hour, we entered the town of Forum Appii. Every traveler knew of Forum Appii by its reputation, which was not good. It was a small post station forty-three miles south of Rome, and the northern terminus of the canal. The town was known to be the home to thieving boatmen and cheating innkeepers. No one chose to tarry there. We walked through the village as quickly as we could, having to push aside street-side hustlers, pickpockets, and beggars alike. The only ones who did not approach us were the numerous prostitutes. Aemilia's glare kept them at bay.

The stretch of the Via Appia north of Forum Appii was not busy that afternoon, and we were the only ones on the road as we crossed the bridge at Tripontium, just four miles north of Forum Appii. The bridge was a marvel of engineering, built straight through the shifting sands of the marshes and under constant assault from wind, water, and traffic of all sorts. Its three enormous arches spanned a wide, shallow river. It was a testament to Roman hydraulic concrete. The bridge had been built by constructing massive pillars of concrete in the river itself. If we had the time, I would have insisted we stop so I might sketch it, as I had done on previous trips with my father.

I was so engrossed in admiring the bridge's engineering that I didn't hear the three men until they were upon us. One, maybe all of sixteen, his face covered in pimples, skinny and rough, came around in front of me, his long knife held low and ready to strike. Another one, a little older, missing two teeth, grabbed Aemilia from behind and held a knife to her throat. The third, middle-aged, perhaps the father, sashayed a pace or two in front of us and grinned.

"Well now, what do we have here?" he said. "A young couple out for a morning stroll. You should be more careful, you see. Some very bad thieves inhabit these parts. Very bad." He gestured to the other two men. "We are good thieves, you see. If you don't make any trouble and fairly compensate us for our time, we'll not harm you. Bad thieves would have just killed you, you see. You were lucky we found you first."

The thieves led us off the main road and onto a small path that curved into a thick copse of trees. As soon as we were in the trees and out of sight of the road, the older man stopped and smiled at us.

"This looks like a nice place to talk," he said. "We won't delay you long. Better for everyone if we can finish this quickly."

"We have nothing of value," Aemilia said. The blood had drained from her face, but her eyes were clear and alert.

"Shut your mouth, woman, unless we ask a question!" the young man holding her said. He tightened the knife against her throat. A drop of blood ran down her neck, and she stiffened.

"No! Don't hurt her. We won't do anything," I said. And, in fact, it was clear there was nothing we could do. The young man holding Aemilia could have easily slit her throat before either of us could move a muscle. I couldn't hear or see anyone on the road. These men had planned their ambush well.

"Careful with the lady there, Scaurus. No harm unless she's trouble," the older man said. He looked Aemilia up and down and smirked. "Let's start with her."

CHAPTER NINE

NULLUS EST STULTUS SEMPER NUNC OMNIS
Nobody's a fool always; everyone is sometimes.

I had never felt so impotent in my life as I did at that moment. If only someone would happen along the road, then I could cry out. The thieves would never try such a thing if help was at hand. Suddenly, I had a thought.

"We're with friends. Friends just behind us," I said with an assurance I didn't possess. The older man turned to study me. I continued, "We have friends who would not take kindly to your harming us."

He let out a protracted sigh. "You have friends. Of course, you have friends. Everybody has friends. Even *I* have friends." He glanced back at the road. "But I don't see them and I don't think your friends will come looking for us."

He turned back and took a stride toward Aemilia.

I was suddenly overwhelmed with rage and lunged at him. I had scarcely moved when something hard slammed against the side of my head, and I was sent sprawling face down in the dirt.

"No!" I heard Aemilia scream.

I lay on the path for a moment and then struggled to my knees. My head throbbed, and the world was spinning. My vision was blurry, but I could see the older man come over and squat in front of me.

"Now look what you've done," he said. "You've made Trebius hit you. I told you, we are good thieves. We won't hurt you if you behave.

You were not behaving." He stood. "Now, stay put." He made a hand gesture such as one would make to a dog. "Stay or next time, Trebius will use the pointy part."

I watched him—or I should say, him and his double, as I was seeing two of everything—walk over to Aemilia. My vision slowly cleared. She stood rigidly as the young man behind her held a knife to her throat, and another drop of blood trickled down her neck from the blade's edge.

"You seem smarter than your husband. You're going to behave, aren't you?" The older man looked her up and down again. "That ring on your finger, let's start with that." He held out his hand.

With the jerkiness of a puppet, Aemilia took off the ring and dropped it into the man's outstretched hand. He turned it over and grinned. "Greek by the look of it. Nice, detailed work." He reached out and pushed back the fabric covering her shoulder, exposing the gold chain I had noticed the night before. "Oh, my, what have we here?" He lifted the pendant and examined it, smiling broadly. Then his eyes widened and his face paled. He dropped the pendant, which swung back against Aemilia's chest.

"Scaurus, let her go," he said in a raised voice.

"But, Father—"

"Let. Her. Go. Now!" The young man holding Aemilia pulled away the knife and stepped back. She sagged and put a hand to her throat.

"We are, ah, so sorry to cause you any problems, lady. Oh, here, don't forget your ring." He handed her the ring and turned toward me. "Trebius, help our friend up. Help him stand." The young man guarding me stared at the older man. "Now, Trebius."

Trebius sheathed his knife, put his hands under my arms and heaved me to my feet, which was a bad idea as I suddenly felt I was going to be sick.

"Father, what is it?" Trebius asked.

The older man didn't answer but came over to me. "You should have told me who your friends were, sir. We didn't mean any disrespect. If we had known…" He let the statement trail off, and then he looked at my head and winced. "And about that, sir, I'm really sorry. I'm sure you'll feel better soon. Hope you don't take it the wrong way. Anyway, nice to meet you."

He turned and motioned to the two young men to follow. Then he glanced back at me. "There really are bad thieves, sir. You and your lady should be more careful." With that, the three men trotted back down the path.

I watched them for a few moments as they returned to the main road and disappeared.

Then I bent over and retched.

***

The world wasn't spinning as badly when I straightened up, and my vision was more or less normal. I put my hand to the side of my head, and it felt sticky. When I looked at my fingers, I saw they were covered with blood. Then I remembered Aemilia. I spun around—another bad idea, as I almost retched again.

She was standing in the middle of the road with a distant look in her eyes. I walked over to her and grabbed her arms. "Aemilia." She didn't move. "Aemilia?" She shook her head.

"Vitruvius." She gripped me in an intense hug, which I returned a little unsteadily. She held me tight. She was shaking, and I could feel her breathing slowing down to a normal rate. We stood like that for a minute or two. Then she pulled back a bit and looked up at me, surprising me with a frown. "What were you thinking, rushing him?"

"I don't know. I just felt angry. I didn't want them to hurt you."

She hugged me tightly again. "That's so sweet… and really, really stupid. How could you ever think that was a good idea?" She pulled back again. "Your head." She moved around to examine the side of my head. "Oh, Vitruvius. Look what you've done."

"I didn't—"

"Now, sit." She pushed me to the ground, the second time that day that I had been reduced to the status of a family dog. She walked back to her boxes and returned with bandages, water, a rag, and another bottle.

I sat by the side of the path while she knelt beside me and cleaned my bloody, battered head.

"Ouch! That hurts!"

"Sorry. This *is* going to hurt a little."

My head was continuing to clear. "Aemilia, why did the thieves leave? What is that pendant you wear? What scared them?"

"Hold still. You're moving too much." With both hands, she forced my head straight. "I don't know. Publicius gave it to me. Well, he loaned it to me. He was the medicus to some very important patrician families. He said the last one he worked for adopted him into the family or something. They gave him the pendant. He thought I could use it for an introduction."

"May I see it?"

She raised it over her head, and handed it to me, then returned to cleaning my wound. The pendant was oval and made of gold, and it held the image of the goddess Venus. Around the outside were the words "*Gens Julia. Nemo me impune lacessit,*" I read aloud.

"No one provokes me with impunity." she responded. "So?"

My breath caught. This was not simply some pendant from a patrician family. It was from the Julii, one of the oldest senatorial orders in the Republic—and also, perhaps, the most ruthless and ambitious in all of Rome. One of them, Gaius Julius Caesar, had been elected *pontifex maximus,* chief priest of Rome, a position, most believe, he attained through massive bribes and not-so-subtle threats. And now he had been elected *praetor,* starting in the new year. He was not someone you would want as an enemy.

"Aemilia, this is a gens Julia pendant," I said in wonder. "The Julii are the oldest family in the Republic. They trace their ancestry to the goddess Venus and Aeneas."

"You're moving again." She pushed my head back around. "Yea, Publicius said it was from a really important family."

"No. It is not just *from* an important family. It identifies the wearer as *being* a Julii. The thieves thought you were a Julii. If they attacked a Julii, their lives would be worth less than a grain of sand."

Aemilia finally stopped. "Oh," was all she said as I returned the pendant.

"Some time ago, Julius Caesar was captured by Cilician pirates. When they ransomed him, he complained that the amount was not high enough, that he was worth more than that. He also told them that once he was released, he would hunt them all down and kill them. And he did, every last one of them. No, you do not cross the Julii."

She finished the bandage and stood up, and I followed—a little too quickly. The world whirled around again, and I retched.

When I finally straightened, she was looking me in the eye, brow furrowed, wiping my mouth with the rag. "You took quite a knock on your head. You're going to take a while to heal. Back into the cart with you. At least you can hang your head over the side. Then, when you become sick, it won't land on my feet."

I glanced down and realized I had just done the unthinkable. "Sorry," I murmured as she shoved me into the cart.

She went back to one of her boxes and returned with her wooden spoon and her hands full of bottles.

***

We had been back on the Via Appia for about four hours and the going was slow. The traffic had become dense as smaller roads joined the Via Appia. We traveled alongside wagons filled with grain, vegetables, and wine, bound for the warehouses outside the city. Processions of slaves headed for the markets passed by the walkway while we waited for a loose herd of sheep to clear the road. The animals scattered each time their herders tried to gather them together.

Of course, we had to be mindful of the official traffic. Our cart frequently had to yield the road, mostly to Legionaries and couriers, which further slowed our pace. I also believe that Aemilia was keeping the cart's speed down to refrain from jostling me.

When we had set out that morning, every bump of the cart had caused the world to spin, sometimes resulting in my decorating the road, but that had mostly subsided. Whatever noxious mixture of medicine Aemilia had given me seemed to have had some effect and I was finally feeling better. I even felt like walking, but when I tried to climb down from the cart, she gave me a severe scolding and threatened me with her wooden spoon, so I stayed where I was while Aemilia led the mule.

"You know, I should really marry you," I told her. "Wives cannot treat their husbands like this, but I have no legal recourse against a perfect stranger."

She laughed, that wonderful laugh. "I'm hardly a perfect stranger, and it wouldn't matter anyway. Husband or not, if you're my patient, I'll decide what's good for you."

"I'm not sure how many patients will appreciate your caring demeanor."

"I don't require my patients to like me. I just need them to heal."

"You still need to be paid."

"True, but if people know I can help them, they'll come." She was quiet for a moment, and then she said in a low voice, "I don't want anyone to lose their family the way I did. I think of them every day."

I thought then of my father and how much I missed him. At least I still had my mother and sister. Her losses must have been particularly hard.

"I'm so sorry," I said.

She gave me a sad, brief smile. "You have to find something else to live for."

She was silent after that, and I left her with her thoughts.

We reached the little town of Tres Tabernae without incident. The town was another post station, just thirty-one miles south of Rome, and contrary to its name, the three main buildings weren't taverns but a general store, a blacksmith's shop, and a large inn that was said to serve good food. The town's sole existence depended on the money spent by travelers along the Via Appia. We were happy to discover that the inn's food was excellent, and it had a large bath complex, which neither of us felt well enough to use—I from lingering sickness and Amelia from exhaustion. For such a small place, the inn was well built and maintained.

Aemilia found us a bright and clean room, with whitewashed walls and a red-tiled floor. It boasted a single couch, a small table, and a bed, and smelled of sage. The mistress of the house brought us a roast chicken, root vegetables, and watered wine for dinner.

The world no longer spun when I moved my head, and it had been hours since I had last been sick. Even the pain in my head had mostly faded to a dull ache, something I was only aware of in the background. I even had an appetite and believed there was a reasonable chance that I would not put the food I ate onto the floor.

I sat opposite Aemilia on the couch as we dined, the food laid out on the table in front of us. The chicken disappeared quickly. When Aemilia caught me watching her, she grinned, and I glanced away reflexively. Then I forced my eyes back to her. She was beautiful, even with her mouth stuffed with chicken. As an eater, she seemed to concentrate more on efficiency than grace.

While I ate, I kept glancing at the single bed in the room's corner. Granted, it was not as narrow as the one in our room the previous night, but it was still only one bed and not all that wide. I wasn't sure how to broach the subject.

Aemilia caught my glance and smiled. "Oh, yes, the dilemma again."

"I can sleep on the floor. With blankets—"

"No! Not with that egg on your head. You'll sleep in that bed. You and the egg need a good night's sleep, or you will spill your lunch all day long tomorrow. We left the mosquitoes and frogs in the marshes, so you should be able to sleep tonight."

"Aemilia, I can't—"

"Medica's orders. End of discussion… husband."

The setting of the sun had pitched the room into darkness. Aemilia lit a candle and put me to bed. Then she rustled about the room, organizing our bags and boxes for the morning. After a few minutes, she blew out the candle, changed into her nightclothes, lifted the blanket and got into bed beside me, putting her head on my shoulder.

"Aemilia—"

She placed a finger against my lips. "Quiet and be still, or you will hurt your head. Medica's orders."

***

I awoke to Aemilia bustling about. She must have just risen as I could still feel her warmth against my side where she had been sleeping. She poured some water from the pitcher into a basin sitting on the small table. She was wearing loose nightclothes and turned her head to look back at me with a smile.

"This would be a lot easier if we *were* married. Please do me the honor of looking away for a few minutes."

I turned my head, realizing as I did that it no longer hurt. The bump on my head was still tender, but that was all.

"All right," she said after a minute or two. She came over to me, now wearing a floor-length tunic belted under her breasts, and a stola, a long, sleeveless garment signifying her status as a married woman. It was part of her costume. Over all of that, she put on a palla, a long, wide, and cloak-like coat for traveling. She was lovely. "Sit up. I need to change your bandage. How does your head feel?"

"Surprisingly good. The world has stopped spinning. My stomach isn't complaining, and my head is tender to the touch, but doesn't hurt."

She let out a long breath as she replaced the bandage. "Good. Head injuries can go either way. Either you wake up just fine or you don't wake up at all. I was so worried last night."

She suddenly sat on the bed beside me and hugged me tightly. When she pulled away, she had tears in her eyes. "Guess we should go."

We returned to the road and started north again. She still forbade me to walk, but she allowed me to speak. After some time, she looked back at me.

"Can I ask you something about your sister?"

"Sure," I answered, a little surprised.

"What happened to her foot?"

"She was born lame. It just doesn't work right."

"That must be really hard for her, but she always seems so happy."

I thought about it. "Yeah, she is. Most of the time."

"I don't think I could do that. I mean, having such a limitation would really change who you were."

"My mother always says that what matters isn't what the gods have granted you. What counts is what you do with what you're granted."

She was quiet for a minute. "Your mother is a wise woman."

"Yes, she is."

The road became steeper as it ascended the Alba Hills. The poor mule was having a hard time of it. Aemilia finally relented and let me walk—for the mule's sake.

Once past the hills, we entered the town of Aricia, which lay near the Lake of Nemi. Aricia was the first post station, sixteen miles south of Rome. Many wealthy patricians had country homes there that lined the hillsides. Several roads joined the Via Appia, and the traffic increased. We continued moving with the flow of the crowd, hemmed in on all sides by buildings and walls.

By midafternoon, it became obvious that we wouldn't be able to make it into inner Rome until well after midnight. We agreed to stop outside the city and time our entry for the next morning. Carts and wagons were only permitted on the streets of the main city after sunset, so we would need time to find a stable for the cart and mule and hire litter-bearers to carry our luggage. Most inns in the city didn't provide accommodations for carts or draft animals.

We looked for a place to spend the night, and fortunately, the choices this close to Rome were much improved. We found an agreeable room at an inn that also provided dinner. We would only have twelve miles to cover the next day before reaching Rome.

The room was small and clean, but it presented the nightly dilemma. Before I could even speak, Aemilia, who was already unpacking, said over her shoulder, "Same arrangement as last night. That means you have to slide into bed first so I can blow out the light and change clothes. You better start getting ready because I'm tired and want to go to bed." She looked back at me, daring me to argue. I was an eighteen-year-old boy, why would I argue with that?

***

I woke up to someone shaking my shoulder. Aemilia was up and already dressed. How had she done that? I hadn't heard her at all.

"Wake up, sleepyhead. The sun's coming up and we need to start moving before the road becomes too crowded."

In the morning light, we could easily see how close we were to Rome. The haze hovering over the city, the result of thousands of hearth fires and the dust of multitudes, was clearly visible in the distance.

We rejoined our role as flotsam in the river of people, wagons, carts, and draft animals of every sort making their way up the road. The city had spilled out of its walls years before and flooded into the surrounding valleys in all directions, even reaching across the Tiber River. The outskirts of Rome resembled one long village center with three and four-story buildings of all descriptions, the walls of which lined the road's edge. I was reminded of my previous trips to Rome I had taken with Father. I missed him so.

Aemilia and I led the mule. The traffic was becoming so intense that we had to sometimes stop and wait our turn to travel ahead. I couldn't imagine having to move in this crowd every day; the struggle to move forward was truly exhausting. We had both been to Rome before, so the sight wasn't exactly new to either of us. Still, the vision of the greatest city in the world remained awe-inspiring. The walls of the city proper stood ahead of us, but we could also see Rome majestically rising across its seven hills within the walls. With the boundaries of the Republic so very distant, the city had no defensive need for walls, but they were still there and gave Rome its definition. The gates now provided access control for policing and tax collection, for what would Rome be without taxes?

The engineers of old had made the walls from red and black tufa from Campania, tufa being a stone that is easily cut from the earth but which hardens when dried in the air. The walls were about thirty feet tall and wide enough for two armed men to pass each other with ease. These walls had been tall enough and wide enough to hold off Hannibal and his army three hundred years earlier during the second Punic War, the last time an enemy had truly tested the walls.

The stop and start of the traffic were caused by the Via Latina joining the Via Appia, which we were on. When we finally made our way through the chaos, we had a full view of the walls and the Capena Gate, where the Via Appia entered Rome. As I looked at the gate, I realized that the trip to Rome was supposed to have been the easy, safe part of my journey. The truly dangerous part would soon begin.

Aemilia must have had a similar thought. "We're almost here. My uncle was right. I was much safer traveling with you." She burst out laughing.

I had to laugh, too. I was alive because of her, and she knew it. "Aemilia, what are your plans here in Rome?"

"Well, first I have to find a place to stay. Then I'll visit the people on the list Publicius gave me. I'll see if any of them will take me on as an apprentice or can help me find someone who will. I've enough money to spend a month here. After that, if I have nothing, I'll have to return to my uncle's. How about you?"

"I have to find a place to stay, also. Then I will visit Quintus Fabius Sanga, the patron of my mother's family, and see if he will help us. At the same time, I'll make some inquiries into my father's death and see where those lead."

"Won't that be dangerous?"

"I won't use my actual name, and I'll try to hire people to ask questions, at least, as much as I can."

Aemilia came around the mule to walk beside me. "Vitruvius, hear me out. We are both safer when we're together. Living by myself here in Rome will be hard for me as a woman. And as for you, no one will look for a married man with his wife. In a different sort of way, my uncle was right. Both *you and I* will be safer if we continue the ruse of a married couple."

"Aemilia, staying with me would put you in far too much danger. You need to stay away from me. You could get hurt. These are powerful, dangerous people. Remember the riders at Lucus Feroniae."

"Vitruvius, we make an excellent team. Your mission is too hard for you to accomplish on your own. Besides, who's going to look after you when you do really stupid things like nearly freezing to death or having your head bashed in? Seriously, I can ask some of your questions. No one would suspect a woman."

I knew she was right. I also knew I wanted nothing to happen to her. Yet my desire for her safety was tempered by the fact that, deep down inside, I was terrified and didn't want to be alone or for her to leave.

"All right, but—"

She hugged me and laughed. "Vitruvius—"

"Wait. Let me finish. You have to agree that if I say our position is growing too dangerous, you'll leave. I don't want to have to deal with the pushy lady with the spoon."

"Whatever you say… dear."

I didn't think she had actually agreed to anything, in fact.

We walked on and when we finally entered the Capena Gate, Aemilia put her hand in mine. I felt the coolness of her grip, but also an underlying sensation I couldn't comprehend.

"We'll have to keep anyone from suspecting who we truly are. It will be essential that we act like a married couple in every way." She looked over at me and grinned.

My face flushed.

CHAPTER TEN

ROMA CAPUT MUNDI
Rome is the capital of the world.

We found a stable where we could house the cart and poor mule while we were in the city. When they asked how long, I had to tell them no longer than the end of the month. That was all the money I could afford. The stableyards also rented litters and bearers. Within minutes, they had transferred all our luggage to a litter and were waiting for us to lead the way.

Entering the city proper when the sun was low and casting long shadows resembled stepping into a man-made canyon. Buildings rose to seven stories along both sides of the street, allowing only narrow sidewalks, so people had to step in and out of the street to bypass the knots of others congregating in front of shops that lined the streets. Layer upon layer of sights and sounds met us as we walked with people speaking different languages, shopkeepers hawking goods, shoppers haggling over prices, throngs entering brightly colored buildings—some covered in graffiti. The litter-bearers followed us through the buzzing streets.

The buildings, the plazas, the streets of Rome were amazing. Shops of every kind and people of every description lined the road. But this part of the city had its dark side too. The hungry stood along the road begging for food, crippled veterans and bankrupt farmers among them. The hour was early enough that we still came across the occasional drunk passed out on the sidewalk from the last evenings revelry. The place smelled like the city of a half-million people that it was, too, with the mingled oder of animals, cooking, and refuse. The stench of urine used to whiten clothes in the *fullonica* we passed was overwhelming. Rome had everything. It was, after all, the center of the world.

"Where are we going?" Aemilia asked.

Her question startled me, both as an intrusion into my musings and for her use of "we." I again felt my face burn.

"I don't have the first idea where to find a room," she continued, unaware of my discomfiture.

"I'm thinking of a place, a nice place, on the Quirinal Hill where my father and I stayed. It is the only apartment I know of. It should do for… for us."

"Won't they recognize you there?"

I shrugged. "I don't think so. I've only been there a few times, and I always kept to myself. I spent my days making drawings of the great buildings. I doubt the owner or workers even noticed me."

We took close to an hour to trek through the warren of streets and alleys on our way to this four-story building that rented rooms and accommodations for guests for extended periods of time. As it came into view, I realized here was where my father had stayed the day they killed him. Grief warred with fond memories of being here with him. I remembered it as bright, clean, and well run, yet the building now bore the dark stain of my father's murder.

After stowing our bags around back in the receiving area, we entered the vestibulum.

"May I help you?" asked a young woman at the entrance.

I forced myself to gaze at her face. "Yes, we need rooms for one to three weeks."

"Follow me."

Aemilia and I followed the young woman through the vestibulum and out into an atrium, where we met an older woman I recognized as the mistress of the house.

"Yes?" she asked.

I hesitated and inhaled slowly. "My wife and I need rooms for a week, maybe as long as three weeks."

"Just the two of you?"

"Ah, yes."

"We are quite full at the moment. I have only one room left. It is on the second floor, in the back, but you can have it as long as you need. It is a nice room, plenty big enough for the two of you, and it is quiet."

I glanced over at Aemilia, and she gave me an almost imperceptible nod. That the room was in the back appealed to me. Rome had banned commercial traffic from the streets during the day, so delivery wagons and carts rumbled through the streets all night long. I never slept well in Rome.

"All right. We'll take it if the price is right."

The price, after perfunctory haggling, was a little higher than I would have preferred, but it was fair, so we took the room. The woman lifted a tablet off a peg set in the wall behind her and picked up a stylus. "Your name, sir?"

How stupid of me. I hadn't thought of a name to use, so I was obliged to invent one on the spot. "Aulus Marrius Scaevola." I had known a Aulus Marrius once. He was a tall, handsome, rugged boy with the sort of body I wished I had been born with. As I am left-handed, Scaevola, added some authenticity as a *cognomen*.

"Placida will show you to your room, Marrius."

Placida, the young woman we had met when we first entered, led us to the room while our bags and boxes were brought up from the receiving area. She deposited us in a light and airy corner room with windows on two sides. It was furnished with a table, two chairs, shelves, and a single bed, all of above average quality. I stared at the bed with some consternation and glanced over at Aemilia, who was also looking at the bed but with an enigmatic smile.

Before I had time to consider her expression, two young boys and a woman, whom I recognized from my previous visits, brought our bags and boxes into the room. The woman paused after delivering her load and studied me with her hands on her hips.

"Vitruvius, is it? I was sad to hear about your father." She looked about the room, taking in Aemilia. "I didn't think you were married."

"I'm sorry, but I believe you are mistaken. I don't know any Vitruvius."

She narrowed her eyes. "You look just like him."

"Well, I'm Aulus Marrius Scaevola, and this is my wife."

"Yes, we're from Brindisi and don't come to Rome very often," Aemilia said in a noticeable Brindisi accent.

"I apologize, but you look just like him," the woman said. She paused at the door, giving me a lingering gaze before leaving.

"What did that look mean?" Aemilia whispered after the woman's footsteps retreated down the hallway.

"I have no idea."

"Do you think she was convinced?"

"I don't know."

***

One reason my father stayed at this apartment was that the public baths were just down the street. They were open most of the day, from the bell around midday until an hour or so past sunset. After our time on the road, Aemilia and I gladly spent the afternoon in the baths to rid our bodies of the accumulated grime and physical insults. I practiced the normal rounds of the baths, starting in the steamy *caldarium*, moving to the warm *tepidarium*, and finishing with a plunge into the icy *frigidarium*. The baths lifted a weight from my shoulders and added a spring to my step. I recall thinking at the time, that were I ever wealthy, I would have a bath in my house and would never leave it.

I now felt better than I had in days. The walk back to the apartment in the crisp afternoon air helped clear my head, and the tasks ahead of me seemed somehow less daunting. When I entered our room, Aemilia was already there, slouching in a chair, drinking from a goblet of wine.

She looked totally relaxed. She smiled at me and handed me a second goblet.

"I bought some wine and food for dinner," she said. "Didn't expect you would remember. You don't often seem to think about mundane tasks like eating. Someone has to look after you."

She was right, I realized. "Yes, I tend to forget about eating until my stomach reminds me… or until you do."

I sat in the room's other chair, mimicking Aemilia's slouch, drinking the wine and eating from a plate filled with olives, grapes, nuts, and some sort of dried meat that tasted as though it had been pickled—and, of course, with no garum.

The wine warmed both of us. Our voices grew a little louder, and our smiles a little broader. Over the next hour, Aemilia explained to me the medical properties of baths, which I had learned, with little enthusiasm, from her uncle. Somehow, her passion and delight for the subject actually made it seem intriguing. In truth, though, I was only half listening. She could have been speaking a foreign tongue, and I would have been equally enthralled. I decided the feeling was only partially because of the wine. She certainly seemed to enjoy talking—something she did a lot of, especially when wine was involved—and I enjoyed watching her while she did. Her mood was contagious. I was completely relaxed and at ease.

"Vitruvius? Vitruvius, are you paying attention?"

Suddenly I realized she had asked me a question and I had no idea what she had said. "Sorry, I was mesmerized by your recitation," I said weakly.

She rolled her eyes. "I asked what your plans were for tomorrow."

"Oh, I will need to wake up early to see Quintus Fabius Sanga. Most senators meet clients in the morning, so I'll join the queue. And you?"

"I have the list of medici that Publicius gave me. I'll see as many of them as I can over the next few days, starting with the easiest tomorrow. I'm saving the Julii for last."

We continued to talk and drink wine until it was gone and the dark loomed about us. After a couple of tries with a flint, Aemilia lit a lamp, and the nightly dilemma returned.

"Aemilia, I can sleep on the floor—"

"No. I will not relegate you to the floor like some servant. We have managed so far to be in the same bed without incident. I see no reason to stop."

I was certainly not going to argue the point, but I had asked anyway, just for the sake of form. "Are you sure?"

"Yes. Everything will be fine. Trust me." She grinned. "But you'll need to slide into bed first so I can snuff out the lamp and change."

I did as I was told. The bed was as comfortable as mine at home, better perhaps. As I slid over to the far side to make space for her, I heard her moving about the room in the dark. Soon she lifted the covers and slid into bed beside me. She put her head on my shoulder and her hand on my chest. I reached my arm around her and froze. She was naked. She giggled as she reached back and put my arm around her, my hand on her breast.

"Aemilia—"

"Shh." She placed a finger across my lips. "I've decided an incident would be good for you," she whispered into my ear. "I assume you don't disagree?"

"No, not at all."

Then she moved up and kissed me passionately.

***

The light of dawn flooded in through the room's east-facing window; the curtains having done little to diminish it. I awoke to find Aemilia's legs wrapped around mine and her head on my shoulder. I feared moving lest I disturb the moment, so I stayed still a little longer, soaking in the memory of the previous night. Responsibility to my family eventually gnawed at me, and I gently tried extracting myself.

Aemilia awoke, blinked, licked her lips, and looked up at me. A moment of surprise passed over her face before she smiled in my direction. At first, the smile was small, but then it broadened into the smile I come to relish.

"I wish you could stay," she said. "I'm too comfortable."

"Aemilia, the wine—"

She put her finger on my lips again. "The decision was mine, not the wine's." She looked at me, concerned. "I hope you don't regret it."

I shook my head.

"Then I think we should try it again. It solves the single-bed dilemma."

"I, I would like that very much." My face grew hot again, but I cupped her chin in my hand and kissed her. "I am sorry, but I need to go now."

She stayed in bed, propped on one elbow, watching me as I collected my clothes from the floor and dressed. I kissed her again before I left.

I had never been to Quintus Fabius Sanga's house. My mother had given me directions of a sort, but navigating Rome is an art in itself. Nothing is marked. Unless you know exactly where you're going, arriving at the correct place is like playing the kid's game of twenty questions, with each answer guiding you a little closer. But the game takes some time to play. By the time I found the house Sanga used while in Rome, it was late morning.

The house was sizable but not ostentatious. It had a certain grace and symmetry not usually found in the homes of the rich. Beauty in most things, but especially in buildings, is produced by the pleasing appearance and good taste of the whole and by the dimensions of all the parts being duly proportioned to each other. This house was beautiful. It struck me as the home of someone who was comfortable with his wealth and reputation, with no need to impress anyone with either. The house and the man who owns it are inextricably intertwined. One always explains the other.

But both house and man have a public and a private side. Like Sanga's illustrious ancestor, Quintus Fabius Maximus Verrucosus, who defeated Hannibal by not fighting him, Quintus Fabius Sanga was known for his caution, composure, and soft-spokenness. He was wealthy from his business deals in Gaul, but he was a good man, and this was a good house.

The surprise for me was that I encountered no long queue of clients about. I feared I might be too late to call on him. I approached a male servant standing by the house's *ostium*. I suspected his severe expression was cultivated to discourage the uninvited, like me.

"I would like to see the master, Quintus Fabius Sanga, at his convenience. I have a letter of introduction."

The servant's expression softened when I mentioned a letter of introduction. "I am sorry, sir. The master is out of town today and is not due back for a while. He will receive visitors in ten days, the 8th day before the *Kalends* of December."

I was sure my disappointment showed. I never even considered the possibility that he might not actually be home. I guessed I should have been happy that he would see people in just ten days. It could have been months.

The servant continued, "Even then, he may not see you. He has many clients. Perhaps, if you leave your introduction, I can make sure he receives it as soon as he gets returns."

I was hesitant to part with the scroll that mother had given me, but this servant was the gatekeeper, and I shouldn't make him an enemy.

"Certainly. I look forward to seeing you in ten days," I replied.

He took the scroll and nodded.

Now what to do? I had planned to deal with the family money problems before investigating my father's death, but I suddenly had ten free days. This seemed a good time to begin my inquiries. But where to start? I knew only three facts about father's death: he had met with Annius, he had been carrying a message, and he had died at the Latiaris stairs.

***

The Latiaris stairs were exactly as I remembered them, eighty-six flat stone steps about a span wide, cut through the hillside. Even at this time of day, they weren't crowded. People trudged up them and scurred down. Most people respected the custom of keeping to the right, but a few didn't, largely because of inattention, I suppose, rather than ill manners.

I went up the stairs. As I did, I became more convinced that even if you weren't paying attention, you wouldn't likely misstep. The stairs were even, solid, and well-spaced. The rule of thumb was that the height of a step was half its width. These stairs were almost perfect.

At the top, the path passed between two buildings. Just beyond the stairs, a small alcove led to a recessed door in the building on the right. I wandered into the alcove and stood back in its shadows. This seemed the ideal place for an assailant to hide.

I tested my theory by waiting for someone going towards the stairs to pass by, someone about the same height and build as my father, then I strode out right behind him. I was behind him for two steps before we started down the stairs, plenty of time to strike him from behind with a hammer. The perfect ambush spot.

People rushed by as I walked slowly down the stairs. I imagined my father falling and tumbling down to the bottom. I scrutinized each step as I descended. Nothing here could have caused such an injury as I found on the back of his head.

Across from the bottom were two businesses: a small inn and a *popinae,* which sold cooked fish. The popinae had a small counter with stools, and I took a seat and ordered a grilled fish.

I sat at the counter and began to practice Syphāx's trick. "What's the news?" I asked the man working the counter when he served me my fish. "Just arrived in town. What's happening?"

"Same old stuff, I guess. Grain prices are going up. People are unhappy about that and I hear news of a fire last night near the Field of Mars. Didn't say what was lost. I also heard something about the Senate declaring Catiline and Manlius *hostes,* public enemies, for some plot or something."

I immediately wondered if this was the plot to which the cipher referred. "Was that about Praeneste?"

"Don't know. Didn't hear what it was all about." He brought me some wine.

"How long have you had this shop?"

"Oh, I only work here. Shop's been here for, let's see, nine years this coming summer."

"Guess you stay busy, being at the bottom of the stairs. Seems to get a lot of traffic," I said between bits of fish.

"Yeah, lots of people pass by."

"Those stairs look steep. Anybody ever fall down them?"

"Those? No. Not since I've been working here these last three years. But you know…" He hesitated in thought. "I did hear a story about a fellow who fell down them a month back. I wasn't working that day. He's the only one I ever heard of—I mean more than a stumble. Don't see how he could have. I've seen old ladies go up and down. Must have had his eyes closed." He chuckled and headed back to his fire.

Anger rose inside of me. If I needed any more proof, this was it. My father's death hadn't been an accident. He had not stumbled and fallen. Now what? The last fact I had to go on was that he had been performing a service for Annius. I needed to find out more about Quintus Annius Chilo and the people who worked for him.

I wandered through the streets until mid-afternoon, my mind working over all the potential next steps. Sadly, none of them seemed good options. Aemilia might be back, so I threaded my way through the busy streets and alleys to our room.

I couldn't shake the ill feeling I had every time I glimpsed the apartment building where we were staying. The dark stain was ever present. I opened the door to our room and froze. Aemilia was in the middle of the floor on her knees, picking up her clothes and belongings and repacking them, her face streaked with tears. The room had been ransacked and all our possessions lay scattered across the floor. Even the bed had been flipped over.

My heart raced. "Aemilia! Are you all right?" I knelt beside her, grabbed her, and looked for injuries.

"Thank the gods! I didn't know what happened to you." Without another word, she threw her arms around me and buried her face in my chest. I held her there. After a short time, she pushed back and looked up at me. "I'm… I'm fine." She wiped her face with both hands. "I wasn't here. I returned only a moment ago and discovered this." She gestured around. "I was so worried about you." She hugged me again. "Who would do such a thing? Why?"

"Thieves, I suppose. What did they take? Do you know?"

"Nothing. That's just it. Nothing is missing. I even had some jewelry, and they just scattered it on the floor. As far as I can tell, they didn't take a thing." Her jaw muscles clenched, and she brandished her wooden spoon. "Argh! If I ever find out who did this, I'll, I'll…"

An icy chill ran down my back, and I shuddered. "They were looking for something. I expect the same people who were watching my house have found me here. That woman must have recognized me and told someone."

CHAPTER ELEVEN

QUIS CUSTODIET IPSOS CUSTODES
Who watches the watchers?

We cleaned the room, putting all our clothes and personal items back in their bags. Aemilia repacked her bottles and jars into her boxes. At least the interlopers hadn't emptied any of them, though one was cracked, labeled *lunar caustic*. Aemilia wrapped it in a small cloth before putting it back into the box. When we were done, we sat on the bed. Neither of us was missing anything.

"Aemilia, if this wasn't the work of thieves, and I don't believe it was, then it must be the people who were following me in Fundi."

She sniffled. "What do you think they were looking for?"

"As I see it, I can imagine three possibilities. First, maybe they just wanted to scare us. But I don't think so. They could find more direct ways to intimidate us."

Aemilia nodded.

"Second, perhaps they aren't sure who I am and were looking for some identifying item. If so, they were disappointed. I had nothing here that could have identified me in the items they searched. I had the documents case with me when I went to Quintus Fabius Sanga's house. How about you? Did you have anything that would identify me? Or even you?"

She sniffled again, sighed, and bowed her head. "No. I'm wearing the pendant, and like you, my documents were with me," she said in such a quiet voice that I wasn't sure I'd heard her. "Not that they did any good."

"All right, then they didn't find any identifying information.

"The third possibility is that they know who I am, or at least suspect who I am, and were searching for something specific, something that wouldn't fit in any of your bottles or jars. They might want the message my father was carrying, but I destroyed that before I left. Either way, they'll be back, maybe to confirm who I am or maybe to find what they're looking for."

I paused and looked over at her to make sure she understood what I was saying. "Aemilia, you're not safe being with me." My gut tightened, and I struggled to continue. "You need to leave, now, and find someplace safe."

She jerked her head around to face me. "What? Wait. No! I can't go!"

"Staying with me isn't healthy. These people are dangerous. They're killers. You need to go. Aemilia, I can't let them hurt you."

"No. No. It's not safe for me to leave, either."

"Aemi—"

"Listen to me, Vitruvius. I'm already associated with you. They're not going to just let me walk away. They'll want to learn what I know."

"We could... we could work out a way to slip you out while they keep their eyes on me."

"No!" Tears welled up in her eyes, and she turned her head away. "No," she then repeated in a quiet voice. "I can't leave. I have nowhere to go. No one to go to. My family is gone. They're dead. Epiphanes is getting old. He won't be around much longer." She turned to face me. "I'm twenty years old. I'm not married, and I don't have a family or a dowry. None of the medici I met with would even give me a chance. They wouldn't hire me as an apprentice. They are all *so* worried about the proper character of a woman my age who doesn't have a family or a husband, and they don't want to be legally responsible for me."

She buried her face in my shoulder and cried. Her body shuddered as she sobbed, and I didn't know what to say, so I just held her. After a few minutes, she stopped crying. My tunic was wet from her tears. In a faltering voice, she said, "No one wants me. You are all I have left. Please don't make me leave."

She had lost her family and now, perhaps, her dreams. I couldn't turn her away. It would be too cruel—and by the gods, I did so want her close to me. "If you are going to stay with me, then we need a strategy."

She sucked in a ragged breath and turned her face up to mine. Her cheeks were wet. She smiled and kissed me tenderly on the lips. She tasted of salt.

We spent the rest of the evening making plans for the next few days. Aemilia was both clever and imaginative, and we made a good team. I wasn't sure I could have made her leave, anyway. I needed her as much as she needed me.

The hour was late when we finally went to bed, but this time she sprang no surprises. Aemilia undressed before she snuffed out the lamp.

***

Roman society operates under a highly stratified social order. One's social position defines the careers open to you, your protection under the law, what you can vote on, and even the clothes you may wear—certainly the clothes you can afford to wear. Everyone in Roman society understands and expects the maintenance of the strict social order. The pursuit of status, making it up to the next level, is the single, all-consuming Roman ambition.

Like the majority of Roman citizens, Aemilia and I were plebeians. We behaved and dressed like plebs. Anyone searching for us would expect to see a pleb matching our physical description. But I still had Hanno's clothes with me, and he was a slave at the very bottom of the Roman order. Everyone who saw him would see a slave and treat him as such, even if they had never met him, simply because of the clothes he wore. In everyday life, slaves were invisible to plebs like us—or anyone of a higher order.

The plan Aemilia and I developed depended on first finding out who, if anyone, was watching us. To do this, I would dress in Hanno's clothes, become invisible, and leave the apartment. Once I made sure I, or rather, Hanno, wasn't followed, Aemilia would walk through town while I kept pace with her and tried to identify anyone following her. Once we did that, we would change places, with Aemilia dressing down and me walking through the city.

"You ready?" I asked Aemilia, and she nodded. I pulled my hood down, covering my head and masking my face.

As I was now a slave in everyone's eyes, Aemilia led me down the hall to the stairs, as an unknown, unaccompanied servant in the apartments would raise questions. We made it to the building's rear door and paused. Two of the house's slaves were stacking stinking baskets of kitchen scraps by the door. Likely, the apartment owners sold the gallery scraps to nearby pig farmers.

"Yes, mistress, I will do that," I said to Aemilia.

She looked at me with puzzlement in her eyes and then understanding. "See that you do, and no malingering, you understand? I need you back by early afternoon."

She continued to give me directions until the two slaves had finished stacking their baskets and moved back down the hall toward the kitchens.

Aemilia glanced around, quickly grabbed my face and kissed me. "Be careful."

"You, too." On a whim, I picked up one of the reeking baskets and went out the rear door. The back alley was already busy by that time of the morning. People were everywhere, but nobody paid me any mind. Most gave the foul-smelling basket a wide berth.

I made my way down the alley and through the warren of connecting streets. As I walked down a deserted little path, I set the basket in a doorway and hurried on. The smell was about to make me sick. I'm sure it would surprise someone when they opened their door. After about twenty paces, I paused and headed back the way I had come. The path was still empty. No one had followed me.

When I arrived at the U-shaped alley that Aemilia and I had agreed upon, I settled into the shadows of a slender niche formed by two buildings that didn't quite meet. I had discovered the narrow alley accidentally the day before while searching for a shortcut on the way back from Sanga's house. No one would enter the alley unless they were going to a building somewhere down it. Anyone tailing Aemilia should be obvious.

***

Tucked into the narrow crevice between buildings, with only my thoughts and the smell of stale urine to keep me company, I began to have misgivings about this entire enterprise. It put Aemilia at too much risk. She was alone in the streets, and Rome is a rough place for the unwary, even when not being stalked by assassins. I wondered if I should go back and check on her.

Footsteps. Someone had entered the alley. A moment later Aemilia passed by, heading along the alley to the bottom corner of the "*U*." As soon as she turned left, I heard other footsteps, and two people passed me, a wisp of a young girl, who looked vaguely familiar, and a hard looking bald man with a scar across his right cheek. They hurried through the empty alley and slowed at the end to peer around the corner where Aemilia had disappeared.

I had told Aemilia to walk halfway along the next alley, the bottom of the "*U*," pause as if lost, as I had done yesterday, and then walk back the way she had come. I watched the young girl and the man with the scar stop and scurry back towards me. The man stopped and appeared to pay great attention to the roofline of the adjacent building, and the young girl knelt to adjust her sandals. Both kept their faces turned away from the alley. Aemilia came around the corner and passed between them, paying them no attention, and then she headed out into the main street. The two waited only a moment before following her. I stepped out of the shadows and strode after them, following the followers.

Aemilia chose a meandering route through the streets of the Quirinal Hill. The two took every turn she did, maintaining their distance. That they would use a girl to follow Aemilia hadn't occurred to me, but their doing so made perfect sense. She could follow Aemilia into places the man could not, such as the baths.

When Aemilia and I had planned this, I had assumed that people concentrating on following someone wouldn't spare the time to see if they were being followed. Neither of the two had yet glanced back. Then I realized, with a start, that neither had I, so I looked back every time we paused.

More and more people joined the throng moving along the street and sidewalks. Keeping track of the two became harder and harder for me. Aemilia's two watchers had the same problem and had to speed up to reduce the distance between them and her. When they made a turn at an intersection, I sped up to close the distance to them, but a man in front of me dropped a sack of figs, and everyone stopped or moved into the street to avoid the mess on the sidewalk. By the time I made the turn, I couldn't see the two followers.

Panic gripped me, and I stepped out into the street and ran about half a block. In my haste, I almost knocked down two women, and they yelled at me to watch where I was going. I stepped back onto the sidewalk and searched for the followers. Rising on my tiptoes, I peered over the heads of the people in front of me, but I still couldn't see them. I was about to make another dash into the street when I realized that the young girl was right in front of me. I was almost touching her. I slowed down and took a deep breath.

As Aemilia continued her walk, she stopped at a few shops along the way and bought various things, as a woman out in Rome would do. The wispy girl and the scar-faced man stopped and gazed into shops every time she did, but I caught them throwing side glances at the store Aemilia had entered. Two of her stops served our long-term plans: the Inn I had found yesterday, the one by the popinae that sold cooked fish at the bottom of the Latiaris stairs, and a nearby transportation vendor that rented litters for freight and palanquins for women.

Just before noon, Aemilia made her way back to our apartment. When she entered the front door, the wispy girl and the man with the scar moved to opposite ends of the block and merged with the crowds of pedestrians on the sidewalks. I walked around to the back door, where Aemilia was waiting to escort a slave up to our room.

"Well?" she asked quietly once we were inside.

I told her about the two who had been following her.

She nodded. "I thought I saw the man with the scar twice." She let out a long breath. "Your turn," she continued.

We both changed, me into my normal pleb clothes and her into a slave woman's rough work tunic that she had just purchased at a shop while walking through town. I realized with a start that one benefit of our new sleeping arrangement was that neither of us was troubled by changing clothes in the presence of the other. When Aemilia caught my glance while changing, she simply smiled.

I escorted her down the hall and to the back door. "Be careful," I told her, and she nodded.

After opening the door a crack and glancing around, she stepped out.

I counted to one hundred to give her time to move into place, and then I strode out into the street through the front entrance and started my walk through town. The route I followed was different than the one Aemilia had taken, but it accomplished the same goal. I went down some empty alleys and backtracked twice. The entire process lasted about two hours. When I re-entered the apartment, I went to the rear door and waited for Aemilia, who arrived soon after.

"How did it go?" I asked once we were back in the room.

She smiled, the one I so loved to see. "Found them. Different people are following you, two of the foulest-looking men I have ever seen. One has a flat, pockmarked face, and the other is tall and rat-faced, with a badly broken nose. They will be hard to miss."

"Yea, I saw the rat-faced one."

***

We rushed to eat and catch a brief nap. Tonight, I would watch the watchers. The idea was simple. We knew who was watching us, but we didn't know who they worked for. That the watchers we had identified would be outside all night was unlikely. Someone might monitor us all night, but not be the same ones. Where did the watchers go when they weren't watching?

I changed back into Hanno's clothes. The slave was going out to watch the watchers. I placed my own clothes in a bag, which I slung over my shoulder. I would follow the two watchers who had been following Aemilia. They were less likely to be on the lookout for me when they were waiting for her.

Aemilia escorted me downstairs to the back door. Fortunately, no awful-smelling kitchen scraps were here for me to take out. I wasn't eager to do that again. She grabbed me in a quick hug. "Please be careful," she said.

"I will. I'll be back before dawn." I passed through the back door and carefully made my way around the building, where I remained in the shadows, keeping my eye on both of Aemilia's followers, who were just visible at opposite ends of the block.

I slowly scanned the street in the faint moonlight, watching both watchers. Just after sunset, movement caught my eye. The unmistakable rat-faced man Aemilia had described stepped out of the shadows only twenty paces up the street from me. I inhaled and backed up, pressing myself hard against the wall, as deep into the darkness as I could. Ratface paused, said something that I couldn't make out, and walked down the street—right past me. I decided to follow him instead of either of the two who were following Aemilia.

He was almost a block away from me before I started after him, and as I followed him, I tried to skitter from shadow to shadow and keep checking behind me. Evidently, Ratface wasn't worried about being followed. He never looked back. He walked down major streets with no apparent care and made his way to the warehouse district along the

Tiber docks. Once there, he stepped up to the front of a warehouse and then thumped loudly on the door. Someone on the inside opened it. As the warehouse's light flooded the street, I heard voices greeting Ratface.

I pulled back into the shadows of a broken building just up the street from the warehouse and settled in to see if he ever came out. As the night wore on, the cold deepened, and Hanno's tunic proved not terribly warm. Men working around the docks and warehouses lit braziers, but I dared not move into their light, so I stayed in the shadows and listened to my teeth chatter.

After what seemed like two hours, three figures approached the warehouse and banged on the door. When it opened, the light illuminated the young girl who had followed Aemilia earlier in the day. I thought that one of the men was the man with the scar, Scarface. The third was probably the other man who had followed me, Pockface. I had found their nest!

That was enough work for one night. While still in the shadows, I changed into my own clothes, and then I stole back to the apartment. I greeted the startled night watchman at the entrance and headed up to our room.

"Aemilia, it's me," I whispered as I opened the door. The room was dark, and for a moment, I thought she must be asleep. Then she collided with me and threw her arms around me.

"You're safe. Thank the gods. Did you learn anything?"

I recounted my evening while I undressed and slipped into bed. She slid in next to me and put her head on my shoulder. We were both so fatigued that we fell asleep almost at once.

***

We spent the next day doing much the same as we had the previous day. Aemilia stayed in the room while I kept an eye on all the watchers hiding in the streets around the apartment. My intention was to use one more day to ensure that we found them all. Once we did, we could start the second part of the plan, the disappearing act.

By mid-afternoon, I was exhausted. How much work is needed to do nothing but stand in the shadows and observe is surprising. The watchers had revealed nothing new, so I headed back to the apartment. As I stepped into the alley behind our building, I recognized the wispy young girl standing by the back door. I darted into a nearby doorway to hide and cautiously peered around the corner, keeping an eye on the girl.

After a few minutes, the woman who worked in the apartment, the one who had recognized me, stepped out of the building and hugged the young girl. Now that I had seen them together, I noticed a strong family resemblance. They must have been mother and daughter. They talked in quiet voices I couldn't hear, and after a few minutes, the young girl left, winding down the alley, away from me, and the woman went back inside.

I waited until the young girl was out of sight before I made my way to the back door and entered. The hall was eerily quiet and empty. The only noise was my pulse pounding in my temple.

"What's wrong?" Aemilia asked when I entered our room. I guess my face must have shown my worry.

"We have a bigger problem than I thought." I told her all about the young girl and her mother.

"So, she recognized you, and she's working with them."

"Yes, it would seem so."

"She was probably the one who ransacked our room. But why all the following and hiding, if they know who you are? What are they after?"

"I have no idea." I sat on the bed. A wave of exhaustion broke over me, and I tried to smother a yawn.

"Why don't you lie down and rest. I'll pick up something for us to eat from that little popinae down the street. We can work it out over dinner."

I was too exhausted to think clearly. "Yes. You're right. A brief rest would do me good," I said as I lay down.

Aemilia bent over and kissed my cheek. "Back before you know it."

Though exhausted, my sleep was deeply disturbing. In my dream, I saw my father's ghost passing through building after building. He was looking for his killer. I chased after him, but I couldn't help him. I didn't know what they looked like. I wanted to help, but couldn't.

I awoke feeling stiff and sore, the way you sometimes do if you've slept in a bad position for too long. The room was dark. It was well after nightfall.

"Aemilia?" Silence. "Aemilia?" I said more urgently, but again I was answered only by silence. "Aemilia!" I lurched up and lit the little lamp on the table. She wasn't there. I didn't see any sign of the food she had gone to buy, either. The room was exactly the same as it had been when I had returned—except Aemilia was missing.

CHAPTER TWELVE

US NON UNI FIDIT ANTRO
A mouse does not rely on just one hole.

The lamp on the table cast an uncertain light over the room, leaving the corners vague and untouched. From the dark outside, I heard the patter of a delicate, persistent rain. Unable to stand, I sat in one of the room's chairs, elbows on knees, head in hands. A hollowness deep inside clutched my chest, making breathing hard. Though I was overwhelmed by a profound sadness, tears wouldn't come. I was stunned. How could I have been so stupid as to let her go out after all we had learned? What should I do? With a start, I realized I didn't even know if she was still alive.

I don't deal well with chaos and disorder. I accept change and am able to react quickly to the unexpected. But this was different. This kidnapping of Aemilia was messy, like scrolls placed carelessly in a library, unsorted, haphazard. I saw no purpose behind this, nothing in its proper place.

Slowly, very slowly, fear replaced my sense of shock. I feared not for my own life but for my future—for Aemilia. I suddenly grasped that what I feared for was *our* future—hers, mine, ours. This feeling was completely foreign to me and altogether unexpected.

As the minutes passed, the steady hum of the rain droned in my ears. An unfamiliar sensation came over me, a fear that my fear was paralyzing me. I had to move. I needed to do something. I must make this right. Only… I had no idea how or even where to start. That realization threatened to replace my fear with despair.

And I knew despair. Anyone who is a farmer and depends on the weather for survival is familiar with despair. My father and I had spoken of it often. He would tell me we do not control as much as we think we do about the world or our lives and we shouldn't dwell on those things we cannot change. Rather, we can recover from calamity and disaster by focusing on what was in our power to alter and then pursue that with relentless energy.

I couldn't control the fact that Aemilia was missing, and I refused to accept that she might be dead. The Stoics hold that if we embrace the wrong understanding of the world, we will behave as if the world differs from what it actually is, and that is a recipe for failure. Aemilia was missing. That was the world as it was.

The Stoics also maintain that sound reasoning protects us from doing nonsensical things. I knew where Aemilia had been going and where my enemies were, so I knew where to look. What I discovered would further refine that search. But how to search? Should Aulus Marrius Scaevola search for his missing wife, as would be normal and expected, or should invisible Hanno search from the shadows?

***

I decided Aulus Marrius Scaevola would search for his wife. But Aulus Marrius Scaevola was no fool. He knew they would watch him and follow him. So, along with my cloak, I took one of Aemilia's dark gray blankets and put it in a bag. What else would I need? A weapon. I searched through my luggage, retrieving my father's pugio, and strapped it on.

I threw the bag over my back and made my way down the dark hallway and stairs, as much from memory as by feel. At the bottom, light cast by torches spilled out from the vestibulum. The night watchman was standing in the door, watching the rain and speaking quietly to a woman. He heard me approach and turned around.

"Good evening," I said.

"Good evening, sir. Master Marrius, is it? Late for going out."

"Yes, Aulus Marrius Scaevola. It is late, but I need to visit a friend who is not well."

"I hope it's not far, sir. Rain's not bad, but it'll still right soak you."

I recognized the woman as the one who greeted people at the door during the day. Placida, I remembered her name to be.

"I'm sorry, Placida, but do you remember when it was that my wife left this evening?"

She looked at me with a quizzical expression. "She didn't come by me this evening, sir. But I was not always at the door. Might have been when I wasn't here, but that would be more like late afternoon."

"Yes, that must have been it," I said. Either she was lying or Aemilia had left by the back door, which was unlikely. We had decided to use the back door only when we dressed down to keep the watchers' attention on the front door.

I shrugged into my cloak, pulled the hood over my head, and stepped out into the light rain. I headed for the U-shaped alley I had used to identify the people following Aemilia. I made sure I was visible, staying as much as possible in the light cast from the torches and braziers used by businesses along the street and moved at a leisurely enough pace for anyone following to become comfortable and relaxed. As I turned into the U-shaped alley, I darted to the slender niche I had hidden in previously, and squeezed myself back into the shadows, and waited.

After a moment, footsteps entered the alley. They stopped for an instant and then resumed at a quicker pace. From my hiding place, I saw the vague shape of someone run past and heard the footsteps go to the end of the corner and then fade away.

Moving quickly and quietly, I left my niche and returned to the main street. I ran to the next alley and turned into it. Then I made a series of switches darting up one alley and down another, putting distance between me and where I had last seen the follower.

After about eight turns, I slowed down, collected my bearings, and headed to the docks. I stayed mostly on the major roads where the constant stream of commercial traffic, the wagons, carts, and litters, all resupplying shops, provided cover and safety. In the rain, most wore cloaks and hoods. No one could have recognized me from a distance.

One thing that I had learned over the last few days was not to make any assumptions. I knew I had lost the one follower, but I didn't know if another was behind me. They seemed to work in pairs. When I came to the next small, dark, side alley, I turned into it and then ran about twenty paces to a doorway with an overhang. Stopping, I pulled out the dark gray blanket, sat in the doorway, and completely covered myself, drawing up my legs to make myself as small as possible. At night, in the rain and the smoky haze of Rome, this alley was blacker than soot. I would appear to be only a slightly darker shadow among other dark shadows. The blanket smelled of wet wool, masking the rotten food stench of the very narrow alley.

I was surprised when I heard footsteps enter the alley, made louder by splashing in the little pools of water in the alley. The feet stepped cautiously down the narrow street, passing by at what must have been only an arm's length away, and then they sped up to the next intersection. They stopped there, and after a moment faded down another alley.

I waited only a moment before jumping up and dashing back the way I had come, stuffing the blanket back into the bag as I ran. From there, I backtracked along the main street for a few blocks. Then I took another ally in the opposite direction.

After a few more turns, I arrived at the warehouse district by the docks and merged into the shadows of the loading cranes that stood like silent leviathans on the waterfront. The night was far too dark to unload boats. The workers would wait until dawn before they returned. I was completely soaked and shivering from the cold, and the dark meant that I couldn't see more than a stride in front of me.

Without warning, I tripped, falling face down on the stone quay. My hands and arms took most of the force, and I skinned my elbows. I had tripped over a line running to a crane. Someone, some idiot, had left the crane in a precarious state. Its lines were still spread out. Wooden spokes and other parts were scattered all about. The wayward line might have killed me if I had been running.

With considerably more caution, I edged along the loading equipment until I came upon the nest I had discovered the night before. The warehouse was quiet, but I could clearly see a figure with a cudgel standing by the door, a night guard. Getting inside to find Aemilia would not be easy.

***

I had studied buildings and I knew them. The warehouse was a common two-story design. I expected they would store most items on the ground floor. A gallery or loft would run around the walls of the upper story, and the middle would be open with a hoist attached to the ceiling. If this was a typical warehouse, a short beam would also extend straight out from the roof with a pulley attached. Workers would use it to transfer cargo directly from a wagon at the side of the warehouse into the loft.

Ghosting through shadows, I felt my way further down the quay and then across the street and around to the side of the warehouse. Yes! I could see a pulley and the loft door was open. The trouble was in climbing up. I wasn't overly athletic, and as the tightness in my stomach indicated, I had a great fear of heights.

A long rope was looped through the pulley with both ends coiled on the ground. I held one side of the rope in my hand. Would it make a noise? Grimacing, I gave it a tentative pull and heard only silence. The pulley was greased and quiet. I relaxed and continued pulling until just a short amount of rope from one side of the pulley remained on the ground. Taking up the long side of the line, I tied knots in the rope, spaced about a foot and a half apart, twenty knots total. Next, I pulled on the short side of the cord until the first knot jammed into the pulley.

Then I tied off the rope. Now I had a knotted rope from the ground to the pulley that I could climb.

I put the bag over my shoulders and started up. Climbing was challenging. Thank the gods no one was watching. I would have died of shame, if nothing else. The rain made the climb particularly precarious. The rope was slick, and keeping my feet on the knots was difficult. I was only a span off the ground when my feet slipped, and I was left dangling from a slippery grip. I scrambled to put my feet back on a knot, but slipped again. After a sickening moment, I finally secured myself, and continued the climb.

I was two knots short of the top when my feet slipped again and my hands slid down to the knot below, rubbing them raw. This time, I was hanging in midair. The rope had canted out away from the pulley at a steep angle, because of the way I was gripping the line, and I needed several tries before I could wrap my legs back around it and get my feet on a knot.

On reaching the top, panic gripped me. I now had to transfer from the rope to the loft. Though this was not a great distance, my fear of heights wouldn't allow me to let go. I was paralyzed. Then, too, the rain had intensified and was no longer gentle. It stung my face, making focusing difficult.

A flash of lightening tore across the sky, followed by the deafening rumble of thunder. Lightening was uncommon this late in the year, I concluded that Jupiter must have been furious with someone. I could only hope that person wasn't me. Just my luck, the weapon of the heavens would strike me, and I would die there, hanging onto that stupid rope. The thought of my having made my way so close to Aemilia and failing because of my idiotic fear of heights was so pathetic that I forced myself to move. I reached up, stretched, and grabbed the top of the beam with first one hand, then the other. Hand over hand, I made my way the short distance to the loft door.

Inside, sacks of wheat stacked two high filled the loft, presumably arranged that way to allow any moisture to dry out. I couldn't see a place to hide anyone up there. Aemilia had to be on the ground floor.

The drumming of the rain on the roof was almost deafening. Even with the rain, wheat dust drifted through the air and I had to pinch my nose to keep from sneezing.

When I moved to the edge of the loft, the floorboards squeaked loudly. I panicked. If anyone had heard, I was a dead man. I waited, frozen, but nothing happened. I slowly let out the breath I had been holding. The sound of the rain must have masked my noise.

I slid the final distance to the edge of the loft on my stomach and cautiously looked over. I could see the entire floor below, which was brightly lit by torches and a brazier. Chairs and a table covered with food scraps were scattered about and tools lay on the floor, including a hammer. Was it possible that my father's killer had been the one who had taken Aemilia?

In the middle of the room, a naked man sat tied to a chair. His head hung forward and his face was bloody and swollen. What a sad, awful sight. In front of him stood a large man I hadn't seen before. His hands were balled into bloody fists. Standing, just off to the side, was Quintus Annius Chilo, whom I recognized from my mother's description. The scar leading from the corner of his mouth was hard to miss.

Panic gripped me looking at the brutal scene. Aemilia! But she was nowhere to be seen. I could view the complete ground floor. Two men sat in the chairs facing the bloody man, one of whom was Ratface. I didn't recognize the other. The wispy girl stood talking to Ratface. But Aemilia was not in sight.

I sat back on my haunches, both deflated and relieved. I'd been certain she would be there. She *had* to be there. All my plans counted on her being there, but thank the gods she was not. Now what? Unless I came up with a better idea, I would have to follow the followers until they led me to her. Time for an alternative plan.

I returned to the loft door, but I paused. I didn't know how to crawl back to the knotted rope. I had not considered that part of the plan. If I thought about it too much, I knew fear would overtake me and make doing anything impossible. I clenched my jaw, held my breath, and launched out and onto the beam.

Moving hand over hand, I made it back to the pulley, where I quickly wrapped my legs around the rope and put my feet on top of a knot. I paused and took two deep breaths, and then released the beam and grabbed the rope. My hands found purchase, but slid painfully down to jam into the next knot. My feet dangled for a moment. I then somehow managed to put my feet back on the rope, after which my climb down was tedious and painful. My arms were shaking from weakness, and the wet rope stung my raw hands. I made my way about halfway down when the strength in my hands gave out, my feet slipped, and I fell, landing very hard with a thud on the paving stones, the pugio clattering out of its sheath.

For a moment, I just lay on the ground in the rain, stunned. I had landed awkwardly on my right leg, and the pain in my knee felt as though someone had stuck a knife in it. Just as I sat up to take stock, another lightening flash illuminated the sky, and I saw that the guard with the cudgel had come around the side of the building and was staring straight at me. I struggled to my feet, grabbed my pugio, and ran.

"You! You there, stop! Stop now!"

I ran with a limp. A sharp pain shot out in my right knee each time my leg came down in a step. I headed back to the quay and into the darkness of the cranes. The footfalls behind me were loud and getting closer.

"Stop! Somebody stop him!"

Finally reaching the shadows, I turned and ran into the darker black. My pursuer was not far behind and gaining. The rope! The one I had tripped over must be just ahead. There it was. I slowed to hop over it and then dashed around the crane, where I picked up one of the long wooden spokes I had noticed earlier. I waited for the guard.

Just a moment later, the guard ran by, and *twang*, I heard him hit the rope. Then he fell face down on the paving stones with a loud, wet thud. I stepped out from behind the crane, ready to strike him, but he wasn't moving. Dropping the spoke, I left as fast as I could, bad knee and all.

Shouts erupted from all across the docks. I'd stirred up the nest.

***

The rain continued, not heavily, but steadily as I limped back. The light rain couldn't make me any wetter than I already was. I was soaked to the bone, and I was freezing, teeth now chattering uncontrollably. The last time I had been wet and freezing, it hadn't gone so well. But for Aemilia, I would have been in bed for a week. Aemilia, I had to find her. I couldn't imagine what I would do without her and I was terrified for her.

The sky wasn't visible, but I thought the time was still a few hours before dawn, and I couldn't do anything until then. Finding Aemilia would be impossible if I had to keep looking over my shoulder. I had to become invisible and slip away.

I made my way back to the dark alley where I had lost my last follower and sat under the short overhang of the doorway. There, I pulled the blanket out of my bag and put it around me. The smell of wet wool was somehow a comfort to me. I would wait there until dawn. I closed my eyes.

I was abruptly awakened when the door I was leaning against gave way and opened. What followed was a tirade in Greek about my total lack of character and moral upbringing. All this from the diminutive elderly woman who evidently lived in the house whose door I was blocking. I struggled to my feet, wincing as I put pressure on my knee, and humbly apologized in Greek. My use of Greek stopped her in mid-sentence, and she peered intently at me.

"Who are you?" she asked, again in Greek.

"Aulus Marrius Scaevola."

"Why are you sleeping at my door?"

What should I say? The truth was probably the least stupid reason I could give. "I am hiding out of the rain from some people who wish to harm me."

She looked at me, head tilted, thoughtful.

"What did you do to them?"

"I followed them. I think they may have hurt a friend."

She stared at me for a moment and then nodded. "Stay here." She abruptly went back inside, and returned a moment later with a steaming mug of *calda*, hot mulled wine, which she held out for me.

"Here. I have to go to work," she said. "Just leave the mug on the doorstep when you're done." She stepped out into the rain, closed her door, and pulled a hood over her head.

I watched her totter down the alley as I sipped the fiery liquid.

The darkness slowly receded with the coming of the day, but the rain and the gray remained. When I could see the shape of the paving stones, I packed up the blanket and put the mug on the doorstep, placing a few coins underneath it.

After limping through the back streets as the city awakened, I came to the top of the Latiaris stairs, where I was again reminded of my father. I knew he would approve of what I was doing. He would have said that the only journey worth taking is one that leads to the truth.

I hobbled down the stairs, across the street, and into the inn next to the popinae that sold cooked fish. Aemilia had visited the inn when she'd made her walk through town. She'd had a purpose for her visit.

A man sitting on a chair in the atrium looked up. "Yes?"

"I am Aulus Marrius Scaevola. My wife secured a room for us a few days ago. I've just made it into town and would like to rest… and dry off."

He picked up a tablet and opened it. "Yes, I have it. She paid in advance for a month. The room's been waiting for you. Can I get your luggage?"

"It will be along shortly."

"Very well, sir. Please follow me."

He took me to a small room on the third floor. It had a narrow bed that noticeably sagged in the middle, one chair, and a small table with a pitcher of water and a basin. But the blankets were clean, and a small window looked out on a courtyard. This was not as good a room as the one on the Quirinal Hill, but I doubted they employed kidnappers.

The room also had a brazier with a small stack of wood, the wood being an extra charge, of course. I lit a fire and hung my clothes on the chair in front of it. While they dried, I cleaned my scrapes and rethought my plan to find Aemilia.

CHAPTER THIRTEEN

FLAMMA FUMO PROXIMA
Where there is smoke, there is fire.

The little room was warm, heated by the red glow of the brazier. Steam rose from the clothes draped over the back of the chair that sat a hand's breadth away from the fire. An hour had not been long enough for my cloak and tunic to feel dry, but they were at least warm and that was all the time I could spare. Few things match the miserable feeling of donning wet clothes when you're finally warm and dry, of course. But every minute idle was a minute lost in the search for Aemilia.

Two hours after dawn, the rain was still falling. The paving stones on the street in front of the inn were pocked with scattered puddles to be sidestepped. The rain was light and feathery now, more of a thick wet mist. My damp clothes wouldn't know the difference. They were capable of absorbing only so much water.

As I crossed the road, I glanced over my shoulder, marking the people behind me. Who was pacing me? Who was crossing the road with me? Who was following me? This was a routine to which I'd grown accustomed. With a start, I realized I didn't need to do it right now. I was free, if only for a short time. I'd slipped away. No one should be pursuing me, at least until I returned to the apartment. A smile lit my face, and I felt giddy at having lost a burden that I hadn't realized I'd been carrying.

Rome was a crowded city. Block upon block of multistory buildings formed manmade ravines that channeled people, livestock, and cargo through like a river flowing through the narrow stone streets and straw-covered alleys. Shopkeepers spilled out onto the sidewalks and into the streets to advertise and sell their wares. Hawkers, holding their goods in raised hands, plied the streets and sidewalks, creating obstructions, like islands, that the stream of people had to pass around.

Pedestrians occupied every free space of the street, which was why the city banned all commercial carts and wagons during the day. Moving during daylight was accomplished on one's own two legs. Litters with poles moved cargo too heavy for one man's shoulders. Likewise, wealthy women not wishing to suffer the indignities of the press of flesh traveled comfortably in curtained palanquins.

Those not wealthy enough to own either litter or palanquin and the slaves needed to carry them could rent them for the day from the many transportation vendors throughout the city. Aemilia had visited one on her walk about the city, when I was identifying her followers. She had secured a palanquin and four bearers for the day, which I confirmed with the owner. We had planned to use the palanquin to remove our baggage from the apartment without notice. This would be part of our disappearing act. We had chosen to rent a palanquin rather than a litter so we could draw the curtains to hide our luggage. The transportation vendor hadn't blinked an eye at the request as palanquins cost about three times more to rent than litters. He was more than happy to take the extra money.

I thought much about our scheme this morning. Aemilia and I had intended to move our luggage with the palanquin, and then, wearing our slave clothes, fade into the crowd, invisible. Without Aemilia, that wouldn't happen, but if I were going to look for her, I still needed to disappear, to become invisible. I couldn't watch the watchers if they were watching me. I still had to go through with that part of the plan.

When I finished making arrangements with the transportation vendor, I braced myself for the rain and trekked back to our old room on the Quirinal Hill.

No one wants to be out in the rain. Everyone moved with purpose and economy, and it took less than half an hour to walk to the Quirinal Hill. Finally, with the apartment in sight, I passed my gaze over the crowd of pedestrians on the sidewalk and briefly glimpsed Ratface leaning against the wall of a wool shop across the street with his arms folded and water dripping from the hood of his cloak. I had to smile, knowing he had suffered at least as wet a night as I had.

"Good morning," I said to Placida, who was standing in the door when I arrived.

"Good morning, sir. Welcome back. You're still in time for breakfast. Would you like me to bring it to your room?"

Eating was the last thing on my mind, but I had to appear as though nothing was out of the ordinary. "Yes, please. That would be nice."

I climbed the stairs to our room and slumped a bit when I entered and didn't find Aemilia. The room was just as I had left it late the previous night. I had fervently hoped that this was all some mistake and that I would find Aemilia waiting for me. Finding the still empty room was devastating.

I stuffed all of my possessions back into my bags and started on Aemilia's things. I had already packed away her medical supplies, so I gathered her personal items: comb, brush, mirror, and nightclothes. At the sight and touch of her possessions, tears welled in my eyes and blurred my vision. I held her nightclothes to my nose and caught her scent. It was almost as if she were with me.

A tap at the door interrupted my dark thoughts. Placida handed me a plate heaped with food: olives, plums, a bowel of wheat porridge, and fresh bread, along with a sizable pool of garum. I smiled, thinking of Aemilia. Probably better she wasn't here for the food. She wouldn't have been thrilled with the amount of garum they had poured on the plate. I, on the other hand, sopped up the garum with the bread and ate with relish.

After eating, I set the empty plate aside and finished packing Aemilia's things. Now came the time to bring back Hanno, so I changed into his clothes. Then I paused for a moment. I was truly grateful they were dry, but they really smelled. Anyone downwind would think I worked in the pigpens.

The palanquin should have been in the back alley by this time as arranged, so I hefted up all the bags that I could carry in a single load and, after checking that the hallway was empty, stepped out of the room and hurried to the stairs.

I was almost at the bottom of the stairs when the woman who had initially recognized me came up from the storerooms below on the stairs to my left. I paused, hoping she wouldn't look up to her right. Hanno's clothes and the bags hid most of my face, but I didn't want her to wonder who I was or where I was going with the luggage. Fortunately, she kept her eyes focused in front of her. She was carrying a breakfast plate back to the kitchen. I froze. The plate that she was carrying up from the storerooms was empty except for some bread crumbs, an empty bowl, and bits of garum soaked bread neatly pushed into a pile on the side of the plate.

***

Think this through, Vitruvius. Any number of people could be in the basement of this building who would create little piles of garum-soaked bread bits on the side of their plates.

How could Aemilia be here? She had left. Well, I had always assumed she'd left. But the two people watching the front door hadn't seen her leave. Of course, I had thought they had lied, but what if they had been telling the truth?

The one detail about abducting Aemilia that had always bothered me was how they had managed to take her away. They could have marched her off at knife-point, not too subtle in the streets of Rome. But how would they have carried her in such a way that no one would notice—

wrapped in a rug, hidden in a barrel? If she had never gone, concealing her wouldn't have been a problem.

Once the woman had passed from view, I continued down the stairs and out the back door. The palanquin and its four bearers were waiting down the alley, where it was a little wider and offered an overhang that sheltered them from the rain.

I found the man in charge. I had met him in the shop where I rented it. "Here is the first load. I need for two of you to come with me to bring the rest of our luggage down to the palanquin. Then wait for me until I return."

"You rented us for the full day. We can stand here until sunset if you want." He looked me up and down. "Why are you dressed like that?"

"I want to fool some friends. I'll explain later," I answered, though I had no intention of explaining.

The two bearers followed me back inside and up to our room. They were muscular young men, their strength a byproduct of their job, and they had no problem bringing the rest of our luggage down the stairs and out to the palanquin. I then walked over to the stairs leading down to the storerooms and looked down.

The bottom was dark but I could see the stairs ended in a corridor that went to both the left and right. A faint light flickered from somewhere down the right side. I was unarmed. As a slave, I couldn't wear a pugio. Looking around, I found only one weapon, a piece of broken broom handle that someone had discarded by the back door. Not much of a weapon, but I took it anyway. I edged down the stairs, landing on each step as quietly as possible. I didn't even want to consider the repercussions should anyone see or hear me.

At the bottom, I peered carefully around the corner to the right and discovered a man I took to be Scarface. He was holding a long knife and sitting in a chair with his head back and eyes closed, but I couldn't assume he was sleeping. Along the hall were six doors, three on each side. Scarface was sitting outside the middle one on the right. All the doors were shut and bolted except for the nearest one on the left which was wide open. I could see it was a small room, maybe two spans by two spans, with a stone floor and barrels along the wall.

Scarface was clearly guarding the middle storeroom. He was five or six strides away, and no way would I be able to round the corner and make it that far without his noticing. What if I lured him to me and then hit him? That would certainly surprise him, but it might not put him down, and then I would be in trouble. What else could I do? All I had by way of arms was the broken broom handle I had picked up.

Then I had a thought. I backed up one step and lobbed the broom handle into the open storeroom across the hall, where it landed on the stone floor with a clatter, shattering the silence like a clap of thunder. I waited. From the flickering light cast in the corridor, I knew the lamp was moving toward me, and I saw Scarface's back as he carried the lamp into the open storeroom. As soon as he was most of the way in, I dashed across the corridor and slammed the storeroom door into him, knocking him forward. Once the door was shut, I slid over the bolt. Muffled shouts, followed by a pounding on the door, echoed in the dark as I ran along the corridor and unbolted and opened the middle door.

The middle storeroom, small like the other, was lit by a lamp on a table, and there I saw Aemilia sitting on a bed!

"Aemilia!"

"Vitruvius?"

"Yes, come on!"

She ran over, grabbed me in a tight hug and then smiled up at me. "What took you so long?"

"What took me so long?"

"I knew you'd figure it out. I just thought you would be a little sooner, that's all."

"I was busy." I grabbed her hand and raced down the hallway. "We have to leave before someone discovers the guard I locked in there." I pointed at the other storeroom where Scarface continued to pound on the door.

We bounded up the stairs two at a time and ran out the door and into the light rain of the back alley. Aemilia, squinting against the daylight, climbed into the palanquin and shuffled our luggage around to make room. I pulled the curtains shut.

"I'm going to take one of the poles for a few blocks," I told the head bearer.

"Your money," he replied and stepped back.

The other three bearers and I picked up the palanquin and put the poles on our shoulders. By the gods, it was heavy. I wasn't sure I could last more than a few blocks, but I'd go as far as I was able. The palanquin also noticeably tilted toward me, since I was shorter than the other men. I hoped Aemilia was able to hang on.

I kept my hood up and my head down in the light rain, checking out the street as we passed in front of the apartment building. I knew Ratface would be watching the front door, waiting for Aulus Marrius Scaevola to come out. They believed Aemilia to be safely locked up, so all they saw was a pampered woman's palanquin carried in the rain by four miserable bearers.

***

The brazier, the center of warmth and light in our little room, crackled and spit. We had made a mess of things, stringing a piece of borrowed rope around the room to create an improvised clothesline. It was early afternoon, and I sat on the bed, my back against the wall. Aemilia lay on the bed, her head in my lap. A bruise colored her cheek. She said that she wanted be warm and comfortable before we exchanged stories. All I had learned so far was that, aside from the bruise, they hadn't harmed her and might have actually treated her well.

She softly hummed a tune I didn't recognize. I looked down at her face. "You don't know how happy I am to have found you and learned you were all right. I refused to believe you were dead, but I really didn't know where you had gone."

"Well, I wasn't worried about it. As I said, I knew you would figure it out."

"I wasn't so sure."

"Sooner or later, you would realize that I hadn't left the building. Then you would find me. After I left you last night, I had just reached the bottom of the stairs when Acaunus Cicatrix, that's Scarface's name, came up behind me and put a knife to my throat." She looked up at me and frowned. "That's the second time that's happened since I started traveling with you. Cicatrix, ah, invited me to continue down the stairs and then down the corridor to the storeroom where you found me. He asked me questions, all about who you were, where you came from, and what you were doing in Rome."

"He didn't threaten you?"

She rolled her eyes. "He was holding a really big knife. Anyway, I stuck to our story of coming to Rome from Brindisi. It turns out he was from Brindisi, too, so he asked lots of detailed questions I could easily answer or improvise. He said he believed me and that he was sorry for scaring me, but he would have to speak with someone before he could let me go."

"That was it?"

"No, of course not. About an hour later—it was really hard to tell time in the storeroom—the woman who recognized you came in with Scarface. I didn't get her name. She said she needed to search me for documents, and she was pretty thorough in doing it. When I protested, she hit me on the cheek. Then she discovered the pendant. She read it and turned white. Well, I think she turned white. It was hard to tell by the little lamp, but it scared her. She showed it to Scarface, and then he reminded her he couldn't read. She told him I was a member of the Julii household. Then he turned white. I could tell that even in the lamplight. They gave me back the pendant, and Scarface asked me to explain. I made up the story that I was a medica for the family and that they had adopted me."

"They believed it?"

"Yes. The woman said she had found the healer's supplies in our room." Aemilia looked up at me with a knowing sort of smile. "She must have been the one who ransacked our room. I noticed a black stain on her fingers. The jar holding lunar caustic was cracked, and the powder stains your skin black when you go out into the daylight. I told her the black stain was a slow poison—it's not—but she became really nervous and left."

Aemilia smiled, clearly enjoying the discomfort she had caused the woman. "Scarface stayed. He said he had been a legionnaire and served under Julius Caesar when Caesar served his *quaestorship* in Hispania. He told me they would have to keep me until sometime tomorrow, that is, today, when someone important would come to talk with me. They never said who it was. I only hoped you would finally figure out where I was and rescue me before he showed up. And you did."

She sat up. "Your turn."

I told her my story of slipping past the followers, going to the warehouse, and escaping, and I ended with how I realized she was still in the building.

"Garum? It was the garum?"

"It was the garum." I couldn't help but laugh at her expression.

"That poor man in the warehouse. Do you think the man doing the beating might have been the one who killed your father?"

"I've been thinking about that. It's possible, even likely. I decided not to stay around and ask him."

She stood. "Take off your tunic."

"What?"

"I wasn't looking at your knee when you dressed. Lift up your tunic."

I was certain I wouldn't like the result, but I took off my tunic as she hunted around in one of her boxes. She grabbed a small bottle and the she rubbed a liniment on my knee. The potion smelled awful but actually made my knee feel better.

Later, we finished the dinner we had bought from the fish popinae next door. Aemilia poured the last of the wine into our cups and sat back, satisfied.

I took a deep breath. "I have to confront Annius. I need to hear what he has to say." I steeled myself for Aemilia's protests, but they didn't come.

"I know, but we better have a solid plan before you do."

"We—"

"Don't even try." She shook her finger at me. "I'm in this as deeply as you are."

I wanted to argue with her, I really did, but I also didn't want her to leave. I convinced myself that she was safer if we were together. And maybe she was.

CHAPTER FOURTEEN

ALEA IACTA EST
The die is cast.

The new room, as we had taken to calling it, wasn't as large, clean, nor quiet as the one we'd left on the Quirinal Hill, yet it was much better. One could charitably describe it as cozy, but the lack of kidnappers more than made up for its other shortcomings. I had been awake for some time but had yet to move. The bed was so narrow and of such poor quality that it forced us to sleep with Aemilia practically on top of me, and I was delighted.

The cold from the raw breeze that blew past the window's ill-fitting shutters was perfectly balanced by the embers in the brazier and the warmth of Aemilia's skin. Had it not been for the weight of responsibility, I wouldn't have moved at all. But that weight distorted everything. I shifted a leg.

"You're awake?" Aemilia asked without moving.

"I thought you were still asleep."

"I've been awake for a while, but I didn't want to move. I'm too comfortable."

"Yes, but I guess it's time to start the day."

"Not just yet," she said as she rose and nibbled my ear.

***

Half the morning had passed, and we had just finished breakfast. The room's only window framed a clear sky, a solid-blue painting hanging on the dingy white wall. The rain had blown through last night, leaving Aquilo to bring cold from the north.

"Are you planning to visit the Julii today?" I asked.

Aemilia bit her lower lip, something I'd never seen her do before. "I should, but I'm not sure I can."

"Why not? It's your best chance."

She glanced down. "It is," she said in a voice that was almost a whisper. "It's also my last chance. I couldn't bear it if they rejected me."

She had her own demons. I understood what she was going through. Quintus Fabius Sanga was my family's last chance, and I dreaded going to see him. I rose to embrace her. She held me and didn't let go for some time.

Finally, I said, "Aemilia?"

"Yes, yes. I have to go."

She shrugged into a woolen cloak pulled from her largest bag, gathered a leather documents folder, and kissed me. "Back before you know it." She paused, her smile wavering. "That's what I said last time, isn't it?"

"Yes, it is, and I got pretty beaten up looking for you. Try not to get kidnapped this time."

She laughed and left.

Our new room was suddenly empty, cold, and bare. I sat with thoughts of my goals unaccomplished. I thought of my mother and sister. They knew nothing of what had happened, good or bad. With nothing to do but wait, they would painfully watch the sand drain from the glass.

Grabbing a blank scroll and ink, I penned them a summary of all that had transpired, minus Aemilia's kidnapping, and where Aemilia and I were currently staying. After sealing it, I put on my warm, and now thankfully dry, cloak and headed downstairs.

As I turned the corner into the inn's unadorned atrium, the owner was speaking in low, conspiratorial tones with another man and gesturing passionately. The two were an unmatched pair. The owner was short, my height, but more than twice my girth. His skin was light, almost ruddy. The other appeared to be a Nubian, dark-skinned, thin, almost emaciated, his hair short and tightly curled. When they saw me, the talk stopped, and the Nubian gave me a slight bow and left.

"Master Marrius, what might I do for you this fine morning?"

"I need to send correspondence to Fundi by the fastest means. Where should I go?"

"That would be Cico Baibius's messenger service, down the left to the glassmaker's and then left again just past the fountain. They can wait for a reply and deliver it here, too."

"Thank you. You seem to know a lot about this area."

"That I do. I make it my business to know everything that goes on around here, everything. Keeps me out of trouble."

He had a hint of a smile on his face that I couldn't quite place. "Well, I'm new in Rome. What's all this about a rebellion or something?"

He thought for a moment. "Well, that would be the Catiline affair, of course."

"The what?"

Before he could answer, the Nubian returned. "Sorry to interrupt," he said to me, and he handed the owner a folded piece of papyrus.

The owner unfolded and read it. His face formed into a frown. "No. That is *not* acceptable. Tell him it has to be what we agreed," he said to the Nubian, who nodded and left again.

"I'm sorry. Where was I?"

"You said something about the Catiline affair, I think it was."

"Yes. That was it. Well, it all started when some of the senators received anonymous letters warning of a massacre in Rome on the 6th day before the Kalends of November and that they should leave town. Cicero told the Senate that he had proof that the letters came from Catiline. He said Catiline's friend Manlius would start a rebellion on that day and Catiline would massacre the patricians and burn the city on the following day. Well, Catiline denied it and the 6th day before the Kalends of November passed with no problems, so everyone started thinking that the fuss was all some plan of Cicero's to grab power. You see, create a crisis and all."

"So, nothing happened?" I said and thought about the cipher my father carried, which called for an attack on Praeneste. That hadn't happened either.

Regulus gave me a wide smile. "No, something happened, all right. Reports came in later from all over the countryside that troops loyal to Catiline were gathering. They even tried to seize Praeneste, but Cicero stopped it."

"Praeneste. I heard about that," I said, and I thanked the gods yet again that I had burned that document. "What happened to Catiline?"

"Cicero gave two long speeches against him, one to the Senate at the Temple of Jupiter Optimus Maximus and one to the people from the Rostra in the Forum. In both, he spoke about how bad Catiline was. Cicero had the Senate declare Catiline and Manlius hostes. Now the Senate is trying to find all those involved in the conspiracy."

"He named them public enemies? Were they arrested?"

"No, they fled town. Some said they went north to Etruria to raise an army, but as hostes, all good citizens of Rome are now bound to do them harm if they are able."

"Interesting, but nothing to do with me. Thank you," I said and left to find my way to Cico Baibius's messenger service.

Back out in the street, I had time to reflect on what I had learned. Clearly, the Catiline plot was what my father had stumbled upon, knowingly or not. Was this what had caused him to be killed? How did Annius fit in? Was he one of Catiline's supporters? How could I find out?

The messenger service took my scroll and promised to have it in my mother's hands in two days—for a price. Knowing what I would feel like in my sister and mother's place, I paid for the quick delivery. I only wished my news were better.

Aemilia was already back when I returned, and she was smiling.

"You look happy."

"I am. The Julii didn't toss me into the street. I gave them Publicius's letter and showed them the pendant. I'm to go back in four days and talk to Caesar's wife, Pompeia, at the Domus Publica, the pontifex maximus residence. They still might throw me out, but at least I'll have the opportunity to make my case." She paused and looked me over. "What was your day like?"

"I learned we're in more trouble than I thought. We have somehow walked into the middle of a plot to overthrow the Republic."

"What?"

I told her what I had learned about the Catiline affair.

***

Since I had learned much about following someone over the last week, I spent the next day discovering the habits of Quintus Annius Chilo. I'd followed him and asked questions, so I learned where he lived, where and when he traveled, and how many people were likely to be with him.

When I met him, I would arrange it to be at a place of my choosing, where I was prepared, and he was not. The spot would need to be open yet crowded enough to cover my escape. The Forum Romanum was the obvious place, surrounded as it was by shops, porticoes, temples, and offices. As an open plaza, it was full of people in motion, the crowded and chaotic heart of Rome. You could meet anyone you wanted there, be they vicious or virtuous, decent or indecent, a place well suited to discussing murder.

I learned that Annius would attend the Senate in the Curia in two days. That would provide my opportunity. I would approach him in the Forum just as he left the Curia. I knew the direction he had to walk. All I needed to do was devise a plan to approach him, talk to him, and then disappear.

I strolled the Forum as Annius would. Starting on the steps to the Curia, I walked west, across the Forum. Someone was always speaking from the top of the Rostra when the Senate emptied, Annius would make his way behind it to avoid the crowd in front and then continue to the alley between the Temple of Saturn and the Basilica Julia. He couldn't go on the north side of the temple because construction there blocked the alley. The temple is also the Roman treasury, which means it is always crowded and guards are about. Annius wouldn't wish to call attention to our conversation in such company, so he would bide his time and do nothing when we met. He would act after I left.

The best place to approach him was from the crowd listening to the speaker on the Rostra. Annius's retinue of clients wouldn't be able to enclose him as he moved through the crowd. They would be strung out and disorganized. I should be able to merge with them. But how would I then slip away? After we talked, he would have me followed by one or both of the guards he usually had with him. He would wish me harm. Running and hiding wouldn't work.

Then I had an idea. If you can't hide, you need to be as obvious as you can.

On my way back to the inn, I stopped at a shop that sold nice yet moderately priced travel cloaks. The shop was clean and well kept, with a variety of cloaks on shelves, organized by color and type. The proprietor, a young man, probably the owner's son, greeted me as I entered.

"Good afternoon, citizen. Can I help you find anything?"

"I'm looking for a long cloak, not too warm. It needs to be distinctive. I don't want to wear the same cloak as everyone else. I want to stand out in the crowd."

"You've come to the right shop. We have many one-of-a-kind cloaks."

"Well, I need a two-of-a-kind cloak. I want to be distinctive, but I want to have two in case one becomes too wet."

"Let me see what I have."

He riffled through the stacks of garments and returned with two cloaks dyed a deep red, not the dark-wine red of a legionnaire's cloak but more the red of an apple, something you would recognize from a long way off, yet something that wouldn't seem out of place.

"Yes. These will do nicely."

My next stop was the palanquin shop. They remembered me and the odd sort of things I had asked of them. When I gave the owner my request, he raised an eyebrow but said nothing. I had become somewhat of a fascination among the palanquin bearers after taking a turn at carrying Aemilia the last time. They seemed delighted to play along with my schemes, viewing them as practical jokes. I suspected they would be less jovial if they learned of the stakes.

I finally returned to the inn in the late afternoon. The owner was in the atrium, where I had left him that morning.

"Good day, Master Marrius."

"Good day to you." I started toward the stairs. Then I had an idea and turned back. "Sir, your Nubian friend."

"Onyebuchi," he said.

"Would Onyebuchi be interested in a small job that might involve some risk? I would pay him well."

He gave me a sidelong glance and a brief grin. "You lead an interesting life, Master Marrius."

"Me? How so?"

"It's not every educated man with money who dresses as a slave and carries a palanquin to avoid being followed by Quintus Annius Chilo's men. You know, that sort of life."

My breath caught, and I froze. He had put together much of my activity. But as I thought about it, I realized, how could he not? I guessed he could see my hesitation, for he continued.

"Sir, as I said, I make it my business to know what's going on around here. Whatever you're doing is safe with me. First, because you are my customer. Second, because I despise Quintus Annius Chilo, and third, I can provide certain services you might wish to purchase."

"Services?" I could only hope he wasn't suggesting some type of blackmail.

"Lookouts, bodyguards, that sort of thing."

Suddenly what he said made sense. This was *his* block. He was the leader of the *collegia,* the trade association for this area. Some of the collegia were less about business and more about business protection, with an emphasis on brute force protection.

"Does that include Onyebuchi's services?"

"Indeed, it does."

Over the next hour, he and I discussed what I needed. We started by speaking in euphemisms and dancing around the subject. Finally, I told him of Aemilia's kidnapping, and how I suspected Annius was behind it.

"I'm impressed. You can call me Regulus. Quintus Annius Chilo is no friend of mine. I trade in information Master Marrius, but never to Annius or his people."

We worked out the details. Regulus would help… for a fee, but I believed him trustworthy in his way. He kept to his own moral code, which, in this case, coincided with my needs.

When I finally made my way to our room, Aemilia was waiting, and she was smiling.

"Pompeia wants me to come back and talk to Caesar," she said in answer to my question about her interview. "She would hire me now, but she says the decision is Caesar's to make. It is up to me to persuade him."

"When do you meet Caesar?"

"In six days."

She was quiet then, and I noticed she was biting on her lower lip again, a gesture I now recognized as something she did only when agitated. I walked over and put my arms around her. She held me for some time and then backed off with a sigh and put her hand on my arm.

"What did you do all day while I tried to avoid becoming destitute?"

I smiled. “Oh, nothing really. Mostly just walked around Rome, you know, taking in the sights.”

She frowned at me. “You never just walk about. You usually hurt yourself. Let me have a look at you.”

***

The next morning delivered a cold, clear winter's day. Even through the haze of Rome, the sky was bright blue with flecks of clouds. I took it as a good omen.

Dressed in my new apple-red cloak, I walked into the Forum, which was already in fine form this late morning with hundreds of people packed in closely, moving in different directions: patricians in togas, plebs in tunics, and slaves in, well, almost anything, or in case of the prostitutes advertising their wares, almost nothing. Most everyone wore a cloak against the late November chill, though the prostitutes had a way of allowing theirs to accidentally fall open as you passed.

I stood with the Rostra in front of me. The Curia, with its imposing bronze doors, lay on my right, its stairs covered in young men and their tutors, all listening to the morning's senatorial debate. A speaker had stepped onto the Rostra and launched into a plea for swift action against the Catiline conspirators. The address was a call to hand Consul Cicero additional powers to deal with the crisis. A crowd formed around me, concealing me within it.

Someone said that Catiline was building an army to attack Rome. The crowd was outraged at what Catiline had done and feared what he yet might do. Speaker after speaker echoed the same sentiments. Caught up in the argument, I almost missed that the Senate had finished its debate and the senators were leaving the Curia. I moved to the edge of the crowd and scanned the senators' faces as they descended the steps in their white togas with purple trim and cloaks open so that we might all recognize their status and give them leave.

I marked Annius. He was easy to find, for he strutted and preened like a rooster among cackling hens. His cloak had been dyed with expensive dye, not the purple dye used for the edges of senatorial togas, but an equally expensive cobalt-blue. Rome had sumptuary laws for the purpose of restraining extravagance, particularly against inordinate expenditures for clothing, and Annius had pushed the rules to the edge. The true effect of the laws was to prevent plebs like me from wearing the same clothes as senators like him. The rule didn't matter anyway, as I could never have afforded a cloak like his.

Annius angled toward the back of the Rostra, surrounded by a small flock of followers.

Walking quickly, I came up behind Annius, shoving my way through the crowd and his retinue of clients. His two guards preceded him, clearing a passage for him through the crowd.

"Senator Annius, could you give me a moment to talk about my father?" I said when I had drawn up beside him.

He did not acknowledge my presence.

I raised my voice to be heard above the noise of the speaker and the crowd. "You were to pay him for delivering some very interesting messages for you."

He stopped and turned to face me, his eyes narrowed and brows lowered. "Who are you?"

"Marcus Vitruvius Pollio."

He stiffened as he studied me for a moment. "Vitruvius, yes. I remember your father. Sold olives, I believe. I know nothing about messages. Cannot say that I remember any business agreement I had with him. I am sure I would remember something like that. Don't suppose you have anything documenting such a relationship? No, of course you don't."

He turned away.

"Because of your messages, he died in *an accident*," I said, emphasizing the last words. "I intend to find out what happened."

He stopped and turned to face me with cold, menacing eyes, and I thought of the poor man in the warehouse. The flow of other senators and their followers parted around us.

"I'm sorry your father is dead," Annius conceded. "He was a good man. He was a little too curious, though. That might have led to his accident. You know, paying too much attention to things that he shouldn't have, above his station, and not enough attention to where he was walking. Make sure you don't do the same. Don't let your gaze wander too far from where it should. It could cause you, or someone close to you, to lose their footing, and we wouldn't want that, would we?" He made a slight nod to the two guards who were a little ahead of him and they moved toward me.

I turned and merged into the crowd and headed along the shops lining the Basilica Sempronia, to the Temple of Castor and Pollux. One glance back confirmed that the two men were following me.

I pulled the cloak's hood over my head and quickened my pace. I was sure they wouldn't come too close, not with all the soldiers around the temple. They didn't have to. With my apple-red cloak, they could safely follow at a distance until I was away from those who might take note—I was depending on it.

When I reached the end of the Basilica Sempronia, I turned right, down Vicus Tuscus that led between the Basilica Sempronia and the Temple of Castor and Pollux. More respectable Romans usually avoided that road. It was said that if you went behind the Temple of Castor, you would run into those who could be trusted to quickly put you out of your misery. But I had friends, courtesy of Regulus.

I turned left when I reached the back of the temple, where Onyebuchi was waiting, wearing the other apple-red cloak. He smiled at me, put up his hood, and walked back out into the alley, heading in the direction where I had been walking. Just beyond him was a palanquin and three bearers in matching tunics. I removed my cloak and hid it under the palanquin's cushions. I was wearing the same matching tunic underneath my cloak. I took my place at the unmanned palanquin pole, and then the we four bearers picked up the palanquin and started moving.

I heard Annius's two men come to the end of the temple and continue down the alley after Onyebuchi. If everything went as planned, he would pull back the hood of his cloak in a minute. They wouldn't need to approach him to verify he was not me. His black skin would make that obvious. Believing they had followed the wrong cloak, they would immediately backtrack, I trusted, allowing Onyebuchi time to make his own escape.

We carried the palanquin along the back of the temple and had just turned left again, toward the open part of the Forum, when Annius's two men ran by the palanquin. One stopped and came back. My breath caught. I would be unable to reach my pugio while carrying the palanquin, but the man just pulled back the curtain, glanced in, and then continued with his friend.

When I finally returned to the inn in the late afternoon, Regulus and Onyebuchi were waiting. Onyebuchi laughed, and handed the cloak back to me.

"This was great fun. Thank you for letting me play," he said.

"You keep it, Onyebuchi. Consider it a down payment. I may need you again."

I climbed the stairs to our room and thought about what I had learned this day. Apparently, my father had suspected something about the message he was delivering and tried to learn more—the curiosity Annius had spoken of. I didn't know if he had succeeded, but I now knew Annius had ordered that he be murdered for fear he had. If I weren't careful, I was sure the same fate awaited me.

CHAPTER FIFTEEN

SPEREMUS QUAE VOLUMUS SED QUOD ACCIDERIT FERAMUS
Let us hope for what we want, but let us endure whatever happens.

I awoke with the thought that only a little over a month was left before we lost our home and lands. Even the presence of Aemilia, her soft skin against mine, the smell of her hair, couldn't push aside the anxiety that weighed upon me.

Ten days had passed, and I could today plead my case to Quintus Fabius Sanga. Like Aemilia with the Julii, he was my last hope.

As I moved, Aemilia stretched, lifted her head, and kissed me. "I'll find us something to eat," she said and slid out of bed.

I dressed as she put two plates of food together from what she had purchased the day before. The meal wasn't elaborate, just bread, olive oil, and figs, but we ate and I made ready to leave.

"I'll be here when you return," she said and hugged me. "May the gods favor you."

I shut the door, still uneasy about leaving her alone. I couldn't stop thinking about how empty I had been when she had been kidnapped.

I took much less than an hour to walk to Sanga's beautiful home. However, unlike the last time I visited, a queue of clients waited outside, the servant acting as gatekeeper.

"Good morning. I would like to see the master, Quintus Fabius Sanga, at his convenience," I said to the servant. "I gave you my letter of introduction when last we met."

"You are, sir?"

"Marcus Vitruvius Pollio."

"Ah, yes. I remember you." He consulted a wax tablet. "Yes, he will see you, but you will have to wait your turn."

I didn't know what I had expected. My letter of introduction had gained me entrance but not favor. "Thank you. I will be waiting."

I walked back to the end of the line, past the others, who looked at me with a smugness that suggested I was no more important than they were. I winced. I had been arrogant to think my need more pressing than theirs and that I should be granted entrance before those who had waited all morning, perhaps even since before dawn.

So, I waited. I could do nothing else. Every few minutes, I took a step forward and returned to waiting. My father would have told me that waiting was a practice in patience. The line moved, but ever so slowly, and several hours passed before I reached the front.

"Master Vitruvius, Quintus Fabius Sanga will see you."

As I stepped into the vestibule, the gatekeeper threw out his arm. "Sir! Always enter with your right foot first. Otherwise, it will be bad luck!"

I had never heard of such a thing, but I left and re-entered, this time making sure my right foot touched the tile floor first. The gatekeeper led me through the vestibule, into the atrium, and on into the tablinum, where Sanga sat at a desk, reading a scroll that I recognized as the letter of introduction my mother had written. "Good morning, Quintus Fabius Sanga," I said.

He didn't answer or look up; rather, he held up a finger to me and continued reading. I waited.

He was in his fifties with grey hair and had to squint to read.

Finally, he looked up. "I remember your mother, a bright star. She says you take after her. That is a compliment, if true." He put down the scroll, clasped his hands together, and placed them on the table. "Why are you here?"

I looked away. Making my request was difficult for me. "We need a loan. Over the last several years, the weather has not been good for our olive farm. My father took out loans from Gaius Gargonius, a wealthy landowner in our town, to tide us over. My father changed our farm so that we could generate a sufficient surplus to pay back our loans, but Father was killed last month, so we haven't had the chance to put his ideas into practice. Our loans are due at the end of the year, and if not repaid in full, we'll lose our land."

"Was killed? Curious phrasing."

"He was here in Rome, seeking a loan last month, and died in an accident."

He closed his eyes for a moment. "I'm sorry about your father, Vitruvius. I realize that taking on the family at your age is a significant burden."

"Thank you, sir."

"How much do you need to cover your debt?"

I told him, and he raised an eyebrow.

"Not a trivial sum, perhaps an indicator of poor management rather than the fortunes of nature."

I was offended. My father worked hard and had a good head for business, but I didn't argue with him.

"I do not believe blame falls on my father. The gods just didn't favor us. But as I said, we have plans that will help us in the future."

"That may be so, but the results are the same, and this is more debt than I can address." He paused for a moment and then picked up a different scroll and frowned. "You were speaking with Annius after the Senate yesterday. What is your relationship with him?" His voice was sharp.

How did he know? More so, why did he care? He must have been observing Annius. I didn't know what to say. I looked down, unable to meet his eyes.

"It is a private affair, sir. I have no relationship with him."

"You are not seeking a loan from him?"

"My father was, but that didn't come to be."

"Well, I cannot help you. But out of affection for your mother, here's a list of others who may be more receptive to your request." He handed me a scroll and nodded to the gatekeeper, who approached. I had been dismissed.

The walk back to the inn was long and slow. The meeting hadn't unfolded as mother had led me to expect. Clearly, Sanga held some affection for her. He said so, but he had brushed us aside, judging us not worth the risk. He had been almost hostile when questioning me about Annius. Obviously, Sanga held no affection for him. Perhaps that was it. He didn't trust Annius, and my family and I had been vilified by association. How many others would feel the same way? If Sanga knew I had met with Annius, likely others did as well. I would need to clear our name before I could approach anyone else.

Aemilia met me when I entered the room. I must have been wearing my emotions on my face, for she said nothing. She just hugged me.

***

When morning broke, I was wide awake, as I had been for much of the night. The weight of my obligation to my mother and sister, already a palpable burden, now seemed overwhelming. Both of the tasks I had set for myself in Rome, finding my father's murderer and raising money to pay our loans, were now linked and even more difficult. The sand was quickly slipping away.

As I dressed for the day, Aemilia rose from bed and wrapped her arms around me. "Please be safe, Vitruvius."

"I'll be back before you know it," I said, echoing her last words to me.

She smiled at my feeble joke, but her eyes looked tired and worried. Given the size of our bed, if I didn't sleep well, neither did she. "Don't get kidnapped," she said and returned to bed as I left.

On the sidewalk outside the inn, I started to walk, but then I realized I didn't know in which direction to go. Annius had told me my father had been too curious. Father had been looking for something, and

Annius had been worried enough about it to have had him killed. What could my father have been looking for? When the woman searched Aemilia in the storeroom, she had been looking for documents, and Annius had said I had no documents to prove my father's business relationship with him. Perhaps a document somewhere tied the cipher to Annius, Annius to Catiline, or both.

If such a scroll existed, it would implicate Quintus Annius Chilo in the Catiline conspiracy. That document would be worth killing for. But who would know of such a document? Perhaps someone who was looking for it. Could I find out from the woman who had searched Aemilia for documents? Maybe.

I made my way back to the apartment building we had previously stayed on the Quirinal Hill. Epiphanes had once told me I was a quick study. Well, I had learned much about moving in the shadows over the last week, lessons more important to me now than physics or rhetoric. I stood across and slightly down the street from the building's entrance and waited for the woman who had recognized me and had searched Aemilia. As I stood underneath an awning, I pulled the hood of my cloak over my head, becoming a shadow in a shadow.

I forced myself to be calm and still by concentrating on my breathing, in and out. Minute after minute. I waited.

Shortly after midday, the woman emerged from the apartment building, walking on the other side of the street but in my direction. I waited until she passed and then I followed her. She didn't hurry. She had an exaggerated sway to her hips as she walked, and she stopped to flirt with one of the street vendors before moving on.

I followed, but then, remembering what I'd learned, when I crossed the road, I glanced over my shoulder and marked the people behind me. Was anyone shadowing me? Did anyone cross the road with me? That's when I saw them: two men walking together, both solid men with broad shoulders, laborers or military men. They crossed the street when I did, and they kept pace with me. Their being on my trail might have been a coincidence, but I was following the woman from the apartment, so my options for confirming that they were after me were limited. I couldn't simply choose a meandering path. All I could do was continue to follow the woman and check again after she had made a few turns.

She walked by the vegetable market, through the River Gate, and on to another street vendor, with whom she flirted, gently touching his face. When she stopped, I did as well, coming to a halt in front of a shop selling lamps. As I pretended to look at the selection of hanging lamps, I kept an eye on her and then glanced behind. Up ahead, she was giving the vendor a kiss on his cheek. Behind, the two men were still there. They, too, had paused at a shop, but they kept looking my way.

She started walking again. So did I. So did they. We headed toward the docks and the same warehouse I had searched the night they'd taken Aemilia. I glanced back over my shoulder while walking. The two were still there. When I turned back around, I collided with a man standing on the walkway. I looked up at his face as he stared down at mine. It was Scarface, the man who had kidnapped Aemilia.

He looked as surprised as I felt, but I recovered more quickly than he did and ran across the street, weaving in and out of the flow of people in the road, as I made toward an alley. From the shouts of people being pushed out of the way behind me, I knew he was following.

As I reached the end of the alley, I spared a glance back. He was just entering it. What I couldn't see were the two men who were following me. Would they try to cut me off? I turned away from the direction they would likely come and ran as fast as my legs would take me. I needed to put as much distance as possible between where they might emerge and where I was. My heart was pounding so hard I couldn't think clearly.

Scarface was big and strong, but he was also slow, and I soon increased the distance between us. I dashed into another alley and through the warren of small chandler shops that served the merchant ships. I turned at random. When I reached the docks, I stopped and headed back toward home. As I passed a pile of discarded baskets, I picked up one, and hoisted it across my shoulders so it rested against my neck, forcing me to bend forward. Then I slowed to a walk and stooped as if burdened, so that I would look different to the eye of someone searching for me, but also because I was exhausted. I had to catch my breath. I was at risk of collapsing under the weight of the empty basket.

I shuffled along the docks with my basket, but I saw nothing of those who followed. Every time I turned, I checked behind me. Twice I completely reversed course to check, but I saw no one following. Finally, I put down the basket and headed back to the inn. The day had been a complete failure.

Regulus was in the atrium when I returned. He never seemed to leave. I was disheveled and sweating, but he merely lifted an eyebrow and shook his head.

When I entered our room, Aemilia was sitting on the bed reading. The wonderful smile she gave me quickly faded into concern. She put down her reading and came over to greet me.

"You are a mess. Where are you hurt?"

"I'm not hurt anywhere," I protested.

"I don't believe it. Show me."

I smiled. She no longer gave me commands as if addressing the family dog. I had been promoted to small child.

***

We were late rising the next morning, as neither of us had slept well once more. We'd spent much of the night talking over our events of the day.

"You can't just show up at the warehouse again. They'll be waiting for you," Aemilia said as she scraped the last of the porridge from her bowl with a spoon.

"No, but I can follow the woman. I think running into Scarface—"

"Acaunus Cicatrix."

"Running into Acaunus Cicatrix was an accident. They didn't have any idea I was following her."

She frowned. "What about the two men following you?"

"Ah, well, that's a problem." I pushed my plate back and put my elbows on the table. "I don't understand how they found me. No one could have known I was waiting. I'm sure of it. But I will recognize them now. I'll keep an eye out for them."

"Vitruvius, she won't lead you to a document. It probably doesn't exist anymore—if it ever did. If Annius is so afraid of it, he would make sure it were destroyed."

She had forced the subject into the open. I hadn't wanted to admit that the document probably no longer existed. "I know. I'll confront the woman and persuade her to tell me what she knows. I was hoping she would lead me to a place where I could talk to her safely."

Aemilia looked up and met my eyes. "Why would she do that? She has no reason to tell you anything, Vitruvius, and plenty of reasons not to. I saw her. She is hard. She would have killed me if ordered to. I could see it in her eyes."

"Aemilia, I, I can't think of any other way." As I said it, an emptiness welled up in my chest that threatened to suffocate me.

She looked at me for some time, her eyes large and dark and filled with feeling. I had to look away.

"Vitruvius, you always tell me that problems have solutions. You just haven't found the solution yet."

"Aemilia, I've—"

"You've not looked everywhere or at everything. An answer exists." She took my hands in hers. "You'll find it. I know you will."

I needed to walk, to be alone, to think. I left the inn and roughly headed down the street towards the glass-maker's shop, not really paying much attention to where I was going.

After some time, I realized I wasn't sure exactly where I was. That's when one of the large men from the previous day came up beside me and grabbed my arm in an iron grip. His friend came up on the other side of me and put his hand on the hilt of a knife at his waist.

"You'll be coming along with us, Master Vitruvius. Someone wishes to talk with you."

CHAPTER SIXTEEN

INIMICUS INIMICI MEI AMICUS MEUS EST
The enemy of my enemy is my friend.

The men on either side of me eliminated any means of escape. Forceful and persistent, but not vicious, they weren't like Annius's other street thugs, the ones I had been following. These two steered me down the street with the practiced ease of professionals, deftly directing me through crowds and around obstacles. They accomplished this with a firm grip and completely relaxed faces. I doubted anyone at all noticed my plight. If they did, they showed no sign. Had these men wanted to move Aemilia through the streets of Rome against her will, they certainly could have. I had been so naive. And so lucky.

I needed some time before I could push the panic down enough to speak. "Who, who are you? Where are you taking me?" My voice was surprisingly steady, given I was about to be killed, but neither man responded. I drew a deep breath in preparation for shouting out when the man on the left backhanded me hard in the abdomen, knocking the air from my lungs.

"Please be still, sir. We don't want to hurt you, but we *will* deliver you to our master, preferably conscious, for your sake."

My breathing had just returned to normal when we took another turn. I recognized the street. This wasn't the docks or the street that led to the apartment as I had feared. It was the street I had taken only the day before. Just down to the right, I could see the graceful house of Quintus Fabius Sanga.

No queue of clients waited outside today. When we approached the entrance, the gatekeeper moved aside, and we passed through the vestibule.

"Right foot first!" the gatekeeper scolded as we entered.

"Please be seated, sir," the man on my left said, releasing my arm once we had entered the atrium.

I sat, so completely confused I could scarcely do otherwise. As the two men withdrew to the edge of the atrium, Sanga entered. He smiled at me and took a seat in the chair opposite.

"I'm sorry that I brought you here in the manner I did, but these are extraordinary times that demand extraordinary measures. I hope you weren't injured."

My head was spinning. "No. I'm, I'm fine." Meeting his eyes was difficult for me. His expression was not unkind, but it was accusative.

He leaned forward. "What is your relationship with Quintus Annius Chilo? Why were you following Narcissa Hostilius?"

"Narcissa Hostilius? I don't know who that is."

He looked exasperated. "Narcissa Hostilius, the woman who works at Annius's Quirinal Hill apartments. The woman who runs his informers. The woman you were following."

"I've never heard her name. I just knew she worked for Annius." Then something occurred to me. "Your men, they weren't following me, were they? They were following her?"

"Yes, they were following her. But why, then, were you following her? When I saw you speaking with Annius in the Forum, I thought you one of his men, perhaps out of necessity because of debt, but one of his men nevertheless. Now he has called for your death, and here we discover you secretly following his people."

My attention to his words stalled at "called for your death." My breath caught, and I swallowed. "He wants me dead?" My voice broke. I had realized such a possibility existed, but only abstractly—until now.

Sanga sat back, and his face relaxed. He reached out and lightly squeezed my forearm. "Yes. He has put out a call for your death. Any drunken thug with a dagger may try to collect. Perhaps you should tell me how this came to be."

How could I tell him? How could I trust him? But how could I not? He clearly didn't like Annius, and I was way over my head and out of options. "I will need to start at the beginning."

"I have always found that a suitable place to begin."

I told him of my family's loans from Gaius Gargonius and how Annius had promised to pay my father for delivering messages.

"What sort of messages?" he interrupted.

I told him of my father's murder and the cipher he was carrying.

Sanga let out a long breath. "We discovered some enciphered messages, too. I would give anything to know what they say. We—"

"Oh, I deciphered it and read it," I said before thinking much about it.

Sanga's mouth dropped open, and his eyes grew wide. He swallowed. "You deciphered it? How?"

I told him how I had counted the letters in the cipher to make a drawing of how they were used and did the same for regular Latin text.

"The drawings all had the same shape, but the cipher's shape was shifted down by three from that of the regular Latin text. So, to read the cipher, I just had to shift all the letters down by three. The cipher *D* becomes an *A*, a cipher *E* becomes a *B*, and so on."

He was silent at first. "Do you remember what it said?"

"Oh, I never forget anything I read. The message wasn't signed or addressed, and it commanded the reader to seize Praeneste by force of arms in a night attack on the Kalends of November. It also gave details on how to access the city, what buildings to destroy, and who to kill, and that they were to hold the town until others could join them."

Sanga was silent again, this time much longer than before. Finally, he said, "Why didn't you tell anyone about what you had found? Surely, you realized its importance."

"I didn't decipher the message until the fourth, three days after the attack was to have taken place, and I hadn't heard of any attack on Praeneste, so I dismissed it as someone's strange fantasy, a joke. Not until I arrived in Rome did I learn of the Catiline business and how Praeneste fit in." I looked down. "Also, I was worried that if I told anyone, they would think me a part of the conspiracy and wouldn't believe me when I told them how I came to know. Would you have believed me?"

Sanga nodded, more to himself than to reassure me.

"Why did you come to Rome, Vitruvius?"

"As I said, to secure a loan." I looked up at him. "And to discover who killed my father and why. I now know Annius had him killed because my father was trying to find out more about the message he was to carry. Annius all but told me that when I met him in the Forum, but I don't have any proof. I was following the woman, ah, Narcissa, to find evidence linking Annius to Father's murder."

Again, Sanga was quiet for some time. "I'm sorry, Vitruvius. You will never discover any evidence to link Annius to the death of your father. Annius is far too clever for that." He paused and leaned forward again. "And you need to stop following his people and remain out of sight. He will have you killed. Murder is one of the very few skills in which he excels."

I shook my head. "I can't just hide. If I don't find a loan, my family will lose our home. We'll lose everything."

"Would you rather lose your home or your life *and* your home? Think about it, Vitruvius." Sanga looked over at the two men who had brought me here, and had stood waiting for his command. "Escort Vitruvius back to where he is staying and make sure he is safe. Treat him well."

***

Absent the threat of imminent death, the trip back was considerably more pleasant than the trip that morning. Sanga's two men were friendly, if not talkative, companions. One walked in front of me, and one trailed behind as we made our way down the streets. I noticed—for the first time, given my small stature—how easy walking through a crowd of people is when you're overly large and obviously dangerous. The crowds just parted as if by magic.

The trip back seemed to take no time at all. When we reached the inn, my companions bade me farewell and, incredibly, admonished me to "stay safe."

Regulus was in the atrium when I entered. He looked up and smiled. "It is good to see you, sir. Your wife has been down here four times since you left, asking after you. I'm sure she will be glad to learn you've returned."

When I entered our room, Aemilia practically tackled me. Her eyes were red, and her cheeks wet. I held her, but she pushed back.

She shook her finger at me.

"Where've you been? I've been sick with worry."

"I—"

"I thought something terrible had happened to you. I imagined, well, I imagined the worst."

"Well, I—"

"Never do that again, going off and not telling me. Well, aren't you going to say anything?"

"I've been trying to." Then I told her all that had happened.

She listened, saying nothing, her gaze unfocused. Finally, when I was finished, she looked up at me with sadness on her face. "He's called for your death and will pay someone to kill you? What can you do? Will Sanga protect you?"

"He won't do anything unless I'm with him." I paused to order my thoughts. "It's not all that bad. They need to find me first and they have no idea where we are among the hundreds of thousands of people in Rome. Also, I'm going to ask Regulus for a bodyguard for me and you."

She frowned. "Vitruvius, he hasn't threatened me. Remember, they suppose me to be a Julii. I don't need a bodyguard."

I felt an ache in my chest and a fluttering in my stomach, but I could not find the right words to say how I felt. "Aemilia, I couldn't live with myself if something happened to you on account of me. I couldn't bear it. I just couldn't. I don't know what I would do. No, you *will* have a bodyguard." I waited for her argument, but she gave me only a small, shy smile. She reached up and kissed me.

I walked down the stairs to speak to Regulus. He lifted his head and looked at me when I entered. "Master Marrius. Going out for a walk, are we? Thought the wife would want to keep a close eye on you after today."

"No, I've come to ask a favor of you."

He smiled. "Do tell."

"You said something about bodyguards, I recall."

"Ah, Master Marrius, what have you gotten yourself into?"

I spent the next hour discussing our needs with him. In the end, I hired Onyebuchi as a bodyguard for me. Regulus said his skills with the knife were the best he'd ever seen. As for Aemilia, Regulus would have a man named Pavo Tragus meet her in the morning. I was told that Pavo, when not protecting vulnerable, unaccompanied women, was a fine cook and the father of three doting daughters. I was uncertain the men were the best bodyguards available, but they might well have been the most unique.

***

Winter blew in while we slept. Even with the still-glowing embers, the room was chilly. I could see my breath and the cold caused us to dress quickly.

"What now?" Aemilia asked as she brushed her hair.

Moving the brush through her hair was a simple act. I watched her hair shimmer in the early-morning light streaming through the window. She was beautiful. I had to shake my head to bring back my focus.

"I don't know. Try to find another source for a loan, I suppose. I have Sanga's list, but I am venturing into uncharted waters." I sat on the bed with her, close enough for our legs to touch. "Regulus said that our bodyguards would be here this morning. We can start with that."

When we entered the atrium, three men were there, speaking in low voices. Regulus and Onyebuchi, I knew. The other must have been Pavo Tragus. He was older than I had supposed, with short gray hair and dark eyes. His weathered face showed the faint scars of fights long forgotten, but his body was still corded like a thick rope. He carried all the marks of a former legionnaire.

"Master Marrius, Mistress, I have the men you requested," Regulus said.

"Thank you, Regulus." I answered as I considered them. "They will do fine."

Aemilia stepped forward. "It is good to meet you, Pavo. I hope—"

She broke off as one of Sanga's big men from yesterday entered the room from the outside. He looked at me.

"Sorry to interrupt, but Quintus Fabius Sanga would like to speak with you. Now, Master Vitruvius. It is important."

"Vitruvius?" Regulus asked as he cocked his head with an eyebrow raised. "The same as the man who died on the stairs?"

"I'll explain later," I told him. "Aemilia, I'll be back as soon as I can."

"Be careful," she replied, and a shadow crossed her face.

Onyebuchi approached. "Stay here," I told him. "I'll be fine in the care of this, ah, gentleman."

"But, sir. Are you sure?"

My response was hard to put into words, but I had met Sanga. I had seen his house. He was a good man, as my mother had said. "Yes, I'll be fine."

I stepped outside with Sanga's man. The other was waiting for us outside. We headed down the street, with one man in front of me and one behind.

We took the same route as the day before, sort of two *L*s in a row followed by a *V*, and when we reached Sanga's house, the gatekeeper opened the door.

"Right—"

"I know. Right foot first," I interjected.

He nodded and led me into the atrium, where two men sat, apparently waiting for me. One was Sanga. The other I didn't know.

"Please sit, Vitruvius," Sanga said. He gestured to the other man. "This is Gaius Julius Caesar, pontifex maximus and now elected praetor. He has some questions for you."

I swallowed and bowed before sitting on the bench opposite them. This was Julius Caesar, one of the most important people in the entire Republic, one of its leaders, a praetor to be, the second-highest position in the Republic. I had felt less intimidated when I thought I was to be killed.

Caesar leaned forward. He had a fair complexion, athletic build, and somewhat full face, but what I most noticed were the lively black eyes that seemed to look into my very soul.

"Sanga tells me you deciphered the message about the attack on Praeneste."

"Yes, I did." I swallowed and had to drop my gaze from the force of his stare.

"Can you show me how?"

"I, I cannot. I don't have the message anymore. I burned it."

Caesar reached into his tunic, extracted a scroll, and passed it to me. I unrolled it to find random text, probably a cipher.

"That is a message we intercepted in late October. We think it is the same message that your father had. Can you show me how you deciphered it?"

If it were the same message, all I had to do was shift the letters down by three. They could have worked that out. Then I understood. If I knew to shift the letters by three but couldn't show how I had figured it out, I would have to be one of the conspirators. This was a life-or-death test.

"All right, but I will need blank scrolls, ink, and some regular Latin text, like speeches." I laughed. "Your speeches will do."

Sanga looked over at a servant standing at the edge of the atrium. The servant brought a tray and placed it at my feet. On it lay blank scrolls, pen and ink, and several scrolls of text. Sanga had remembered everything from my explanation the day before.

On hands and knees, I laid out the scrolls on the floor. It took a little less than an hour to recreate the drawing I had made for the first cipher.

"This is a picture of the letters in the cipher, their number." I showed them the scroll. "See, it looks like a mountain range with two peaks, one at *H* and one at *M*. Before, between, and after the peaks, there are these little valleys which are of three different heights: low valley, high valley, peak, low valley, peak, high valley." I pointed to the features as I spoke. Then I spent an hour making two drawings of normal Latin using the speeches they provided.

"These are the drawings of normal Latin." I held them up. "See, the peaks of normal Latin drawings are at *E* and *I,* vowels, rather than at *H* and *M,* consonants, as in the cipher's drawing. But they have the same shapes of peaks and valleys, just shifted left by three."

On the side of one scroll, I wrote the two alphabets, one above the other, but one shifted left by three letters.

```
DEFGHIKLMNOPQRSTVXYZABC
ABCDEFGHIKLMNOPQRSTVXYZ
```

"This is the key that unlocks the cipher. Look here. The letters are just shifted down by three. I can use it to decipher the message."

On a fourth scroll, I wrote the deciphered message using the key I had just made. Then I laid out all four scrolls on the floor of the atrium. The scroll was, indeed, the same message my father had been given. Sanga and Caesar stood beside the scrolls and studied them.

Caesar, who was actually quite tall, began pacing back and forth along the scrolls, studying them. Finally, he looked over at me and shook his head.

"Vitruvius, this is amazing. How did you learn to do this?"

"I didn't learn it. I just do it. I see pictures in my head. I've always been good with pictures."

Caesar looked over at Sanga, who nodded.

"We tested your key last night on this cipher, and it worked, as you just demonstrated," Caesar said. "We needed to see how you did it because we discovered another cipher two days ago, and your key doesn't work on it. We tried shifting the letters down by every possible amount. They enciphered it in some other pattern." He reached into his tunic and handed me another scroll. "We need you to decipher this message if you can. It may be very important."

CHAPTER SEVENTEEN

EX NIHILO NIHIL FIT
Nothing may come from nothing.

Caesar's words froze me in place, and he continued to stare at me with his hand extended, holding the scroll. Yes, I had deciphered the Praeneste scroll, but that was because I had recognized the pattern. I possessed no general understanding of solving ciphers. I had been favored by the gods.

"Vitruvius?" Caesar's question prompted me back to the present.

"I'm not sure I can," I replied. "I may not see a pattern in a different cipher."

"Well, you won't know until you try, will you?"

My mother's words came back to me: *You do not know what you can change until you have tried.* I took the scroll and unrolled it on the floor. The text appeared to consist of random letters, but was written in a different hand than the last cipher—one not as sure or as steady, an older hand, perhaps. I grabbed a blank scroll and counted letters. Caesar and Sanga sat, watching, waiting as if I would suddenly announce the solution. Their scrutiny made me self-conscious, but I couldn't exactly tell them to go away. That would be like a mouse ordering a pair of bears about. Then I thought of Syphāx's words, uttered now so long ago. This mouse would simply pretend the bears didn't exist. I focused on my work.

When I finished two hours later, I sat back. My drawing had two peaks, one at *N* and one at *R*. It also had valleys, but the overall shape was wrong. It looked nothing like the normal Latin drawings.

"Well?" Caesar asked, walking over to me.

"I don't know. The shape is wrong. It has been enciphered by some different pattern."

Caesar sat back in his chair and sagged. Everyone was quiet.

Sanga exhaled a long breath. "I guess believing that you could just sit down and provide us the answer, son, was too much for us to expect. We thank you for trying."

Caesar sat up and leaned forward, his brow furrowed. "How long did it take you to decipher the first message?"

"Two days. I had to think about it overnight."

He smiled. "Sanga, bring this boy some food and wine and let him think."

"I'm not sure the process works that way," I said. "Last time, the thought merely came to me that the cipher picture and the regular Latin picture looked the same, only shifted down. Perhaps the gods guided me, but I haven't always found their help very reliable."

Caesar stood and moved his chair closer to me. He leaned near and said softly, almost in a whisper, "Look at them, Vitruvius." He pointed. "Take a deep breath and look at them. Do they look the same now?"

"No."

"Not at all? Nothing is the same?"

"Both pictures have two peaks, but the valleys are all wrong."

"Is anything else the same? Anything at all?"

"Not really." Then I noticed something. "The two peaks are four letters apart in both drawings, *N* and *R* in the cipher drawing and *E* and *I* in the normal Latin drawing."

"What does that mean?"

It meant something, but I wasn't sure what. The cipher had two peaks like normal Latin, and the peaks must represent *E* and *I* and… "*I* follows *E* by four letters, so the peaks in the cipher must be *E* and *I*. It is just the rest that doesn't fit." I stood and stared at the drawing on the floor.

"What do you mean, it doesn't fit?" Caesar asked.

"Well, in the normal Latin drawing, there is a high valley, really a sort of shadow peak, caused by *A* just before the *E* peak, with a low valley in between. And see here." I pointed. "A high valley near the end in the normal Latin drawing is caused by *R, S, T,* and *V*. But in the cipher drawing, the shadow peak that should be near the beginning is near the end, and the high valley that should be near the end is near the beginning. It's like everything is backward... everything is backward. Everything is reversed!"

I dropped to my knees and looked for another blank scroll, but I couldn't find one. "Where, where? I need another blank scroll!"

Sanga leaped up and ran off, not even troubling to have a slave go. A moment later, he placed a pile of blank scrolls beside me. I unrolled one and wrote the alphabet across the bottom and the reversed alphabet above it. But what I had was wrong. The cipher *R* peak was over the regular Latin *G,* and the cipher *N* peak was over the regular Latin *L*. They should have been over *E* and *I,* not *G* and *L*. I stared at the picture.

```
ZYXVTSRQPONMLKIHGFEDCBA
ABCDEFGHIKLMNOPQRSTVXYZ
```

"Vitruvius?" Caesar asked.

Then I saw it. "It's reversed and shifted by two... No. No. No. They are using the old alphabet, the alphabet we had before we added the Greek *Y* and *Z*. This is two letters short. See, the cipher has no *Y*s or *Z*s. That's because those letters aren't in the alphabet they used."

Caesar and Sanga looked confused.

"Look, let me show you." I wrote a new reversed alphabet above the ones I had already written, but I started with *X,* not *Z*. Now the cipher *R* peak was over the normal Latin *E,* and the cipher *N* peak was over the normal Latin *I*. "It works. That should be the key."

```
XVTSRQPONMLKIHGFEDCBA
ABCDEFGHIKLMNOPQRSTVX
```

I took another blank scroll, and using the new key, I deciphered the message. Caesar and Sanga stood on either side of me, reading along as I wrote. Like the Praeneste cipher, this message was neither addressed nor signed. It directed the receiver to make a list of all foreign tribe representatives in Rome who might be persuaded to rise against the Republic in their homelands in exchange for forgiving all debt owed to Rome. The message's recipient was then told to be prepared to deliver a message to those representatives.

"By Jupiter's name!" Caesar exclaimed and shook his fist in the air. "They are trying to raise an insurrection in the provinces. The army would have to be called away from Rome to deal with it, leaving Rome defenseless. A very clever plan."

"Yes, but who are they?" Sanga asked. "It doesn't say who sent it or who was to receive it."

"We know who sent it," Caesar replied.

"Yes, but we have no proof. We need proof," Sanga added.

"We'll find proof."

The two smiled at each other. Suddenly, Caesar seemed to remember that I was in the room. He put his hand on my shoulder. "Yes, Vitruvius. This was an amazing piece of work. You have done Rome a great service, but this must stay beneath the rose, very secret. If any should learn of this, all may be lost. You must tell no one." He looked over at Sanga. "I will inform the consuls. Cicero must be told. I'll take my leave of you, Sanga."

He glanced back at me with an enigmatic smile. "And you, too, Vitruvius. We will meet again."

***

Sanga walked Caesar out, and I was left alone, sitting on a chair in the atrium. The tiled floor was covered with scrolls, inkpots, and other debris. It looked like the aftermath of a great storm, and the silence somehow emphasized this. The shock of the day had left me drained, and the hour was but midday.

Two servants entered and directed me to the dining room, where Sanga was waiting, sitting at a table spread with food. Also seated was a woman I assumed to be his wife.

"Please join us, Vitruvius. You should let us feed you before you go. It is the least we can do," Sanga said.

I realized how hungry I was. Aemilia and I had planned on having breakfast after we met our new bodyguards. "Thank you. I will."

Sanga indicated the woman at the table. "This is my wife, Trebonia."

"I'm happy to meet you, Madam." A slave put a feast on my plate, several slices of meats, and some fruits and vegetables. One of the meats was lamb, an expensive delicacy for someone of my station.

"My husband says you are a very bright young man, Vitruvius," said Trebonia. She glanced at Sanga. "Perhaps the brightest he has ever met."

I feel my face flush. "Madam—"

"He takes after his mother," Sanga said and smiled, "and Caesar wants to collect him."

"Oh, my. Him, too," his wife replied.

I was confused. "I, I don't understand."

Sanga bent forward, moved his plate out of the way, and put his arms on the table. "Caesar makes a habit of surrounding himself with the smartest people he can find. Not a bad strategy. In fact, that is to be admired, unless one considers the purpose."

"The purpose?"

"Many in power surround themselves with smart people so they can outmaneuver potential rivals. It is a common tactic. Crassus does it. Pompey does it. Caesar does it. They bind the intelligent to them and put them to their own use."

I considered his words. "Why should they not? They would be fools if they didn't seek advice. That is the purpose of the Senate, is it not?"

"Yes, it is, and they ask the Senate for advice. But they ask their own advisers for a different kind of advice. Advise not shared. Advice for their own political benefit."

"I don't understand."

"You see, you will never understand people like Crassus or Pompey, or even Caesar, unless you burn with ambition. And Caesar burns much hotter than most. I have seen it, and Cicero has seen it. Caesar wants it all. Beware, Vitruvius. The poor man who enters into partnership with a rich man makes a risky venture."

I laughed at the absurdity of the notion. "I doubt Caesar will remember my name after a few days. I'm hardly of any consequence to him or his plans, whatever they may be."

"Mark my words, son. He knows your name."

***

I walked slowly back to the inn from Sanga's house, the best speed I could make. I was stuffed. I hadn't eaten so well since… well, ever, and it had merely been a quick lunch. Being rich certainly helped. I was just sorry that Aemilia hadn't been with me to enjoy it. I wasn't sure I should tell her. Describing the elaborate food might be too cruel.

Sanga's two men were escorting me again, but our relationship had changed. They were now deferential and cheerful. The one in front was Davus, and the one behind, for some unknown reason, Nasus, yet I saw nothing remarkable about his nose. They had slowed to a comfortable walking pace for me, but they still effortlessly parted the tide of people on the sidewalk, allowing us to make good time on our return.

When we reached the inn, they smiled, bade me goodbye, and left. Inside, I found Onyebuchi sitting patiently in the atrium with Regulus. They rose when I entered.

"You are well?" Onyebuchi asked as he looked me up and down. "I would hate to lose a contract before it even starts. Such an outcome would look bad for business."

"No, I'm fine. Those two are… friends."

"That is good. No one should have enemies that large."

I laughed and turned to Regulus. "Do you know if my wife is upstairs?"

He gave me a lopsided grin. "Yes, she is upstairs... Master Vitruvius."

Vitruvius? Yes, Davus had used my name that morning. How could I explain? "Well, ah, about that."

He held up his hand to forestall my explanation. "She told us your story, sir. It's better that we know since we are to protect you two."

I caught my breath as my heart raced. Better for him or one of his men to kill me and collect the payment, too. Regulus must have noticed my discomfort.

"Don't worry, Master Vitruvius. No amount of money would be worth betraying you to Quintus Annius Chilo. He's no friend of ours. Tried to run me out of business two years back. Tried to take over the entire block, the whole collegia. I wouldn't throw him a rope if he were drowning. Onyebuchi and Pavo feel the same."

"We do," Onyebuchi said, nodding.

"Thank you, Regulus." I couldn't think of what else to say. His words had lifted a great weight from me. I hated deceiving these men. I turned to go upstairs.

"I'll be here when you need me," Onyebuchi said.

I hadn't thought about what to do with him when we were not out in the town. I guessed this was the custom.

"Where is Pavo?"

"Your mistress sent him home, as she was not going out and Regulus and I were here. Pavo will be back for tonight. Then I'll go home for a while," Onyebuchi said.

"That's the way it works," Regulus said.

I nodded and headed upstairs, while weighing the coins in my shrinking purse.

***

"What did Sanga want with you?" Amelia asked when I closed the door to our room. "You were gone an awfully long time."

She sat on the bed, holding a rolled up scroll she had been reading. I kissed her on the top of her head, sat beside her, and started my tale. I decided to leave out the bit about dinner.

She listened attentively while I told her how I deciphered the message, but, as Caesar had commanded, I didn't tell her what it said.

She spotted the omission instantly. "So, what did the message say?"

I grimaced. "Caesar ordered me not to tell anyone."

"I'm. Not. Anyone," she said and put her hands on her hips, a gesture usually followed by her hitting me with a spoon. Fortunately, at present, she was unarmed.

"Aemilia, I cannot tell you."

"Marcus Vitruvius—"

"Aemilia! It's, it's far too dangerous. Just knowing what the message said could get you killed. I won't put you at such a risk. I will not."

She was quiet for a moment, but I could see her jaw clench and fire light her eyes. I was surprised she didn't ignite. Finally, she said, "Sanga thinks that Caesar will want you? For what? Or is that something you can't tell me, either?"

I ignored the jab. "I don't know. I cannot imagine that Caesar would want me for anything. He can have his pick of anyone in Rome. He would hardly need me to spend my days reading ciphered messages for him. I'm just a farmer's son, and he is a descendant of the gods. No, he'll forget me soon enough."

She was quiet and bit her lower lip, something I had seen her do when she was agitated. She looked up. "Remember, I'm meeting with Caesar tomorrow about a position as a medica for the Julii. Pompeia told me I'm the one who has to persuade her husband. I've been reviewing everything I can about healing, but I don't know what to say to him. Any ideas? Should I tell him I'm with you, or is that secret too?"

I sighed and I thought back to my impression of Caesar when I met him. "First, you may certainly be intimidated by him. I was. He is a contradiction, tall and muscular as a soldier yet meticulously dressed and every hair in place. He presents a powerful presence, and his eyes seem to see into your soul. Just be ready for that. He is also a handsome man. Like a good building, you know, perfectly proportioned. You could draw a circle or a square around him and he would fit it exactly.

"Second, as Sanga said, Caesar is ambitious. Tell him you can help him succeed somehow, maybe by keeping him healthy. Show him you are the smartest medica he has ever met. As to mentioning me, no, my meeting with him isn't a secret, but I'm not sure if your knowing me is a good or bad thing. I hope I made a good impression, but I'm not sure if I'm an asset or a liability for you. Perhaps the problem is that he may remember me."

She was quiet for a long time, her eyes not really looking at anything. Finally, she grabbed me and buried her head in my shoulder. "This is my last chance. I don't know what I'll do if he says no."

Later that night, as we lay in bed, I could tell that Aemilia wasn't asleep. Her breathing was shallow and her body tense. I thought about my family, and that I had made no progress in securing a loan. I was in no position to offer comforting words to her, though she needed to hear them. We were both running out of options. All I could do was hold her.

CHAPTER EIGHTEEN

HIC FUNNIS NIHIL ATTRAXIT
This line has taken no fish.

The weather turned so wicked the very next morning that my breath formed clouds in the frigid air of our room. Sleet pelted the stone street and rattled the roofs. My memories of Rome were of her bathed in the warm sunshine of late spring, not that day's foul display.

Aemilia had been up for hours, agitated, pacing. She had changed her hairdo twice and was considering yet another style. With each alteration, she sought my opinion. I learned after the first two that the question was a trick. If I agreed with her own opinion, I was told that she wanted to know what I really thought. If I disagreed, I had to defend my choice under strenuous cross-examination. I honestly told her she looked lovely, but she replied that this was not a useful judgment.

"Humph," she said as she looked into the hand mirror. "It will have to do."

"Are you sure you don't want me to come with you?"

"No. I need to do this by myself. I think my looking self-confident is essential."

"I'll walk you downstairs, at least."

She exhaled a long breath, steeling herself, and we left the room.

When we reached the atrium, Pavo was waiting. He wore a legionnaire's cloak, now so worn as to be unrecognizable, were it not for its distinctive cut. I caught the hint of a sword beneath the cloth.

"Good morning," he said.

Amelia kissed me on the cheek and pulled up the hood of her cloak.

"The gods be with you," I said.

She glanced back and gave me an apprehensive smile.

"I'll make certain she is safe, sir," Pavo said, drawing up his own hood.

Then they stepped out into the heavy sleet and disappeared down the street.

I spent the day with Onyebuchi learning how to kill a man with a knife, a subject of study my tutors back home had been remiss in not teaching me. I had never really thought about the pugio my father wore and I now had belted at my waist. The dagger had been a weapon only in an abstract sense, but with Onyebuchi's guidance, I learned how to use it for its intended purpose.

Aemilia returned in the early afternoon, soaking wet, her cloak shedding beads of water in a trail on the floor. I helped her hang her wet clothing on the ropes we had fashioned around the warmly glowing brazier. She shivered but smiled, which I took as a good sign. Then she wrapped herself in a blanket and sat down, stretching her legs toward the fire. I waited patiently in the silence that followed, knowing she would speak when she was ready. The crackling of the brazier's embers was the only sound in the room; the burst of sparks the only movement.

"It was an interesting meeting. I guess it went well," she finally said.

"You guess? You don't know?"

"I don't really know. I met with Caesar. A servant took me to him as soon as I arrived. No waiting, no line, just right in. He sat at in the tablinum at a table piled with documents. I sat on a chair opposite him."

She looked down, obviously recalling a memory, and then glanced back at me. "You were right about his eyes. They were so intense, dark, piercing. I could hardly return his gaze. He asked about Publicius. Said he had a great fondness for 'the old man,' as he called him, and was sorry Publicius had left the family's service. He said the letter of introduction from him was the only reason he agreed to see me." She pulled the blanket tighter and stretched her legs closer to the fire. "He told me he didn't want a medica. He had always had men treat him."

"Then why did he agree to see you?"

"I'm getting to that. He supposed a woman might be of use to the women of the family if she were of good training and character. He pointed out that I was not married. Then he asked about my coming to Rome and where I was staying. I could tell what he was thinking, the same thing I heard from the other medici I met with. I told him about the death of my family from disease, coming to live with my uncle, and studying under Publicius. My story didn't move him. I could see it on his face. He was about to dismiss me."

She paused and then said, "I took a gamble." She grimaced. "I hope you don't mind, but I told him you had escorted me to Rome and were looking after me while I was here."

"What did he say?"

"He completely changed, as if I were a different person. One moment I was about to be dismissed, and the next I was an old friend. He smiled and called for a servant to bring me a cup of calda. While I blew the steam from the mug, he started asking me questions about you, where you came from, who your parents were, what your family was like. I answered as best I could. He just grilled me, none of which was about medicine, all about you. He asked me if you had told me what the cipher had said. I told him you had refused. He laughed at that. Then he had a servant come and take me back to the vestibule."

"That was all? He didn't give you a decision?"

"As I was putting on my cloak, he came into the vestibule and told me he had been thinking. The thought occurred to him I might be of use to the women of the family. If I was of good training and character, he might consider hiring me as a medica for the Julii, but he would have to think about it." Aemilia opened her document case. "Then he gave me this and said I was to give it to you."

She passed me a folded sheet of papyrus with a clay seal. "What is it?" I asked.

"I don't know. It's sealed."

I broke the seal and read the letter. "He asks that I come by the Domus Publica tomorrow at the sixth hour and meet with him. It doesn't say why."

***

The next morning, Onyebuchi, wearing the apple-red cloak I had given him, this time held in place with a lion's paw clasp, was waiting for me in the atrium. The whipping wind of the previous night had blown the sleet out, but the gale had died, too. Now the air was as still as the dead.

"You ready?" I asked as we stepped outside.

"Yes. I am ready." He drew back the cloak to expose a long knife in a leather sheath at his waist.

"Pray to Minerva, we won't need that."

He grinned. "Maybe, but this is what you are paying me for."

We walked in silence along the streets, Onyebuchi beside me, his gaze roving everywhere.

Caesar had lived in an old, modest dwelling on the slopes of the Quirinal Hill, but when he had taken office, he had moved to the Domus Publica, the official residence of the pontifex maximus. This was anything but modest, situated at the far end of the Forum, behind the Regia and between the House of the Vestals and the Via Sacra, in the very center of Rome and Roman life.

We arrived at the start of the sixth hour, with the sun directly overhead, and stepped up the stairs to the building's doors. One stood open, and a man dressed in a spotless toga stood at the threshold.

"Marcus Vitruvius Pollio?"

I nodded. "Yes."

"This way, please. The pontifex maximus is expecting you." He turned to Onyebuchi and pointed to a man standing off to the side.

"That man will see to you. He will feed you and take you to a place to wait."

Onyebuchi hesitated, looked at me, and I nodded. Surely of all the places in Rome, I would be safe here. The man then led me through the atrium to a dining room and held out his hand, bidding me enter.

When I went in, I saw Caesar sitting at a simple military field table with a modest lunch spread on it.

"Vitruvius, I'm so pleased you came. Please, join me for lunch while we talk."

The meal before me was simple, fruits, bread, nuts, all of excellent quality but not lavish in either selection or quantity. But plenty of wine was at hand.

He noticed my gaze. "The food is from the residences' kitchens. It is quite good." He picked off a grape. "I wanted to thank you for deciphering that message. It has been very useful in helping us identify the agency of treason the Republic now faces. I am sorry Rome cannot yet acknowledge or reward your service. Perhaps that will come in time."

"I didn't do it for a reward. I have no love for those wishing to harm the Republic." In truth, I could hardly have done otherwise with both Sanga and Caesar staring at me.

"I'm sure, but you came to Rome for money, yes? Or at least, that was one reason you came."

"Yes, that *is* part of it. I need to find a loan. Otherwise, I will lose my family's land."

He took a date and pushed the bowl to me. "Please, eat one of these excellent dates and drink some of the wine. It is very good." He reached over and filled my cup with wine. "Sanga told me some of your situation. The sum you seek isn't small. It will be hard to find without good connections or prospects, and you have neither."

"I know," I replied, my eyes downcast. What else could I say? I took a sip of the wine to cover my embarrassment and found it quite strong. It was undiluted. Did Caesar wish me drunk?

"Perhaps that, too, will come in time." He paused eating and stared at me, his brow furrowed. "Sanga said that you believe someone murdered your father here in Rome and that Annius ordered it?"

"Yes, my father was murdered—"

"How do you know that?"

I explained to Caesar how the wounds on my father's head had led me to consider murder and then told him what Annius had said when I'd confronted him in the Forum.

He was quiet for a time, eating, his eyes focused somewhere in the distance. Based on what I now know of him, his thoughts would have been equally about what I had said along with how he could use the information to his advantage. I came to understand that Caesar never made a decision which wasn't carefully considered and directly beneficial to himself.

"I suspect you are correct, Vitruvius, but you will never prove it. If you want justice, it will have to be of your own making." He took a handful of olives from a bowl as a servant picked up our empty plates. "Tell me of this woman, Aemilia. She said you are looking after her."

The change in subject caught me completely by surprise. "Ah, yes, I am. Her uncle, Epiphanes, was my tutor. He asked that I look after her during the journey and here in Rome."

"Look after her? She is a charming young woman and not married and—"

"No, no, it's nothing like that. She is an honorable woman." I could feel my face flush.

"I did not mean to imply otherwise. But you are fond of her?"

I hadn't thought of it in quite those terms, but yes, I was fond of her. Like Aemilia's questions that morning, this was a trick. I could hardly say that I was not "fond" of her. "Yes, I am fond of her."

"Is she a good medica?"

"Yes. The best I have ever known. She studied medicine for several years, and Surius Publicius tutored her. I'm not sure I would have made it to Rome without her. She saw me through both illness and injury."

"Should I hire her for the family?"

"Absolutely! She could take care of anything. I know it."

He said nothing at first, just grinned. I thought I caught a glint in his eyes as they searched mine.

"Thank you, Vitruvius. Rome owes you a debt that I hope it can reward, and I thank you for telling me about Aemilia. I will have to think about it. Please tell her I will give her my decision soon."

He stood and motioned for a servant. "Teaus here will lead you out."

Onyebuchi was waiting in the Domus Publica's vestibule, and we made our way back to the little inn. As we walked, I pondered Caesar's purpose for the meeting. I suspected it was but a part of some larger plan.

***

Still, no wind stirred as we walked back to the inn. A pall of eye-stinging blue-black smoke clung to the city, billowing from the thousands of cook fires and braziers. I love Rome, but it is a miserable place in the winter. Not everyone has a refuge indoors, and some of the truly poor are left out in the cold and wet. Many don't make it through the winter. As we walked back to the poorer area where the inn was, Onyebuchi and I passed men collecting the bodies of those who had died during the night from exposure or disease. The sight was a bleak reminder of what it meant to be so destitute that you couldn't find a place inside to sleep. Some become desperate enough to sell themselves into slavery for a roof and a meal. Such was the potential fate of my mother and sister if I failed. I always had the option of joining the legions.

Regulus was sitting in the inn's atrium, as was his custom, only this time under a blanket. He rose when we entered.

"Master Vitruvius, this arrived for you. It was delivered by Cico Baibius's messenger service." He held out a scroll.

It was a message from my sister. I broke the seal at once and read it.

Marcus,

It was wonderful to receive your message. We are making ends meet but were having problems getting workmen to repair the barn. Apparently, Gaius Gargonius had threatened everyone we contacted, but Epiphanes put a stop to that by convincing the entire town to publicly condemn his behavior. I think Epiphanes has made an enemy of the Gargonii. I know you are working hard to find a loan, but we are afraid. We feel time is running out. I make an offering to Fortuna every day for your success.

I am hesitant to worry you further, but I must be honest with you. Mother has taken ill. She never fully recovered from Father's death, and I know she is worried sick about you, perhaps literally. She does not eat and speaks little. She is wasting away. Epiphanes had Syphāx take her to Publicius's house, where she is now being looked after as a favor to Epiphanes. I am deeply worried about her. I have never seen her this way.

I have included a small bit of stone from our lararium. It is a token of our family's Lares. May our house spirits protect you there as they would here. May they protect you there as they protect our home and lands.

Write again when you can.

Vitruvia

CHAPTER NINETEEN

AUT VIAM INVENIAM AUT FACIAM
I will find a way, or I will make one.

That night was long and black, with neither of us sleeping. Our restless thoughts came to the fore when I shared my sister's letter with Aemilia after dinner. Then we talked until dawn, sharing our insecurities and fears of failure. Neither of us could see a clear future beyond a handful of upcoming dawns. Sometime that night, amidst the small talk, tears, and mutual comfort, I understood how deeply I loved Aemilia. She was the flame that lit up my heart. I wanted a future with her in it, though I couldn't put the feelings into words. Not that I didn't want to tell her. As during many times in my life, I was unable to bring myself to speak it. Every time I started to tell her, my throat just clamped shut. How could telling her how I felt be so hard?

The dawn came, and we both resolved to take our destiny back into our own hands. Aemilia's destiny hung on Caesar's nod. She vowed to find a way to approach Pompeia again and win her as an ally. My fate depended on somehow convincing someone on Sanga's list, a person I had never met, to loan me a not-so-inconsiderable amount of money. All that could be said for the plan was that at least I had something I could do, however unlikely my success.

"I'm coming with you," Aemilia said, and she had that "it's not negotiable" expression she wore when giving out medicine. "I need to send a letter to Pompeia requesting an interview and I can't do that until tomorrow."

I had previously learned that arguing with her was futile at best and possibly painful at worst. Besides, I actually wanted her company. Just having her near kept my desperation at bay. I smiled with acquiescence.

Pavo and Onyebuchi were waiting when we walked into the atrium of the inn. Regulus was there as well, of course. They stood as we entered.

"We are going out together this morning. We'll need only one of you." I looked them over. Judging from Onyebuchi's baggy eyes, he had been there all night. "Onyebuchi, why don't you get some sleep? You look tired."

He nodded. "I am tired, but I can still go, sir."

"No. You need sleep. We'll be safe with Pavo."

He smiled. "You have your knife?"

"Yes," I replied, patting the spot where the pugio lay hidden beneath my cloak.

"And you remember your lessons on how to use it?"

"I think so. Keep light on the balls of my feet. Keep out of range. When I strike, thrust to kill and slash to disarm."

Onyebuchi smiled, lighting his whole face.

With Pavo in the lead, we stepped out of the inn and into the morning flow of people. Though the day was bitterly cold, the slight breeze cleansed the air of the smoke and haze. The gray sky was laden with the rain or sleet that would soon fall. Aemilia, sensing my mood, put her hand in mine and gently squeezed. I felt its delicate shape, its soft touch, and it seemed to suck the tension from my body.

I had looked again at Sanga's list. At the top was, as expected, Marcus Licinius Crassus, by far the wealthiest man in the world. He had acquired his wealth by fire and war, making public calamities his greatest source of revenue. Over time, he had developed the sole fire brigades in the city, but they would only put out a fire if the owner sold him the burning property at a deep discount. Consequently, many rumors suggested that Crassus's men set the fires in the first place. No, he was not my first choice.

I decided instead to visit Lucius Aemillius Quintilianus. He was near the bottom of Sanga's list but was known to be more approachable than the rest. At least he had a reputation for being honest and open to new clients. He lived back on the Quirinal Hill, close to the infamous apartment we had used. Instinctively I checked behind us as we crossed the street. We were too close to the old apartment.

We continued towards Lucius Quintilianus's villa. By the time we arrived, a queue of clients already stretched from his door. That meant a great deal. An empty house bespoke a homeowner's decline in power just as clearly as a bustling one signified his ascent.

A servant with thin gray hair, mangled ear, and eye patch stood, writing tablet in hand, guarding the entrance.

"I would like to see your master, if I may. I am Marcus Vitruvius Pollio. Quintus Fabius Sanga sent me."

"What?" he asked. "You'll have to speak louder. I don't hear so well."

Raising my voice, I repeated, "I would like to speak with your master, if I may."

"You are?"

"Marcus Vitruvius Pollio."

"Who?"

"Marcus Vitruvius Pollio," I said loudly. "Quintus Fabius Sanga sent me."

He read down his list. "You're not one of his clients, are you? He only sees clients."

"I've been told he would consider taking on new clients."

"What?"

I paused to tamp down my annoyance and raised my voice. "I said, I've been told he would consider taking on new clients."

"Yes, of course he takes new clients. Everybody knows that."

Keeping my voice raised, I asked, "How do I become a new client?"

"Oh, that. You write him a letter and tell him why he should see you. Bring it to me when you're done." He opened up his writing tablet again. "Who are you? I'll make a note of it."

"Marcus Vitruvius Pollio," I said again, practically shouting, partially to be heard and partially out of frustration.

As we left the villa, Aemilia leaned in close and said in a quiet voice, "Why does Lucius Aemillius Quintilianus tolerate such a man as him for that position?"

Pavo, in the lead, looked over his shoulder and answered, "Rumor is, that man saved Quintilianus's life when they were in the legions."

Aemilia met Pavo's gaze. "I'm sorry. I should have thought it would be something like that."

As we headed back to the inn, we walked along the main road and through a connecting alley. The route took us to the Latiaris stairs. Though it was the fastest route, I had been avoiding it. The stairs brought back too many memories. I gripped Aemilia's hand as we crossed the street to enter the alley and glanced back. I couldn't break the habit I had developed when Annius's men had followed us everywhere. That's when I saw them; three thugs had blocked the width of the alley and were fast approaching. By the look of them, they weren't the most friendly sort.

"Pavo!" I yelled.

***

The three men realized I had spotted them and rushed forward, drawing knives. Pavo sprang like a cat, turning and charging the men. As he rushed past Aemilia and me, he stooped to pick up a loose brick on the pavement and threw it at the lead attacker. His target, the fat one in front, put up both arms to fend off the incoming brick. *Thud.* The brick glanced off the fat one's head. Dazed and bleeding he staggered and swayed, trapping the other two men behind him. Pavo drew his gladius from underneath his cloak and lunged at him, plunging the short sword into the fat man's belly. Then he used the impaled weapon to steer the fat man into the older man following behind. The two fell to the ground in a heap.

The third attacker, the youngest, either more cautious or more skillful, had veered around the tangle of the other two, and he hesitated only an instant before leaping at Pavo from the side. Pavo saw him as he put his foot on the first attacker's middle and, with a sucking sound, pulled his gladius out of the man's stomach just in time to deflect the third attacker's knife thrust. Pavo had the advantage, his sword against his attacker's knife.

I stood awestruck at Pavo's speed and skill. As he traded thrusts with the last attacker, the second attacker, the older man, recovered from underneath the fat man's dead body and rose to his feet. He stared at me, and the pure rage on his face finally released my paralysis. I drew the pugio from underneath my cloak and stepped between him and Aemilia.

"Run, Aemilia! Run!"

To my surprise the older attacker didn't come at me. He yelled, "I'm coming son," as he turned and lunged at Pavo just as he disarmed the young amateur.

"Pavo!" I yelled. Without thinking, I struck at the older attacker.

"No, Vitruvius!" Aemilia shouted.

Pavo heard my warning. He kicked at his young opponent and turned to meet the older attacker. Ducking under the man's knife thrust, Pavo stabbed up and struck him in the chest just as my pugio went into his back, glancing off of a rib, and sinking to the hilt in the older man's flesh. The father collapsed.

Pavo turned back to the young attacker, who had retrieved his knife and was lunging at Pavo. Pavo brought his gladius around too late. Though he diverted the attacker's knife down and away from his chest, the blade slashed across his flank.

I had pulled out my pugio from the older attacker's back as he was falling, and in desperation, I lunged forward to stab the young one in the throat before he could strike Pavo again. I saw his eyes go wide with surprise as he brought up both hands to stop the blood spraying from his throat.

"Mithras!" Pavo grunted, invoking the god of Roman soldiers, as he sagged to the ground, clutching his side.

Aemilia rushed by me and dropped to her knees beside him. "Give me your knife, Vitruvius," she demanded as she took off her cloak.

I handed her my bloody blade, and as she cut the bottom of her cloak into wide strips, I turned aside to vomit. The reality of what I had done hit me. Two men—a father and his son—would meet the ferryman tonight, and I had sent them.

Aemilia bound Pavo's wound. "We have to take him back to the inn. He needs attention. Help me carry him."

Amelia and I put Pavo's arms over our shoulders and lifted him. He could bear some of his own weight, and we half carried him through the gathering crowd of spectators and back to the inn.

***

The sleet that had been threatening since the morning fell, and our feet slipped on the paving stones as we struggled to support Pavo, almost dropping him twice. He was losing consciousness, so we had to carry more and more of his full weight.

Regulus's smile at our return changed to alarm as he took in Pavo and the stream of blood and water, running down his side and onto the floor. "What happened?"

"We were attacked," I said. "By three men."

"Pavo needs a room where I can see to him," Aemilia added.

"The men, are they following?" Regulus asked as he dragged out a long cudgel from a drawer in the table.

"No, I think we killed them all," I replied.

He looked at me sharply. "We?" he asked, and seeing my face, he nodded. "Bring him back here." He led us from the atrium to a small room in the back. It had a single bed, a few chairs, and Onyebuchi's apple-red cloak hanging on a peg in the wall. Obviously, the room was used by Pavo and Onyebuchi when we were upstairs.

We laid Pavo on the bed, and Aemilia probed his wound.

"Vitruvius, bring me my medical supplies," she said.

"I'll summon a medicus," Regulus said.

"No! I am a medica," Aemilia replied in an acidic tone. "I will care for him."

Regulus glanced over at me, his eyebrows raised. I nodded to him and left to gather up Aemilia's boxes.

She spent the afternoon cleaning Pavo's wound, packing a poultice into it, and binding it tightly. Pavo was unconscious, but he was breathing steadily and deeply. Finally, she stood and stretched with her hands on her lower back. "Well, it's up to Hepius now. It is only the gods that stand between Pavo and death."

"How is he?" Onyebuchi asked.

I jumped. I hadn't noticed him enter.

"The next day will tell," Aemilia answered without lifting her gaze from Pavo. "He has lost a lot of blood and survived." She put a hand on his forehead. "If he doesn't run a high fever, he'll make it."

Onyebuchi and I walked into the atrium to sit with Regulus, leaving Aemilia in a chair at Pavo's bedside.

Regulus cleared his throat, getting our attention, and then said in a quiet voice. "I had some people check on your assailants. They confirmed that all three are dead." He cast a quick glance at me before continuing. "They were simple street thugs and not unknown in the lowest parts of the city. Mostly they prey on the drunk and unwary at night. Annius's bounty must have made them bolder."

I thought about that. "Someone must have heard my name when at Aemillius's house and tipped them off."

"Probably," Regulus agreed. "I wouldn't go back there if I were you. Too many eyes and ears about."

"And do not go out alone, you or your lady," Onyebuchi added. "Someone may have followed you back here. You were hard to miss, carrying Pavo."

Regulus sighed. "You're right. I'll have to put some eyes on the block and make sure no strangers are skulking around."

I had just stood when I heard several feet approaching. I reached for my dagger.

"Where is he?" a young girl demanded as she entered the atrium. She was fourteen or fifteen years old. Two younger girls were with her—one maybe seven, and the other, perhaps, four. Both struggled to hide behind the older girl's cloak.

***

"Pavo's daughters," Regulus said, glancing at me. "I sent word to them." He shifted his attention to the three young girls. "I'll show you."

I followed behind the girls as Regulus led them back to Pavo's room.

"Papa!" the youngest of the girls exclaimed as all three scrambled to the bed.

Aemilia, surprised, futilely sought to block the girls from hurtling into the bed, but the three girls weaved and ducked, dodging her arms. "No. No. Don't jar him. Be careful!" she pleaded. She turned to me, a cross look on her face. "What is this?"

"Pavo's daughters."

Her scowl faded as concern and sadness appeared in her eyes. "Where's their mother?"

Regulus answered in a quiet voice, "She died giving birth to the little one. Pavo's been raising them with some help from the older one."

"What's wrong with Papa?" the smallest asked.

Aemilia bent to one knee, bringing her eyes level with the little girl's. "Your father has been hurt. He'll get better soon, but he needs to sleep and not be moved around."

"How bad was he stabbed?" the oldest asked, her voice nearly breaking.

Aemilia looked up at her. "It was bad, but I think I can heal him."

"Are you a medica?" the middle daughter asked.

Aemilia smiled. "Yes, and I can help your father." She stood and gestured to the girls. "And you can help too, by letting your father sleep. I'll tell you when he's awake."

"We'll stay here. We're not leaving him," the oldest said, her defiance obvious.

"I'll set up a room for them," Regulus said. He took the three girls and left the room.

"Is he really going to recover?" I asked quietly.

Amelia nodded. "I think so. Fortunately, the knife missed everything important. It hit a rib."

She resumed her vigil in the chair next to Pavo, and I spread a blanket on the floor to lie down close to her.

***

I jerked awake and reached for my knife, and panic set in as I found I didn't have it. Then I realized that I was still lying on the floor in Pavo's room and Aemilia was shaking my shoulder. I had been dreaming of men with knives creeping up behind us.

She looked down at me with dark eyes. "It's nearly midnight. You should go upstairs and go to bed."

"What about you?"

"I'll stay here a little while longer. You go up. I'll be there soon."

I had just managed to stand up when Onyebuchi came in. "Those two big fellows who work for Sanga are in the atrium. They said they are to take you to him. Didn't say why."

As I entered the atrium, I saw he was right. Davus and Nasus were waiting for me.

"Evening, Master Vitruvius," Davus said. "Master Sanga has need of you. He said it was important and that you should come right away."

"Now, in the sleet and the dark?" I asked. "It's almost midnight."

"Yes," they answered in unison.

CHAPTER TWENTY

SCELERE VELANDUM EST SCELUS
Crime must be hidden by crime.

I walked between two hulking shadows, Davus and Nasus, for in the dark and sleet, that is all they looked to be, vague shadows. The hour was late, and I was cold and drained by the day's developments. I hoped that what Sanga wanted was really important. With Davus looming ahead of me, I couldn't see where I was going. I put one foot after the other and followed in the shadow of the shadow in front of me. Focused on ignoring the gusts of sleet-filled wind, I was surprised when a familiar house emerged from the gloom.

Sanga greeted me at the entrance. I put my right foot forward, and he quickly ushered me inside to his tablinum and bade me sit in a chair placed close to a glowing brazier.

"I didn't know if you would come. I am so glad you did. We have need of you."

I couldn't recall his men giving me a choice. If they had, I surely wouldn't have come. "I am honored that you called," I simply said.

He just looked at me, his head cocked slightly. I suspect some of my annoyance showed on my face. He said nothing.

I broke the silence. "I assume you have another cipher?"

His eyes seemed to focus on me. "Yes, we do. Much has happened, and this may be important."

"What happened?" I bent forward.

"You deserve to be told. What you are doing is making a difference." He took a deep breath and paced. "None of what I say must leave this room, Vitruvius. It is all sub-rosa, for your ears alone. Caesar says you can be trusted, and he doesn't say that of everyone." He paused for a moment as if gathering his thoughts. "After the last message you deciphered, we sent agents to all the tribal representatives in and around Rome to find if any of Catiline's men had approached them. We found the conspirators reached out to the representatives of the Allobroges."

When he saw my furrowed brow, he explained. "They are a tribe from Cisalpine Gaul and owe Rome a considerable amount of money in yearly tribute. The Allobroges agreed to help the conspirators by creating a diversion in Gaul to draw troops away from Rome. Lentulus and others gave the Allobrogean envoys letters and pledges of support."

"How—"

"Wait. There's more. After the conspirators left, the Allobrogean envoys decided acting as spies for Rome would be more beneficial, so they made it be known to me. I'm their patron, you see. It is my duty to look after them. I took them to meet with Cicero, who persuaded the envoys to feign interest in joining the affair. They told us they will be escorted from Rome to Faesulae to meet with Catiline and Manlius tomorrow evening by way of the Mulvian Bridge. Cicero has ordered the praetors, Quintus Pomepeius and Lucius Valerius Flaccus, to ambush the entourage at the bridge. We should obtain the proof we need. Your deciphering the message set all that up."

"Then why do you need me now if you have the proof you need? What else do you want?"

"We intercepted two ciphers as they were being delivered from Catiline to some of his supporters here in Rome. What we do not know is who his fellow conspirators are. We hope these ciphers will help shed some light on them." He sighed and seemed to deflate. "Remember,

Catiline planned to murder many in the Senate. All of us fear a knife in the back from his unknown supporters."

He reached into his tunic and withdrew two scrolls. When he held them out to me, my gaze dropped to the smear of blood that ran along the outside of the larger one.

***

I took the scrolls to Sanga's table in the tablinum. The time was near the end of the twelfth hour and the beginning of the new day. Sanga retired to snatch a few hours' sleep, citing the exhausting events of the day, leaving me with a pile of blank scrolls, ink, and more scrolls containing writing in normal Latin. One of his slaves stood silently in the room's corner, with instructions to fetch anything else I needed. I was filled with apprehension that Sanga expected me to solve both ciphers by the time he returned.

I unrolled the scrolls. The larger one contained a long message, consisting of twice as many letters as either of the previous two ciphers. Unsurprisingly, the smaller one contained a short message, much less than half the number of letters of the other ciphers. I stared at both while stifling a yawn, forcing my eyes to focus. My day had been exhausting, and I would have to struggle to resist falling asleep. I wasn't sure I could even think clearly.

I took a deep breath and picked up the longer message. Though the reality may seem counterintuitive, solving a longer cipher is easier than solving a shorter one. Take a short message of only five words, when its letters are counted, not enough letters are available to show the shape of the peaks and valleys. The more letters available, the more detail the drawing has to reveal the cipher's true shape.

I took a blank scroll, wrote the alphabet along the bottom, and counted the letters in the longer cipher. The drawing that developed was unlike either of the previous two ciphers. It had peaks, but they were at *A* and *G*, six letters apart, not four letters apart like normal Latin or the other ciphers. Three lesser peaks emerged at *C*, *S*, and *T*. The expected valleys were there, roughly three different heights, but they were all in the wrong places. Whatever mechanism this cipher used, it did not keep the letters in the same order. They were scrambled up somehow, not just shifted or reversed. This was something altogether new and different, and I had no idea how to solve it.

At first, I just glared at the drawing, anticipating I would see something I had missed, but nothing materialized. I knew the two peaks must be the real Latin letters *E* and *I*, so I tried to think of any scheme that would lead to them being six letters apart instead of four. Again, nothing came to me.

Suddenly, I jerked awake to find Sanga's hands on my shoulders and my head on the table.

"Vitruvius, wake up, son. You've fallen asleep."

I straightened, feeling a crick in my neck and struggling to suppress a yawn. "Sorry. I didn't realize it."

"How are you doing? What have you found out?"

Rubbing my eyes, I told Sanga what I had discovered, and that I didn't know how to find a solution.

"The first time you solved the cipher, you figured it out after you had slept, didn't you?"

"Yes, but—"

"I think you need a fresh mind. Why don't you sleep for an hour and then try again? I should have realized you needed to sleep, too. Casus, take Vitruvius to Mirus's room. I'll wake you in an hour."

***

I had scarcely closed my eyes before Sanga shook me awake. He said I had been asleep for a little over an hour, but I didn't feel that I had slept that long. The mug of calda he handed me probably did me more good than the much-too-short nap had.

I followed him back to the tablinum, softly stepping over the sleeping slaves in the hall. I sat at the table and stared at the drawing. The light cast by lamps on each end of the table created overlapping shadows on the pile of scrolls and ink. The only other source of illumination was the brazier against one wall.

What was I missing? I expected to find a pattern to indicate how the letters were changed, one that was easy to remember. Otherwise, the sender and receiver would both need to have a written copy of the cipher alphabet, the key to decipher any messages. However, having a written copy of the key would be as risky as having the messages themselves.

To decipher the previous two messages, I had made a drawing of each cipher's letters so I could perceive a pattern. But that only worked if the letter's relative positions were the same. Clearly, that was not the case with this cipher. But what if the pattern was in the key itself? What if the key had some simple pattern that was easy to remember? How would you see a pattern in the key, though? What did I know?

I took a new scroll and wrote the alphabet across the bottom. Above it, where I would normally write the cipher alphabet, I put a dash in place of each letter. I took a second scroll and filled it with dashes, one for each letter in the cipher's message. The cipher's *A* and *G* must be the normal Latin *E* and *I*, so I wrote *AG* above the normal Latin *E* and *I*. I also wrote *EI* on the second scroll everywhere an *A* or *G* occurred in the cipher message. Still, I saw no apparent pattern.

What else did I know? The next three tallest peaks, *C*, *S*, and *T* in the cipher, would have to be *A*, *T*, or *V* in normal Latin, so I did the same for them. Normal Latin has distinct word endings depending on the noun's declension and the verb's conjugation. For example, while an *A* or a *V* would be common as the next-to-last letter in a word, *T* would not.

Each time I confirmed one choice, I eliminated another, and each piece led on to the next one. Slowly I filled letters in the dashes representing the ciphertext and the corresponding cipher key. Then I saw the pattern. The creators of the cipher had used a word as the pattern in the cipher alphabet. I could make a reasonable guess that the cipher alphabet began with *COLEGIVM* and was then followed by the letters not used in the word.

COLEGIVMABDFHKNPQRSTXYZ
ABCDEFGHIKLMNOPQRSTVXYZ

It made sense. Their keyword, *COLEGIVM,* designated them as a brotherhood or an association. What better way to remember the key?

Sanga had been quietly sitting in the chair by the brazier, with only half his face visible. He came over then as soon as I sat up and smiled.

"Vitruvius?"

"I have it. I've found the key."

"The key?"

"The way to unlock the cipher and read it."

"What does it say?"

"I'm deciphering it now."

I chose another blank scroll and, applying the cipher alphabet key, deciphered the message. It was from Catiline himself to Senator Lentulus, and it detailed the names of seven other people and the positions they held in the conspiracy. Noted at the top of the list was Gaius Cornelius Cethegus, whose job was to acquire and store weapons for the conspirators' use.

But what caught my eye was the name at the very bottom of the list: Quintus Annius Chilo, responsible for messages and communication. The man who had murdered my father. Even half asleep, I smiled. I would have my justice after all.

***

I gave Sanga the deciphered scroll. As he read the message, his eyes grew wider with each line. "This, this is astounding, Vitruvius." He glanced up at me and beamed as I yawned back at him. "I need to take this to Cicero now. It cannot wait. With this, we'll obtain confessions. Give me all your work so I can explain to Cicero how you deciphered it, should he ask."

"I still have the small cipher," I said as I gathered up all the scrolls. "It will be much harder to decipher if it uses a different key. What do you want me to do?"

He thought for a moment, peering at the wall as if he could see through to the outside. "It is just into the second hour. Why not spend a few more hours on it. I doubt it will tell us anything new." He placed his hand on my arm in a gesture that reminded me of my father. "Go home after that, son, and get some sleep. I'll let you know if I need you again. Davus will be here to take you back. Just ask for him."

He collected all my documents and left me sitting at the desk. I glanced around and noticed the slave he had left to fetch things for me still standing in the corner.

"What's your name?"

"Aquilius, sir."

"Well, Aquilius, why don't you sit in the chair by the fire? It's tough to work with you standing there."

"Sir, I'm not—"

"Sit. If anyone asks, I'll tell them I told you to."

With an involuntary sigh, he sat.

***

I picked up the small scroll and counted the letters. When I finished, I had a drawing of sorts. As expected, none of the peaks or valleys seemed very pronounced. The message simply didn't have enough letters to show a good definition. I saw two peaks at *E* and *V*, and those were probably *E* and *I*. Beyond that, I couldn't see any form.

The two peaks at *E* and *V* meant this cipher, like the last, was not shifted or reversed. And having a peak at *E* was curious. I doubted anyone would choose a keyword where the cipher *E* was a real Latin *E*, so I assumed, at least for the moment, that the cipher *E* was really the *I* and the cipher *V* was really the *E*. Using that as a starting point, I began trying letters for word endings.

Over the next couple of hours, I made spotty progress until I noticed a curious set of letters in the message. I worked out that the cipher *A*, *V*, and *Q* were actually the real Latin A, *E*, and *S*. In the message's text, I then noticed *_AESA_*, and the unknown letters on either end were middle-level valley letters. Perhaps because he was on my mind, the name Caesar stood out. I tried the C and the *R* in my solution. Pieces fell into place, first a little, then more and more until I found the solution. The key word was *AMICVS*, followed by the rest of the alphabet. All the letters lined up. I wondered at the significance of using a word for friends as a keyword.

```
AMICVSBDEFGHKLNOPQRTXYZ
ABCDEFGHIKLMNOPQRSTVXYZ
```

The deciphered message was another letter from Catiline, addressed to Lentulus. In it, Catiline reminded Lentulus that if Lentulus needed help, he should contact Gaius Julius Caesar. Catiline had discussed the issues with Caesar two months earlier, and while Caesar had not committed to becoming involved, he had expressed sympathy for their cause. Catiline's opinion was that Caesar would come to their aid if needed.

What I read stunned me. I knew Caesar had worked to expose the conspiracy. He had helped me decipher the second message and argued against the conspirators in the Senate. Caesar had just been elected to a lifelong position as pontifex maximus in Rome and praetor for the coming year. Perhaps he had once supported their cause but had backed out before its designs and some participants were discovered. He didn't need to endanger his political career by associating with the participants in the affair. His support for the conspirators made little sense.

What, then, of this message? It said that Caesar hadn't actually joined their cause. But he had known about it before it came to fruition. He had known about a plan to murder senators and overthrow the Republic, yet he had told no one. Perhaps he didn't think the insurrection would ever come to pass.

But if I made this message known, it would destroy Caesar's political career. A whisper of scandal was often louder than a shout of truth.

Moreover, in the back of my sleep-deprived head, in a place far removed from Republic politics and beyond the balance of good and evil, I well knew that Aemilia needed Caesar. Without his nod, her prospects vanished.

CHAPTER TWENTY-ONE

VERBA TRANSEAT PER MUROS ET LAPSU PRAETERITI CLAUDERE ET CLAVIS

Words pass through walls and slip past lock and key.

I followed Davus as he led me back to the inn, struggling not to fall asleep even as I trudged one step at a time. He slowed his pace and kept glancing back. I must have looked as bad as I felt.

I had left a note for Sanga telling him I had not yet been able to decipher the second scroll but would continue to work on it after I slept. I was in no condition to decide whether I should reveal its contents and the small lie gave me more time. I desperately hoped that a clear head would bring a clear choice.

When I entered the inn, Regulus was holding court with two men in the atrium. He turned away from them to greet me with a broad smile, which quickly receded into concern as I drew near.

"Master Vitruvius, you look to have had a long night. I hope it was successful."

"I assume so. Time will tell."

"Well, while you spent the time frolicking with your high-class friends, your lady tended Pavo all night."

"How is he?"

"Much better. He woke up and ate some soup about two hours ago. That's when Mistress Aemilia finally allowed herself to retire." He paused and scratched his head. "Your lady, she has the blessing of Hepius, she does."

"She's in our room?"

"Yes, and you should join her by the look of you."

He was right. I was so tired all I could do was nod.

I entered the room as quietly as I could and found Aemilia asleep in the bed, but not alone. Lying with her, with arms wrapped around her, slept Pavo's youngest daughter. The sight touched me deeply and in an unfamiliar way, and I had to smile until I realized what it meant. With a sigh, I took a spare blanket and rolled up in it to sleep on the floor next to the brazier.

I awoke a few hours later, sometime in late morning, with Aemilia kneeling over me, her hand resting on my shoulder.

"Come to bed, Vitruvius. I took Mia back to her room downstairs."

She helped me up and led me to the bed.

The next time I roused, I heard Aemilia stirring about. She was sitting on the chair by the brazier, washing her face. As if sensing I was watching her, she looked back at me over her shoulder.

"Go back to bed, sleepyhead. I'm going to check on Pavo. I won't be long."

I don't even remember if I acknowledged her before falling asleep again.

When I finally awoke, it was late afternoon, judging from the shadows on the wall, and I was alone. Aemilia hadn't returned, or at least, not that I was aware of. My head was finally clear, but my body felt stiff, as though I had slept on the floor again.

***

I found Aemilia in the room where Pavo lay. She was sitting in a chair, her head propped on her hand, her elbow on her knee. She peered at Pavo, who was apparently sleeping. Her face, normally radiant, looked tired and puffy. I was not the only one who had a long night.

"You're up," she whispered.

"Yes. Long night, but you don't seem to have had it much better."

"Oh, I'm fine. Just tired."

"How is he?"

She stood and indicated the door. Once we were outside the room, she said in her quiet bedside voice, "So far, good. If he doesn't run a high fever and the wound doesn't fester, he'll be fine. Otherwise, he'll die. Tonight will tell."

"His daughters?"

"They're back at home. Regulus found a woman to look after them. I told them to come back tomorrow morning. I didn't want them to be here if his blood turns bad." In the pause that followed, she searched my face. "You're troubled. What happened last night?"

"Sanga had two more ciphers for me."

"Was Caesar there?" she asked with a note of hope in her voice.

"No, no one but Sanga."

"I wish Caesar would tell me something. Surely, he's made up his mind by now. I don't know what I will do if he says no, but this waiting and not knowing is eating at me."

"He has been a little busy with the Catiline business."

She glared at me. "That doesn't matter. I deserve to know."

"Yes, you do. I'm sorry."

Her shoulders sagged, and she looked down. "It's not your fault. I'm... worn out." She let out a deep breath and looked back up at me. "Were you able to read the ciphers?"

"Well, yes and no." She raised her eyebrows in a question, and I looked down at the floor, unable to meet her gaze. "I can't talk about it."

"But it troubles you. I know you well enough to see that. You're upset."

"It's just something—"

"Water." Pavo was awake.

Aemilia and I moved back inside the room. She poured water into a cup from a pitcher and handed it to his outstretched hand. Then she put her hand on his head and wrist. "No fever. How are you doing?"

"I've been worse," he said, smiling. "I'll live."

"I suppose you just might. You hungry?"

He seemed to consider the question as if it were something he needed to decide. "Yea, I am."

"Well, good, then. I'll have Regulus bring you some more soup."

"A bit of meat would be better."

Aemilia rolled her eyes at him.

I sat in the chair facing Pavo. "Glad to see you so much improved."

"That's a good lady you have there," he said when Aemilia had left the room.

"Yes, she is."

"You did well, too, with the knife and the last man, I mean."

"I was scared out of my wits. I was lucky I didn't stab myself. You were the one who did all the fighting."

He shrugged, and the gesture caused a wince of pain. "It's what I do. The legions trained me well. I was a centurion. I held *pilus prior* before a wound turned me out. Never thought I would fight again, but I pulled through, good as new, I did. Fighting's all I know, and I do love it so."

"Why'd you not return to the legions once you were able?"

"My girls. When Pella, their mother, died, I had to take care of them. Sometimes you have to put family ahead of what you want or what you believe. That's all you can do."

Pavo was right. I thought about the other cipher, the Caesar cipher. I had really only one answer.

***

Aemilia returned with soup for Pavo followed by Regulus who carried a scroll.

"This came by courier for you," he said as he handed it to me.

It was from my sister. I broke the seal and read it.

Marcus,

I have much to tell you. Two days ago, while Syphāx was out at the mecellem, two men approached him who do occasional day labor for many of the farms. They told him they, and others, had been hired by the Gargonii to attack our home that evening. Gaius Gargonius the Younger would lead the attack. The two laborers didn't want to take the job, but needed the money, so they agreed. They told Syphāx they intended to go through the motions of the attack, but would not press it home. They didn't know if the other attackers were serious.

We spent the rest of the day making what preparations we could. When night fell, we sent Caster and Lepidus to the roof with buckets of water in case they tried to burn us out, and armed everyone else with the weapons we had, including Mother, Epiphanes, and me.

They attacked close to the twelfth hour. We had reinforced both the front and back doors. Clearly, they had hoped to surprise us. Our being ready for them upset their plans. When they found the doors blocked, they threw torches onto the roof, but Caster and Lepidus were able to extinguish the flames before they could spread.

One attacker tried to climb up to a window, but Syphāx stabbed him. The noise and flames alerted many of our neighbors, who thought we had a fire and came with buckets, causing the attackers to flee.

We are all fine and no damage came to the house, but we will have to stand watch each night until you return.

Epiphanes had the idea of spreading the word that our house gods, our Lares, were too strong and Father's murder had angered them. He told everyone that accidents and sickness would come to any who trespassed on our land. All know of Epiphanes's lack of regard for the gods so the town saw his words as particularly significant.

A man might be ready to fight his neighbor, whom he can see, but not his neighbor's ghosts, whom he cannot see.

We hope you will be successful and can find a way of dealing with this when you return.
Vitruvia

***

What was left of the day passed quickly. All I could think about was the attack on our home. I had to find a solution. I had to. I was so upset and tired, I scarcely remember going to bed. I woke briefly when Aemilia slipped in by my side and put her arm around me. I squeezed her hand. She said in a quiet voice that she thought Pavo would be fine, no fever. Then she dropped off to sleep.

I jerked awake at dawn with an uneasy awareness that someone else was in the room, and reached for my pugio. As I turned my head, my eyes met the deep-brown eyes of Pavo's youngest daughter, standing at the side of the bed. Aemilia had said the girls would be back in the morning. Before I could say anything, the little one crawled under the covers and snuggled up to Aemilia, who didn't wake up. The situation was too much to deal with, so I went back to sleep.

A persistent knocking at our door woke us all up sometime later.

"Yes?" I asked.

"Sorry to wake you, Master Vitruvius, but those two big men from Master Sanga are downstairs and wish you to go with them."

"Very well. I'll be down shortly." I looked over at Aemilia, who was staring at Mia.

"How?" she asked, her puzzlement easy to see.

"She showed up at dawn and climbed into bed. You set a bad precedent." I couldn't help but smile at Aemilia's expression.

"Yeah, well, I'll have to put wedges under the door from here on." She switched her gaze to me. "You have to go?"

"Afraid so. No idea when I'll be back." I kissed her and finished dressing.

The trip to Sanga's seemed to take no time at all. Amazing what a full day and night of sleep can do. Sanga was waiting at the entrance when we arrived, and led me into his tablinum and to the same chair by the fire I had used the last time.

He looked at me expectantly. "The other cipher, son, were you able to read it?"

I swallowed under his gaze. "No, sir. I was not. It just wasn't long enough for me to discover any pattern. I'm sorry." I glanced down, and quickly added. "But I can keep working on it."

He gave me a strained smile. "No, you've done your best. No one else could have done what you did. The one you were able to read has been invaluable."

"What happened?"

"The ambush at the Mulvian Bridge last night was successful. The Allobrogean envoys, as we planned, gave up without a fight. Titus Volturcius, the messenger carrying the letters from Lentulus and the others, surrendered. They seized the letters and brought Volturcius and the envoys to Cicero's house for questioning. Cicero has summoned the Senate to an emergency meeting at midday, but he wishes to speak with you before then."

I needed a moment to understand what Sanga had just said. "Me? Cicero wants to meet with me? Why?"

He smiled. "Yes, Marcus Vitruvius Pollio, you. He seems to think you had something to do with all we've accomplished and wants to speak with you before he puts the evidence before the Senate to determine if he has missed anything."

***

A contingent of armed men met us just outside Cicero's residence. Based on their insignia, they were part of the training garrison at the Field of Mars. Sanga exchanged words with their commander, and they permitted us access. We passed more armed men on display, close to a cohort, as we walked down the road to the house. At the entrance, Cicero's secretary met us and showed us to the atrium, where Cicero was arguing with Julius Caesar, who was clearly angry. As soon as they spotted us, they fell silent.

"This is the boy?" Cicero asked Caesar.

"Good morning, Vitruvius," Caesar said as he approached me. "Thank you for coming."

Cicero came over as well and stood in front of me, his head cocked slightly and with an enigmatic smile on his face. Then he turned and said to Tiro, his secretary. "Clear the room please."

Tiro ushered everyone, including the guards, out of the room. All except Sanga, Caesar, Cicero, and me.

When we were alone, Cicero turned back to me. "So, you are the oracle."

"The oracle?"

"The one who reads secret messages."

"I was fortunate enough to be able to read a few, yes."

"Tell me how, starting with the first one."

I started at the beginning, with my father's murder and the Praeneste cipher and ended with the message detailing the conspirators and their duties.

"What of the last cipher? We believe Catiline wrote it in his own hand to Lentulus."

Pavo's words about family, and Aemilia's dependence on Caesar's nod, had decided me. Remembering what the message had said, I glanced over at Caesar. Perhaps he would understand. "I could not decipher the last message. If I had been able to, then I could have known if it came from Catiline and who the message was about."

Cicero frowned. "What was so different about the last message that you couldn't read it?"

"It wasn't long enough to show a definite pattern of how the letters changed. It would have taken a very lucky guess to have found a solution with so little known."

"You are confident about the other solutions?"

"Yes. The correct solution is the only one that will make sense."

"Well, you were right about the conspirators. We searched the home of Gaius Cornelius Cethegus and found a number of weapons, including spears, knives, and swords, just as the message said. Between the messages you read and the testimony of the Allobrogean envoys, we know of nine conspirators and took five of them into custody. Some of the others may still be in Rome. The Senate is to be convened at the Temple of Harmony and Concord in an hour to discuss their punishment. That leaves us with you."

"With me?" My heart froze.

"Vitruvius, what you did was, well, unbelievable. I certainly didn't believe it until Sanga showed me your work. Rome owes you a great debt. Yours is also a great power and, in the wrong hands, deadly. What you have done here must be kept secret, buried deep beneath the rose. It must not be spoken of or written of, ever, outside of us four. The power to know what your enemies may write in secret is only a power if the ability is kept secret. Rome needs that power. We must have it. We have many enemies, both inside and outside the Republic. I know of your debt, but Rome can do nothing publicly to reward you. We must keep you out of the public eye, for your sake and Rome's. I talked with Caesar about this. He will be praetor for the coming year. We will see what we can do in the new year."

Tiro came back into the room and noisily cleared his throat.

"Yes, Tiro?" Cicero asked.

"Master, the others are waiting."

"Yes, yes. I'll be there presently."

He turned back to me. "I will address the people from the Forum after the Senate adjourns. Come and hear. Then find me. We'll talk afterward."

With that, he left, followed by Caesar and Sanga. I stood alone for a few moments, expecting someone to give me instructions, but no one did, so I went back to the inn by myself.

***

When Aemilia and I arrived at the Forum later that day, the sight of thousands of people packed in and around it waiting for Cicero's address took us aback. We had never been part of such a crowd. Some had been there since morning, so serious was thought the day's oration. Desperately trying not to lose Aemilia's hand, I pushed and elbowed our way to within a stone's throw of the Rostra.

Much was already known, as rumors of the Senate's deliberations had spread like fire through the city. Volturcius and the Allobrogean envoys had testified. Lentulus and four others had confessed in the Senate to writing the letters. They had named four additional citizens as participants in the affair, totaling the nine listed in the cipher. The Senate had found all nine guilty without a trial, a move indicative of the patricians' fear. Lentulus, Cethegus, Gabinius, Statilius, and Caeparius were to be detained until their punishment could be decided. The other four, including Quintus Annius Chilo, were still at large despite a massive search for them, all of them implicated in the deciphered messages.

A stillness fell over the multitude as Cicero stepped up to the Rostra. He motioned for silence. His gestures were mere theatrics, for the crowd was already quiet and waiting.

"You see this day, O Romans," he began, his voice echoing off the buildings surrounding the plaza. "The Republic, and all your lives, your goods, your fortunes, your wives and children, this home of most illustrious empire, this most fortunate and beautiful city, by the great love of the immortal gods for you, by my labors and counsels and dangers, snatched from fire and sword, and almost from the very jaws of fate, and preserved and restored to you…"

He continued for some time, making his case as to the dire threat posed by the conspirators and defending the Senate's actions against them as both right and just. By the end, he had won the crowd over. They would have put the conspirators to the sword then and there if given the opportunity. Cicero claimed he had discovered all the intricacies of the plot through his own diligence and divine providence instead of naming specific informers or revealing the corroborating evidence of deciphered documents. I had expected nothing else, yet his was a brilliant performance of oratory, the likes of which, in all my later years, I would never know again.

The jubilation and cheering from the crowd was nearly deafening when he finished, and a mob surged forward to congratulate him as he stepped down from the Rostra. Aemilia and I, borne along by the throng, fought our way to the podium. How were we supposed to find him? His bodyguards already surrounded him, and the lictors were in front, wielding their fasces to clear a path through the crowd. Everyone was crying his name. I could think of no other way he would hear me call it, so I shouted my own name, "Vitruvius!"

He glanced over, saw me, and spoke to one of his bodyguards.

The moment vanished. The crowd swept us away while he retreated in the opposite direction. Then I felt a tug on my collar and heard a voice in my ear.

"Follow me. I'll take you to Cicero."

With Aemilia's hand in mine, I grabbed the bodyguard's sword belt with my other hand and stayed with him as he cut westward across the Forum and up to the Temple of Concord stairs.

When we stopped, he glanced at Aemilia. "He said nothing about bringing anybody else."

"She has to come. I can't leave her here, in this," I said, pointing to the swirling mass of the crowd.

"All right. He said for you to wait in the temple. He'll be here within the hour."

In truth, only half that time passed before Cicero entered the temple. His lictors stood by the door, barring entry to the crowd still seeking him.

Cicero approached me and gripped my shoulder. "Let us step over here." He glanced at Aemilia. "I'm sorry, but I need to speak with Vitruvius alone," he told her. He led me to an alcove at the back of the temple. "As you are doubtless aware, we convicted the nine on the list. Yes, we presented other proof, but your deciphering told us where to look for that proof. I thank you on behalf of Rome."

"Do you think you might find other conspirators?"

"I think we have all the big fish. Now we find the little ones. Accusations and insinuations will be set forth to settle political grievances, but thanks to your list, we know who is and is not a conspirator. During another meeting of the Senate late yesterday, Lucius Tarquinius claimed Crassus was involved in the affair. That charge was so obviously for political advantage that the Senate did not believe him. In addition, Quintus Lutatius Catulus and Gaius Calpurnius Piso claimed Caesar was involved. With no evidence, their allegation was quickly dismissed. This, too, will die down over the next few days."

I couldn't help but think of the second cipher. Was Caesar involved? Did Catulus and Calpurnius know something? Had I miscalculated and made a horrendous mistake?

CHAPTER TWENTY-TWO

INTER MALLEUM ET INCUDEM
Between the hammer and the anvil.

The clamor continued the rest of the day, following Cicero's speech. All of Rome was abuzz with crowds swarming the streets and shops, speaking and shouting in angry voices. The people called Cicero *pater patriae,* father of the fatherland. He had saved Rome from disaster. However, not all shared that view. A small but growing faction hoped to see Catiline's vision realized. They grumbled in the background and moved in the shadows as Aemilia and I went to bed that night.

By the next morning, the city had settled down. The crowd, which had gone to bed drunk on righteous indignation, awoke with the inevitable hangover of conscience. They began to question the Senate's actions. A different tone echoed in the streets and shops, one of caution, one of accusation. But the Senate was to meet again, and most were content to await the outcome.

We paid no attention to the furor. Aemilia and I stayed indoors, tending to Pavo, who, though still weak, was now sitting up in bed, and taking meals. That was the simple part. Pavo's daughters were another matter. The smallest, Mia, wouldn't leave Aemilia's side, literally hanging onto her dress as Aemilia moved about the room. The middle daughter, Mona, sullenly complained about everything and the oldest, Sabrina, upon discovering I had studied in Athens, displayed an intense passion for Greek culture manifested as a never-ending interrogation on the subject. What was at first touching became taxing. I was approaching wit's end, even as Aemilia kept glancing at me with eyes pleading for patience.

That was how we spent the day. By day's end, the city was quiet, seemingly holding its breath for the Senate's resolution. Aside from checking on Pavo, we slept undisturbed.

***

The next day we were up with the sun and went downstairs to check on Pavo, where we remained for most of the morning. He was noticeably better, but still in some pain. Aemilia busied herself with a mortar and pestle preparing more medicine for Pavo. I recognized what she worked with from Epiphanes's teaching as a tincture of the poppy.

A little after noon, I sensed something. At first, I heard only a low rumble, an indistinct noise, but slowly grew. By the eighth hour, the rumble was strong, the sound of thousands of voices filtering in through the windows and walls. I had decided to find out what was going on when Regulus opened the door.

His eyes were wide with shock. "The Senate is out," he said. "They executed them. All of them."

"What?" I wasn't sure I had understood him.

"They executed them. They say the senators worried about rescue attempts. Cicero persuaded the Senate to order Lentulus and the others executed immediately. They took all of them to the Tullianum—"

"What's the Tullianum?" Aemilia interrupted.

"An old building in the Forum that used to be a well house. They sometimes hold people there. They took the five of them into a small room and an executioner strangled them one by one with a noose. Just like that, all of them, dead."

Aemilia looked pale. "Can they do that, I mean, without a trial?"

"I've never heard of it before," replied Regulus, "Certainly, a trial is customary, and I think lawful. But Cicero used his emergency powers to force the decision and skip a trial. Only Caesar argued against it."

Only Caesar, I thought. If I had any leverage with him, it was slipping away. They all had been so pleased to tell me how much Rome was in my debt and how they would find some way for the Republic to show its gratitude, but our loan was due in less than a month. I would have to act quickly. This was my last chance.

"I'm going up to the room for a moment. I'll be back."

Once in the room, I copied the solution to the last cipher and put the original and all the work scrolls in a bag. Then I wrote a quick note to Sanga explaining how I had solved the last cipher. I added the note to the bag, tied it with a cord, and sealed it.

I set aside the copied solution and wrote a note to Caesar requesting a meeting and telling him I had something to share.

Back downstairs, I gave Regulus the note to Caesar. "Have someone deliver this to Julius Caesar as quickly as you can. And this." I handed him the bag. "Keep this someplace safe where no one will find it. If something were to, ah, happen to me, make sure it gets to Sanga."

He studied me for a moment. "Vitruvius, are you sure you know what you're doing, my friend?"

"No, but I'm out of options."

***

The next morning, Regulus brought Caesar's response up to our room. I read it and handed it to Aemilia.

She studied it. "He doesn't say much, just to come to the Domus Publica in the fourth hour. Do you think I should go with you?"

I had expected her to ask. "No, this will be about the ciphers, and he won't let anyone else in the room."

"He doesn't say that."

"Trust me. It's about the ciphers. I'll press him about your position, too. I won't leave until I get an answer for you."

She sat on the bed, biting her lip. "Vitruvius, I *need* an answer. Not knowing is driving me mad. I don't want the answer to be no, but it's even harder not knowing at all."

I wrapped my arms around her. If I had any leverage with Caesar, she would get that position.

***

Onyebuchi and I climbed the steps to the Domus Publica at the appointed time, and the man at the door led us directly inside. As for the previous visit, a servant took me to meet with Caesar while Onyebuchi remained with the staff. This time Caesar was sitting in the atrium, reading.

"Vitruvius, you are doing well?" he asked when I sat opposite him.

"Yes, thank you, sir."

An uncomfortable silence followed, broken by Caesar.

"You said you had something for me, I believe?"

"Yes, I solved the last cipher."

He cocked an eyebrow. "Why bring it to me?" he asked as I handed him the scroll. He unrolled it. "Ah, I understand. Who else has seen this?"

"No one. *Yet,*" I replied, dangling the last word. "I solved it at Sanga's when I solved the other cipher, the one with the list of conspirators. I knew that what they wrote there would hurt you politically, particularly as I heard what Catulus and Piso claimed of you. I needed to give you a chance to explain before deciding what to do with this cipher."

Caesar was quiet. A flash of anger crossed his face as his eyes bored into me. I felt he wanted me to flinch or to see if he could sense some deeper motive. I met his gaze, not even needing Syphāx's trick.

He started to speak then stopped. Finally, his posture relaxed, and he spoke. "I defeated Catulus for pontifex maximus and I once prosecuted Piso, but yes, I supported Catiline during his failed candidacy for the consulship. I regarded him as a ruinously debt-ridden patrician with a seriously unstable character. Yet he possessed considerable charm and an idea that was fundamentally good."

"To murder the Senate was fundamentally good?"

"No, of course not." He scowled, the anger momentarily returning. "That was a stupid and reckless plan for achieving a noble goal." He stood and started pacing. "People like Cicero idealize the Republic and its values without realizing that those values have become distorted by time. Corrupt oligarchs now rule the Republic while they keep everyone else desperately poor and mercilessly attacked by bailiffs, with no prospect for a better future. Catiline wanted to cancel all debts, enact a large-scale confiscation of property from the wealthy, and redistribute the land to the working poor and ex-soldiers. He wanted universal voting for all public offices and the priesthoods. Rome would return to the Republic it once was. Was that such a terrible goal, Vitruvius?"

I had to agree with what he had just said because I could see it was so, even in my own life. "No, those were good ideals, but that is not what he did."

"No, that is not. I was sympathetic to his early ideas. Many of us were. We judged him morally and intellectually weak, but we thought we could guide him and mold him. As soon as those ideals changed to something else, something personal and sinister, I and many others, distanced ourselves. I wanted no part of it."

"Yet you didn't sound an alarm."

"No, I didn't. It was nothing but talk. We all thought that if everyone withdrew, he would come back to his senses or just fade away into the shadows." He paused his pacing, turned to face me, and thrust out his arms. "Look at Rome! What do you see, Vitruvius? I will tell you. War and debt have ruined farmers. This, you have seen. Slave-run pastures and plantations owned by the very rich spread onto public lands and compete with family farms. Many in the Republic do its bidding but never obtain the full privileges of citizenship, including the right to vote. Is that justice? Is this the Republic we want? The fault is not in what Catiline *wanted;* it was in the *way* he chose to acquire it, by violence when he should have sought it by the vote and the law."

"But still, you argued against the conspirators being put to death."

"Yes!" Caesar caught himself and took a deep breath, unclenching his fists. "Regardless of the crime, what the Senate did was not legal. Roman citizens have the right to a trial no matter how great or how small their crime. Under the state of emergency we granted, the Senate can decree just about anything, even if it is otherwise illegal. We cannot tolerate such a loophole in our democracy. Cicero and I have argued about this."

He was quiet for a moment. Then he sat in the chair facing me. "So, Vitruvius, what will you do with this?"

He held the scroll out to me. It rested heavily in his hand. This was the time I had to choose. Caesar was so persuasive, so sincere, I believed him. More than that, at that moment, I believed *in* him.

"Do with what? As I told Sanga and Cicero, I could not decipher that last scroll. Not enough message was present to find a pattern."

He smiled appreciatively. "Thank you. Now I apparently owe you a personal debt, along with the one Rome owes you. But you knew that already, didn't you?" He half stood and dragged his chair closer to me. "What do you want, Vitruvius? Why are you *really* here?"

I swallowed. The moment had come. "I need to ask two favors of you. You, Cicero, Sanga, all claimed that Rome would recognize the debt you think I am owed, and I appreciate that. But my family must pay back a loan in three weeks, or we lose everything. I don't have the time to wait on Rome. I need your help, or we will be one of the farms you spoke of, destitute from debt."

"And the second?"

I swallowed and took a deep breath. "Aemilia needs that position of medica with the Julii and you would all benefit from her knowledge and labors. I know this as surely as I know anything."

For the first time in our discussion, Caesar smiled. He clapped his hands, and a servant appeared. "Bring some food and drink for Vitruvius and look after him until I return." Then, looking at me, he said, "I understand you now, and I have some ideas, but I will need to check something first. Please remain here. I may not return until the afternoon."

He left me alone.

***

They fed me well, Caesar's servants and staff, but you can only eat so much, and my stomach was so unsettled that I wasn't sure that what I had eaten would stay down. So, I sat alone for hours and waited. I memorized the placement of every tile on the floor and every flaw in the columns. I could see that one must have been hurried into place. It lacked the detailed work of the others. Yet the column was there and had been long before any in its chamber had walked the earth. Even with the flaws, buildings endure long past the lives of the mortal men who built them. To construct a building is to grasp immortality.

Finally, Caesar entered carrying a sheaf of documents and sat in the chair opposite me. He smiled. "I met with Cicero. Given the events of the last few days, getting his ear was not an easy achievement. You present us with an interesting dilemma, Vitruvius. On the one hand, we have to keep you out of the public eye, yet on the other, none of us wishes you to stray too far from our sight. You are too important and, forgive me for saying, too dangerous. We found a way that may meet all our needs."

Relief flooded through me, and I sank into the chair. "Thank you. And—"

"Wait," he said, raising a hand, palm out to me. "Hear me out. You have to agree to the conditions. I will personally pledge you the money you need to pay back your family's loan by the date you need, but you will have to work for it."

"Work for it? I thought I had?"

"You did, and you will continue to do so." He held out one of the documents he was carrying. "This appoints you an apparitor, a Roman official supporting Cicero for the few remaining weeks he is consul. And this document"—he pulled out another—"appoints you as an apparitor supporting me when I'm praetor for the coming year. You will be a scribae, the most senior level of apparitor. It is a well-paid position, paid from the public treasury. You are charged an initial fee to take the position, but Cicero has agreed to pay it for you."

"What would I do?"

"Whatever I need, but as a start you will find the rest of those who supported Catiline. We seized documents and correspondence from the conspirators' homes. Put that mind of yours to work and show us the pattern in the conspiracy. If more ciphers are among the documents, we want you to solve them. We both know you will be able to read every one of them."

This was not the profession for which I had studied my whole life. The offer was a munificent one and a great honor, but I wanted to create beautiful structures. I wanted to build things. Caesar saw my hesitation.

"Vitruvius? This is a generous proposal."

"I know, and I am really honored by it. It's just that, well, I've trained my whole life to be an engineer and architect. I may be able to solve ciphers, but I did it out of necessity. I was born to be an engineer."

Caesar sat and studied me for some time, but I could tell he was focused on something else. "All right," he finally said. "Then I have another deal for you. After my term as praetor, I'll be given a military governorship. It comes with an *imperium*. I can command an army and appoint its officers and staff.

"After your year as an apparitor, I will appoint you as a military engineer, a *scriba armmentarius* or something. In time, you could become Praefect of the camp. It is the best apprenticeship you could hope for. You'll come with me. That will give you the opportunity to practice your art with the army. You can build for Rome, bridges, walls, buildings."

"Yes, that, that would be perfect." I couldn't contain my enthusiasm.

"But..." Caesar went on, emphasizing the word with a finger pointed at me. My mind was racing. He had said this was a deal, hadn't he? So, what did he want me to agree to?

"When I make you an engineer, you will keep the duty of gathering and understanding information on Rome's enemies, whether they are tribes at our borders or conspirators in our streets. You will report to me. Agree to that, and I will also grant your second favor."

Second favor? Aemilia. He would hire Aemilia. I felt tears in my eyes. I didn't like the idea of collecting secrets for him, but he was talking about Rome's enemies, such as the conspirators who murdered my father and those who would attack the Republic. And I thought of Aemilia. This would give her what she wanted and what I needed.

"I agree."

"But I have one last thing you must agree to before I can hire her, and it is not negotiable."

***

Regulus looked up with concern when Onyebuchi and I entered the atrium in the late afternoon. Then he caught my grin and softened.

"Out of the lion's lair, Master Vitruvius?"

"Out of the den, Regulus."

His face brightened. "Excellent. Glad to hear it. So what should I do with the bag you gave me?"

"I'll take it back when you have the time. Is Aemilia upstairs?"

"Yes, sir. She was with Pavo until about an hour ago."

"How is he?"

"Doing much better. He even got up until your mistress yelled at him and threatened him with a spoon."

I chuckled at that. Amelia was intimidating when armed with her spoon. "And the girls?"

"Home. Pavo sent them home."

Aemilia was asleep on the bed when I entered the room. I sat beside her.

She glanced up and yawned. "You're back." Then she sat up. "Are you all right? You were gone a long time. What did he want?" What did he say? Did he say anything about me?"

"Slow down. Everything's fine, and yes, we spoke about you."

She stared at me, narrowing her eyes.

"Caesar and Cicero talked. Caesar will cover my family's debt if I accept the job of apparitor for Cicero, a scribae, for the rest of the year and for Caesar the next year. After his praetorship, when Caesar becomes a military governor, he will appoint me as a scriba armmentarius, an engineer."

She beamed and hugged me, squeezing with surprising strength. "What did he say about me and the position?"

"He will give you the position—"

She shrieked, pumped her arms, and hugged me again, crying.

"But, but…"

She sat back, her face a mask of apprehension. "But what?"

"The position has a condition attached. He said that for the sake of propriety, you must be married before you enter his service."

Her joy evaporated. "That's no dif—"

"Amelia."

"—frent than what—"

"Amelia!"

She stopped talking and eyed me.

"I'll marry you—if you'll have me, that is. Caesar said that if you marry me, he'll give us a place to live here in Rome as a wedding present."

She stared at me for some time. Then she murmured. "Vitruvius, you're serious? I don't have a dowry. I cannot marry you. Everything I own is in those two bags. A woman is supposed to bring something to a marriage, something to start a home. You won't be getting much."

I looked into her eyes. "I'll be getting all I want. Since I won't be given the home unless we're married, you can think of it as a dowry."

"You'll really marry me?"

"Yes, I will. I, I love you, Aemilia."

"Epiphanes would need to agree. He has patria potestas, but I don't think he'll object. He likes you."

"So, that's a yes?"

She rolled her eyes. "Of course it's a yes."

We remained there for some time, just holding each other. My life had passed from the verge of total despair to relative bliss. Not bad for a day's work.

"What does an apparitor do for Caesar?" she finally asked.

"I'm not altogether sure. Nothing interesting, as long as I remain an asset instead of a liability." I knew that the five men Rome had just executed had been valuable until they became liabilities.

CHAPTER TWENTY-THREE

FACTUM EST ILLUD FIERI INFECTUM NON POPTEST
It is done; it cannot be undone.

That night, I slept better than I had since my father's murder. Yes, I knew I had subjugated myself to Caesar, but I would worry about the ramifications of that later. For the time being, my family and I had a future.

I detected a smile on Aemilia's face as she slept, and after she arose in the morning, the smile remained.

"You look happy today," I said. "I'm so glad you have the position. You deserve it. Knowing that must make you feel better."

She looked at me and shook her head slowly, her eyes sparkling. "Yes, I'm glad I have the position, but you do recall that I'm getting married, don't you? That's why I'm happy." Then she narrowed her eyes. "You do remember, don't you? You're not backing out, are you?"

This caught me unprepared. "No. No. I mean yes. I remember, and I'm not backing out. Of course not."

She smiled again and uncovered two small loaves of bread that Regulus had left outside our door.

We quickly finished our simple breakfast of bread and olive oil. Even though we were both now employed, our purses had yet to see any earnings, so we continued to husband our resources and lead an economic life, including eating sparingly.

The first thing I needed to do was to write to my mother and sister. I could imagine the anxiety they must be feeling, not knowing if I had been successful or not. As I sat with quill and scroll, I thought of what had just transpired. Some things, I dared not put to papyrus, for their sake and mine. My life was now filled with secrets.

That was when I realized that my life had changed in a subtle but irreversible way. From then on, I would have a public life out in the open and a private life of secrets hidden from view. Staying alive depended on my discretion.

I wrote to my mother and sister, telling them that I had secured money to pay back our loans and would be home before the end of the month, and that I would have news about Aemilia and me. The rest would have to wait until I could tell them in person. I dropped the letter off at the courier service. Then Onyebuchi and I headed to work.

The first step in my new life was to go to the Temple of Saturn, where the Aerarium, the Roman treasury, was located. It and the Tabularium were the center of civil administration and records. There, in the Tabularium, I would officially take up my duties as an apparitor, a scribae, for Cicero. The Tabularium kept the records of Rome's history. Its primary purpose was to hold the official copies of the Senate's decrees, which only became valid after they were deposited in the Aerarium and stored in the Tabularium. To become law, decrees had to be filed under the guardianship of a god, in this case, Saturn. The Tabularium had the offices of the Roman administration and such records as Rome kept.

Onyebuchi and I climbed the long steps to the Temple of Saturn, a massive building on the Forum, opposite the Curia. The steps were busy with people coming and going, all of whom seemed to carry documents of one sort or another. I stepped through the imposing door and into organized chaos. People moved in all directions, but all conveyed a sense of purpose. All except me. I had no idea where to go. I looked about and spied a severe-looking servant, who seemed to be the *ianitore,* the doorkeeper, standing in the center of it all.

"Excuse me," I said.

"May I help you," he replied in a nasal voice, making a point of glancing at my disheveled tunic. Ouch, I probably should have worn my toga.

"I'm looking for where I turn this in." I handed him my appointment and enjoyed watching his eyes grow wide as he read it and saw Cicero's signature and seal.

"Yes, of course. Please follow me."

We followed him out of the temple and to the left, up the slope of the Capitoline Hill to the Tabularium and then up a flight of stairs to a room where a white-haired man sat at a table covered with scrolls.

"Master, Marcus Vitruvius Pollio, appointed apparitor for Cicero."

"Ah, there you are, Vitruvius. I've been waiting for you. You're late." His greeting took me aback, but then I spotted his grin to show me he wasn't serious. "I am Servius Sentus. I lead the *decuriae*." He noticed my incomprehension. "The association of apparitores. Welcome to the *decuriae.* Cicero paid your fee. If you need anything, you come to me—except pay, that is. The pay master is in the Aerarium, where you came from."

He pulled a document out of one of his stacks and passed it to me. "You need to sign your acceptance. This will also register you with the Treasury so you will be paid." While I signed, he pulled something from a cabinet against the wall behind him. He took the signed acceptance from me and presented me with a medallion on a deep crimson ribbon. "This is the sign and seal of your office. Wear it when you are out performing official duties. While you wear it, you are an official of Rome. Any who disregards it does so at their peril. Now, let me show you where you will work."

"Where I'll work?"

"Yes. Cicero and Caesar insisted that you have your own room. You are one of very few apparitores who do. They wouldn't say why."

I dismissed Onyebuchi and followed Servius Sentus down a long hall to a door guarded by two bored legionaries, who straightened as we approached.

"This is Marcus Vitruvius Pollio. Mark him well. He is the only person allowed in this room by order of Consul Cicero." The old man handed me a key and waved me to the door. I unlocked it and entered alone.

The room was small and lit by a window high up on the back wall. It was furnished with two floor lamps, a chair, and a long table, on which were eleven stacks of documents. Each pile had a note on the top held down by a stone. One note said *Legal Documents*, the first of which was *The Disposition of Seized Property*. Each of the other ten piles had either Catiline's or one of the nine guilty conspirators' names. These were the correspondence and ledgers belonging to the conspirators that the Senate had seized. One of the piles of documents on the side of the table drew my eyes. The note on the top identified the pile as documents seized from Quintus Annius Chilo.

***

I walked alone to work the next morning, after putting on my toga—which I should have worn the day before—going to my first paying job ever. Without Annius's offered bounty, it was unlikely that anyone would attack me. More importantly, I wore the apparitor's medallion. I knew I was the same person who had walked to the Tabularium the day before, but I admit to feeling a selfish pride. My father, of course, would have warned me that pride is a trap we set for ourselves.

The two guards at the room were the same as the day before, and they merely nodded to me as I approached. I unlocked the door, went in, and just stood, staring at the great heaps of documents. Where to start? The answer was obvious. As much as I wanted to read Annius's documents, I needed to start with Catiline's. That was what they were paying me to do.

His pile was by far the largest. I spent most of the day reading and making notes. I made a timeline across the side of one scroll and recorded the key statements made, with lines connecting statements and the actions they caused.

Caesar had been right. When Catiline had begun, his goals had been noble, though largely motivated by his own debt and frustration that the wealthy patricians wouldn't allow him to rule. But as time passed, he'd changed. His loss of the consul election to Cicero was a devastating blow. His writing became bitter, vindictive, even manic. Some of his supporters abandoned him. I found the evidence of Caesar's early withdrawal. He had spoken the truth. He was among the many who had abandoned Catiline. Their departure seemed to have pushed Catiline beyond reason, perhaps beyond sanity.

But I was interested in those who hadn't left him, the ones still hiding in dark places. Slowly, I discovered them. The number of conspirators increased from the ten known to the Senate to seventeen. The new names played only minor roles, but they all knew what Catiline had planned. They all had condoned murder. They all were guilty.

After Catiline's documents, I carefully read the documents belonging to Lentulus, Cethegus, Gabinius, Statilius, and Caeparius, the five the Senate had executed. Their documents confirmed their involvement. I noted a phrase here, an allusion there, but when these were taken as a whole, the pattern stood out clearly. I identified six more conspirators, bringing the total to twenty-three. Again, none of the new ones played a significant part. They were, as Cicero called them, little fish.

Though the work was tedious and often difficult—some of the handwriting was abysmal—it was also fascinating. Time sped by. I didn't realize the day was gone until the light began to fade and I could no longer read the documents. I had made it through the writings of the first six big fish. The documents of the other four conspirators who were still at large, Umbrenus, Longius, Publius, and Annius, were for tomorrow. When I would read Quintus Annius Chilo's documents, my father's spirit would be there with me, reading over my shoulder, and the thought made me smile.

***

The next morning, Aemilia woke early. She was to meet with Pompeia to discuss what her duties would be once she became their medica, which would be after we married. We stepped out of the inn together, and I watched her leave with Onyebuchi acting as her bodyguard. I could see she still wore the full-faced smile of the day before, and just maybe, she had a little swagger in her stride.

I made my way to my room in the Tabularium and began reading the documents in the remaining four stacks, saving Annius's for last. I had almost finished with the first of the four when a knock on the door jarred me out of my concentration.

I am uncertain what I expected, but Cicero's standing came as a surprise. I was speechless. Here was the most powerful man in the Republic, gently tapping on my door.

"May I come in?" he asked with a grin.

"Yes, certainly. Enter."

He waited for the door to close before continuing. "Well, Vitruvius. What have you found?"

I presented my notes from the day before and described how I had identified the additional thirteen little fish.

He read my notes for a few moments and then looked up. "Excellent, Vitruvius, very good. We will include these names on the Senate's list. As a minimum, the Senate has already authorized the seizure of all property from anyone who knowingly took part in the conspiracy and has reserved the right to exile them after we review their individual cases."

He rolled up my notes and glanced over at the piles of documents I had made all over the floor. "This position suits you well. I'm glad Caesar found a solution to our common dilemmas. Send me a report when you have finished up with those." He indicated the piles of documents on the table.

After Cicero left, I went back to the stacks of scrolls. I took four hours to finish the next three, leaving me with the final stack, Annius's documents. I moved these to the center of the table and started reading.

One of the first documents was a letter from Catiline to Annius. From what I read, clearly Annius handled the conspirator's communications. Catiline was obsessed with secrecy. Given what would happen when they were caught, who could blame him?

Quintus Annius Chilo was the one who had suggested using ciphers for their messages, assuring Catiline that even if they were intercepted, no one could read them without guessing the method used, and that was unlikely. Annius told Catiline that he knew how to create unbreakable ciphers. That last made me smile. Quintus Annius Chilo had been a victim of his own pride, and I, Vitruvius, had beaten him.

Other documents detailed how the conspirators would pass messages. They would use merchants and farmers to evade the notice of the authorities. These messengers would be kept unaware of the messages' content and the nature of the conspiracy. Annius called them "the sheep." My heart pounded. Plainly, my father had been one of his sheep—and he was sent to the slaughter like a sheep.

Annius wrote the way he spoke, with arrogance and self-importance. I could easily see why he had joined Catiline. Both men showed disdain for the Senate, who they felt kept people like them from their rightful power. But unlike Catiline, Annius made no pretense of caring for the debt-ridden merchants and farmers. He was only interested in personal gain.

I was practically at the bottom of the stack of Annius's documents when I discovered it—the document that finally explained my father's death. In the pile was a letter from Gaius Gargonius to Annius in which Gargonius suggested using my father as one of Annius's sheep. Gargonius explained my father's debt and suggested that Annius offer to pay it if my father agreed to deliver messages. But what really caught my eye were the last lines, *"You need not actually pay his debt. We can easily find a different solution, which would save you the money and allow me to gain his property."* Gaius Gargonius was one of the little fish and he had set up my father for murder!

I sat back in shock. Gaius Gargonius was a murderer. He had lit the spark that had set the blaze. While he hadn't swung the hammer, he had put the hammer in the assassin's hand. My heart pounded in my head as anger flooded through me. Then my rage turned to ice as a plan formed in my mind. I added Gaius Gargonius to my notes and timeline, the final conspirator. The final little fish.

Before leaving that evening, I pulled four documents from the legal pile and took them with me.

***

I devoted the evening to reading the legal process for seizing property and came up with an idea. My solution would require Cicero's blessing and Caesar's participation. Such had been the change in my fortunes that I could contemplate schemes that required the agreement of the first consul and the pontifex maximus. I swam in deep waters indeed, but I did swim.

Before I went to bed that night, I sent Caesar a request for a meeting, and his response was waiting for me at the Tabularium in the morning. He would see me just before midday.

The walk was a short one, down from the Tabularium across the Forum to the Domus Publica, where the doorman ushered me in to meet with Caesar.

Caesar looked up from his reading. "So, Vitruvius, you discovered something?"

"Yes, sir." I told him of the work I had done on the documents and about the additional thirteen names I had given Cicero.

"So Cicero informed us late yesterday. The Senate has already moved to seize their property and detain them for trial—if we can find them."

"Well, I found one more." I explained how I had identified Gaius Gargonius.

"Isn't he the one your family owes a debt to?" he asked, eyeing me with a raised brow.

"He is, and I have an idea." I told Caesar my plan.

Caesar listened, and when I finished, he laughed. "Vitruvius, you are brilliant. Yes, it will take Cicero's authority, but I don't think the Senate will object." He was quiet for a moment, his eyes focused somewhere in the distance as if he were charting a course I couldn't see.

He looked back at me and smiled. "Vitruvius, I will get Cicero to agree, but you need to do something for me." He must have noticed some reticence in my expression. "Oh, don't be so glum. You'll enjoy it. While I speak with Cicero, I want you to write up a plan as to how you will go about gathering information on Rome's enemies, both at our borders and in our streets. You agreed to do this for me. Now tell me how. I should be back in a couple of hours."

He called for writing materials and left me alone again. I already recognized every tile on the floor, so I decided I might as well work on the problem. I admit, I had been thinking about how to do it since I had first agreed. Writing down my ideas took me about an hour. Afterward, I resumed counting tiles.

Caesar returned shortly thereafter and looked approvingly at my endeavors.

"I see you are keen to start. Cicero has agreed. I'll make all the arrangements. What do you have for me?"

I held up the scroll I had written. "My strategy is all in here, but in summary. The people who know what's going on in Rome are the societies, the merchant societies, not the guilds. Some of them are open to other work, as they call it. Bringing a few into Rome's service and having them send regular reports would be ideal."

"You can find such societies?"

"I know of one I believe would be happy to take the job, and I expect they could introduce me to others."

"And outside Rome?"

"Thieves and highwaymen."

"What?" He stared with incredulity.

"*Good* thieves can be found. Well, thieves who follow a code and will do a fair day's work for fair pay. I have encountered some and could probably find more."

Caesar grinned. "You are full of surprises, but I wouldn't trust even *good* thieves in the provinces. They are too likely to work for Rome's enemies."

"I agree. Beyond Rome's firm control, I suggest we use the *fuumentarii*. They handle the purchase and distribution of grain for the army. Because they move around so much in search of supplies, they accumulate a great deal of information. We just need to organize them and train them to report what they learn." I handed Caesar the scroll.

He skimmed the scroll and then looked up. "Good, Vitruvius. Very good. I'll recommend the Senate act on this at once. You have about three weeks before the end of the year. When are you planning to return home?"

"I'd like to leave as soon as possible. My mother and sister must be frantic by now."

"I will require a week to set this up. You can leave then, but don't become too comfortable at home. I want you back here when I am praetor."

CHAPTER TWENTY-FOUR

FORSAN ET HAEC OLIM MEMINISSE INVADIT
Perhaps even these things will be good to remember one day.

Over the next week, I finished my reading of the conspirators' documents and wrote my report for the Senate. Following Cicero's and Caesar's orders, I made sure my name did not appear anywhere on the report. I was a ghost, unknown to all but them.

Word reached Rome of massive desertions in Catiline's army once news of the conspirators' fate became known. The size of his army fell from about ten thousand men to a mere three thousand. We also learned Catiline was marching what was left of his ill-equipped forces toward Cisalpine Gaul, hoping to attack Rome. In response, the Republic had sent an army to meet him. Everyone knew that as long as Catiline remained at large, his followers posed a threat both outside and inside the city. The senators' fear of a knife in the back was palpable. Most of them were willing to turn a blind eye to both the means used to apprehend the conspirators and the strict legality of their punishments.

The Senate found everyone on the list of conspirators guilty and ordered their property seized. For those whose whereabouts were known, the Senate dispatched officials to detain them, pending trial—all except Gaius Gargonius. That task, they gave to Caesar, and he, in turn, gave it to me. And I was looking forward to it.

Caesar persuaded the consuls and the Senate to implement the plan I had given him to gather information on Rome's enemies, internal and external, though, again, my name was never used. I remained in the shadows. The Senate approved a budget for this, and Cicero quietly placed that budget in my office. Given the Senate's justified paranoia, they had allocated quite a large sum. I now controlled more money than my father had made in his lifetime. It represented wealth and power unknown to a plebeian in Roman society, and as such was intoxicating. I would have to remain ever vigilant against its effects lest I become one of those officious bureaucrats I so disliked.

Aemilia and I were to leave for home the next day, yet unfinished business remained. Part of that business was settling up with Regulus. When I came downstairs, he was sitting in the atrium, talking with two men. He reminded me of a spider sitting in his web, sensing the small vibrations of events in the far corners of his domain.

As I entered, he glanced up and motioned the two men to leave. "Master, Vitruvius. I arranged for a litter and bearers to be here tomorrow at dawn to collect your luggage."

"Thank you, Regulus. It is time for us to settle up. What do I owe you?"

He grimaced as he chose a scroll from the shelf behind him. "It is not a small amount, my friend. You paid in advance for the room, but charges for firewood and services have been added. I wish the final amount were less, but this is business."

I read through the itemized invoice and winced. The price was high, but the accounting was in order. I placed an uncomfortable pile of coins on the table, a not-insignificant portion of my salary. Regulus counted the payment and grinned.

"It has been a pleasure doing business with you, Master Vitruvius. You have been the most interesting customer I have ever had. I will miss you and your lady. It will be positively boring without you."

"About that. I would like to offer you a deal."

I made my proposal to Regulus. I would provide a small stipend if he took note of out-of-the-ordinary people and events within the blocks under his control. He agreed without reservation. He also agreed to give me an introduction to other collegia who were likely to be interested in doing such as service to the state.

As I climbed the stairs back to our room, I realized I would miss the inn. While the building was old and cramped, I had friends here, something I hadn't really known before.

***

Aemilia looked up when I entered, her expression pensive.

"Aemilia?"

"I want to talk about Pavo and his girls. I've been thinking."

"Oh?" I said, dreading what was to come.

"Pavo won't be well enough to be a guard again for several months, and I'm worried about his girls."

"The little one has taken quite a liking to you." That the affection was mutual was obvious.

A small smile touched the corners of her mouth. "Yes. I need to do something for them. Pavo was injured saving our lives, and he is a good man."

"What'd you have in mind?"

Hesitantly she told me her plan. I had reservations, but this was plainly something she thought important, and she was unlikely to be persuaded differently. After some discussion, I relented, or more precisely, I gave up.

Pavo was sitting on his bed in the small room when we called on him. He was weak, but alert. "I haven't been moving, mistress. I promise," he said defensively. One did not cross Aemilia in her domain.

"I understand," she said irritably, "but you must be careful. You'll knock something loose, and you'll be flopping around like a fish."

"Pavo, I need to pay you what we owe you," I interrupted.

"No, sir. You don't owe me anything, not after the care the lady gave me. I'd be dead without it."

"And we would be dead but for you. No, we owe you your fair wages." I handed him a small sack of coins.

He took them without counting. "I admit I welcome the money, sir. The girls need it. I have to think about them. It'll be some time before I can take another job. I'll fill in at cooking where I can, but this will come in handy."

Aemilia stepped closer and put her hand on his arm. "Pavo, we would like to talk with you about something." She nodded to me.

"Pavo, when we return, Caesar will give us a small place to live that has more room than we will need. Granted, it's in the *suburra,* not the best part of the city, but I would like to invite you and your girls to live with us. You would be the cook, and once you're better, our guard as well. I can pay you only a little, but you and your girls would have a roof and food."

Pavo looked at Aemilia, then at me, and then back at Aemilia. "I don't know what to say. I would never impose myself, but my girls, they need a good place to live. Are you certain about it? They can be a bit underfoot, if you follow me."

Inwardly I grimaced. I wouldn't choose to have my peace destroyed by three young girls, but when I saw Aemilia's pleading eyes, I realized how important this was to her.

"Yes," Aemilia answered. "We are sure."

I forced a smile.

Settling with Onyebuchi was much simpler. He had already told us he was taking a job for a few months in the new year with his cousin in Sarnus, the port for Pompeii. When I paid him off, he tried to return the red cloak I had given him, but I refused. He had more than earned it. I told him that he was always welcome back. I hadn't finished my knife training.

***

We left the inn at dawn. The four men Regulus had hired brought down our luggage and the small amount of stores we had purchased and lashed them to a litter. Then they waited while we said our goodbyes.

Out on the street, the day was surprisingly warm for the last of December, and only high clouds flecked the sky, a good omen for our trip. I took in the city as we wandered down its narrow streets.

Rome's assault on my senses had always overwhelmed me. Everything ran together: the smells of cooked food, animal dung, unwashed bodies, and the urine used by the fullonicae to do the laundry; the cacophony of voices, construction, and bellowing livestock led to the slaughter; plus the haphazard placement of the graffiti-covered buildings. But my recollection was different now; the novelty was gone, the luster tarnished.

I finally understood the city better. It made sense in its own way. It followed its own rules. During my stay in Rome, the town had not always been hospitable. The weather had been mostly cold and wet. People had tried to kill me. Even with all that, I had obtained money for the farm, secured a job—even if not the one I had wanted—made friends, and found a wife. The city had nourished me. I realized with a start that the city hadn't changed; I had. Rome was in my blood now.

Our first stop on our trip south this early morning was the stables, where long ago it seemed, we had left the cart and the poor mule. I had to return them to the livery in Fundi. The litter-bearers transferred all our bags and boxes to the cart as I paid the bill. With Aemilia on one side of the mule and me on the other, we led the cart out into the street and pointed it south.

We went through the Capena Gate, officially leaving the city behind, but we took Rome's authority with us. Just outside the gate lay warehouses and freight yards where commercial traffic had to wait until allowed to enter the city at sundown. That early in the morning, the warehouse yards were largely deserted except for one yard where a wagon pulled by two horses waited. Along with it were two of Cicero's servants, eight legionaries in full armor and six light cavalrymen. They were waiting for me, courtesy of Caesar and Cicero. The wagon held the box of silver *denarii,* the money to repay my family's loan, along with supplies for both the men and horses.

As we approached, a servant hurried over to take charge of the cart, and Aemilia and I clambered into the wagon and took seats on a bench just behind the driver.

A cavalry officer drew his horse alongside us and saluted. "I'm Jovinus Fulcinius Domitius, commanding your escort. Are you ready to leave?"

I nodded, and our *little* procession pulled onto the Via Appia, heading south. The cavalry rode in front, carrying an official standard, followed by the wagon, the cart, and the infantrymen. Unlike our trip north to Rome, this time *we* were the official traffic. Everyone else pulled to the side, allowing us to pass, the cavalry being none too gentle with those who were too slow in yielding the road.

We traveled at a good pace, stopping only occasionally to let the horses and men rest. Legionaries could march forty miles in a day, but our poor mule and cart would slow us to just twenty-five. The trip to Fundi would take three days.

In the late afternoon, we stopped at an inn in the town of Aricia for the night after crossing the magnificent viaduct. The town was the first main posting station for an overland journey from Rome to Southern Italy on the Via Appia. As it was rather near to the capital, and favored with a fresher climate, many of Rome's *patricii* chose Atricia as the location for their leisure villas. This meant excellent inns were here to cater to their guests.

The inn we chose was one regularly used by Roman officials traveling south. After being led to our room, I could understand why. The accommodations were clean, bright, spacious, and furnished with quality mosaics and paintings. One particularly beautiful mosaic depicted the Greek goddess Diana and the god Virbius in an array of blue hues.

Later that evening, I spent an hour sketching the mosaic and thinking about my good fortune. I could never have afforded such an inn, but my circumstances had changed. I was on official business now, and this was what Rome paid for.

Five of the cavalrymen with us stayed on the road and continued south for the other part of our mission. On Caesar's authority, I had sent out a few people over the last week to find the *good* thieves who had tried to rob us on our way north. Word came back that they were operating out of a small house just south of the town of Tres Tabernae, where Aemilia and I had spent the night after they knocked me on the head. The five cavalry soldiers would ride through the night, surprise the thieves in the morning, and detain them until we arrived.

The cavalry officer remained behind, taking a room at the inn so he could guard the money. Rome would spend the money on an official and an officer, but the rest of the men camped in the inn's side yard, as was their policy.

***

The cavalry officer formed up our company at dawn, and Aemilia and I were the last to step out into the yard. Her dark cloak blended into the deep shadows. As I climbed into the wagon, I couldn't help but feel guilty at the sight of the infantrymen, who had spent the night outside while I had been warm and comfortable in the inn. I didn't like it, but that was how Rome worked, and I couldn't change their traditions.

By law and custom, Rome treated you according to your social status. The cavalry officer was of the equestrian order, so called because he was wealthy enough to equip himself with a cavalry horse and all that entailed.

Aemilia and I were plebs, but an extraordinary turn of fortune had elevated me to the social status of an apparitor, somewhere between an equestrian and a pleb. More than that, I was an apparitor for Cicero, a consul, and I derived a considerably higher status from that association. When Aemilia and I married, she would take on the same status as I had. But unlike patricians and equestrians, my status was at the pleasure of my patron, Caesar. It would last only so long as I remained in his good graces.

The weather was unseasonably warm and clear, in line with the day before, feeling more like early autumn rather than early winter. Near midday, one of our detached cavalrymen cantered up from the south and saluted his officer.

"We found them, sir, the father and the two sons. They set camp in a glen about ten miles down the road. You should be on them in two hours."

The officer nodded. "Good work, Agrius. Any trouble?"

The cavalryman laughed. "No, sir. The old man snores so loudly a herd of cattle could have crept up on 'em."

Right on cue, we approached the glen two hours later. I put on my medallion of office, and Aemilia brought the Julii pendant out from underneath her clothes as a visible reminder of our first encounter. The three thieves were shackled and surrounded by the four cavalry soldiers, who had their swords drawn. Sejanus Terentius, the father, stood slightly apart from his two sons, Trebius and Scaurus. All three were wide-eyed and pale, no doubt contemplating just how painful their deaths would be.

Recognition spread over them as they saw Aemilia and me, and if it were possible, the rest of the blood drained from their faces. Trebius sagged to his knees.

"Good afternoon, Terentius. I see you remember me. I was hoping to find you."

His eyes went from my face to my medallion and back to my face. "Sir, I didn't know. You didn't say. We would never... We didn't hurt you. Well, only a little. Please, sir."

Though I had relished exacting some small revenge in on him, the scene made me ill.

"Terentius—"

"Sir, please, have pity on my boys. They only did what I told them to do. I—"

"Terentius!"

He finally stopped speaking. "I'm not here to arrest you or harm you or your sons. Actually, I have a business proposition for you." I motioned to the nearest soldier. "Unbind him."

Terentius stared at me, his face blank, uncomprehending. I took him by the arm and led him over to a tree, away from the others. "Terentius, I am an apparitor for Cicero, and starting next year, I will work for Caesar." Terentius inhaled sharply. "We are tracking down the rest of Catiline's supporters."

I locked eyes with him. "Terentius, I would like you to help us keep track of unusual movement on the road, such as groups of people going north or south, that sort of thing. Discreetly, of course. I will pay you for good information. Not a large sum but a regular amount if the information is detailed and timely. Are you interested?"

As I watched him, I knew what he was thinking. "And no. If you choose to continue your, ah, occupation, I won't be able to help you if you are caught. Maybe you could make a living a little more reliably and a little less dangerously working for me. It's your decision."

He looked over his shoulder at his boys and then turned to me, scratching his chin. "How much are we talking about?"

I had to admire his recovery, which was an excellent trait for this sort of work. I told him what I was willing to pay.

He thought for a minute. "All right. If you're serious, I'll do it."

I brought out a small purse and put it in his hand. I closed his fingers around it. "This is payment in good faith. Keep an eye out for anyone still supporting Catiline. I want regular reports, even if you haven't seen a thing. I want to know you are looking."

After we worked out the details, Terentius gathered up his two sons, and I watched them slip into the forest. Just before they disappeared, Terentius turned and waved.

The company assembled back on the road and continued south. We soon passed the spot where Aemilia and I had first encountered Terentius and his sons. I recognized the little path they had taken us down. It would be a good place from which to watch the traffic. Perhaps they would use it.

After our time spent in Rome, I didn't find the bridge near Tripontium as impressive as it had seemed the last time here, but I still drew a quick sketch of it as we passed. Someday, I would build better bridges.

The four miles to Forum Appii passed quickly. We planned to stay the night at an inn there despite its dubious reputation. When planning this trip, the apparitores I had questioned had said this would be the best place to stay when heading south as long as I had at least ten armed men with me. The official standard at our lead and the threat of sharp steel kept the hustlers and pickpockets at a respectful distance. We only had to deal with the innkeepers.

Two inns were said to be passable. Both were old and not well kept, yet they managed to charge a premium for official visitors. Here was another form of robbery practiced by the town, just a more polite one. As the innkeeper eyed the wagon and cart entering his stableyard, the cavalry officer smiled at him and doubled the night guard.

***

My sources had been correct. No one tried to rob or molest us during our stay. Twelve armed men made a difference.

The sun was just above the horizon when we mounted up and pulled out of the inn's yard. Aemilia had been quiet all morning, saying little beyond the morning's pleasantries. She was biting her lip again. I didn't ask her about it. I decided to let her tell me when she was ready.

Only when we passed Terracina in the seventh hour did Aemilia finally speak. "What if they don't like me?"

She said it so softly that I almost missed it. "Who?"

"Your family. Your mother and sister. I'm too old, and I'm not exactly the domestic type most mothers would want to have running their son's home. I'll never be a model Roman matron."

"They'll love you. I wouldn't worry."

"Of course *you* wouldn't worry. It's not about *you*."

Ouch. I hadn't said that right. "Aemilia, my mother and sister aren't the domestic types, either. They're both better educated than most of the men I know, and neither is shy about giving their opinion." She didn't reply. "Actually, they are both a lot like you." She still didn't reply. "I'll tell you what I'm worried about."

She looked over. "You can't be worried about Epiphanes. He likes you."

"No. No, I'm not worried about Epiphanes. I'm worried the three of you will gang up on me and I won't have a chance."

She laughed. She didn't realize I was serious.

"You need women telling you what to do, Vitruvius. Otherwise, you get yourself into trouble."

We passed the shops and houses, and rode out onto the dike that ran around the sheer cliffs. The sunlight reflecting in the ripples of the calm blue water danced over the bay. On the other side of Terracina, the road turned east, and we put the harbor behind us for the final fourteen miles of our trip to Fundi.

Long shadows grew across the road as the sun lit the tops of trees and buildings with a warm amber glow. Our column, led by the cavalry and their standard, entered the outskirts of Fundi near the path to Publicius's house, where I had fallen leading the mule on the way out of town what seemed a lifetime ago.

We needed to attract as little attention as possible, so we couldn't enter with the full company, not yet. As we stopped and moved the money box to the mule cart, four of the legionaries pulled their long *caracallus* cloaks over their armor and clothing. The rest of the company, cavalry, infantry, servants, and wagon, went up a narrow path off the road to a small clearing to set up camp until called for.

In the very last of twilight, stars just visible overhead, the jingle of the mule's harness and rumble of the cart were the only noise as Aemilia and I led what remained of our company into town. In their dark cloaks, the four soldiers following at a discrete distance were almost invisible. No one took any notice of us.

Finding our way, even in the gathering dusk, was easy. Fundi hadn't changed. Little towns like Fundi take years to change anything. Still, it seemed smaller than I remembered. As we turned down the street that led to the farm, I knew, even if I had the choice, I would never be content to stay in this place. One look at Aemilia, and I believed she felt the same. How could you stay in Fundi once Rome had seeped into your being?

CHAPTER TWENTY-FIVE

QUI TOTUM VULT TOTUM PERDIT
He who wants everything loses everything.

The moonless night was as black as soot by the time we reached the house. We dared not use torches and reveal the group to curious glances. I led the small party by memory only. Then Syphāx was the one who opened the viewport when I knocked. He squinted at me before breaking into a broad grin as the glow from the atrium lit my face. "Master Vitruvius!" he exclaimed then opened the door.

"Syphāx!" I had missed that man. To my eyes, he hadn't changed at all.

"You're back! Oh, sorry." He opened the door all the way. I entered the house with Aemilia, and Syphāx's eyebrows shot up as the four soldiers followed, two carrying the money box. He threw me a questioning glance.

I put my hand on his shoulder. "Later. Can you see to the mule and cart and bring in our baggage?"

"Yes, sir."

"Who is it, Syphāx?" my mother called from somewhere further in the house.

"It's me, Mother. I'm home."

"Marcus!" Mother appeared, in her night clothes covered by a robe and her face bright with pleasure. She looked frailer than I remembered.

Her clothes hung just a bit too loosely and her face seemed thinner, her eyes sunken. Her smile slipped as she took in all the people standing in the vestibule. "Come in, all of you." She led us into the atrium, lit at night by lamps in wall niches and two braziers. "Cinna, bring everyone some wine." As an afterthought, she added, "some food too."

"Marcus!" my sister cried as she came in from the back of the house.

"Vitruvia!"

I hugged her. Epiphanes had followed her into the room, and Amelia rushed forward from behind me to embrace him.

"You said you were coming, but we didn't know when," Mother said. She looked around. "We need some introductions."

"Yes, of course. Mother, Vitruvia, this is Aemilia, Epiphanes's niece. Aemilia, my mother, Philona and my sister, Vitruvia."

"Your uncle has told us so much about you, but he didn't tell us how beautiful you are," Mother said.

Amelia blushed and bit her lip.

Vitruvia stepped forward. "I remember you from the market. You were always so kind."

My mother turned to the four soldiers. "And you are?"

I motioned to them. "You can take off your caracallae." As they pulled off their cloaks, their segmented *cuirasses* armor reflected the light of the lamps and fires. "These are four of the legionaries who escorted me, Arruntius, Ramirus, Melitus, and Tatian. They are here to guard that." I pointed to the money box. "That is the money to repay our loans."

My sister was wide-eyed. "How did you enlist legionaries to help you?"

"It's a long story. We'll tell the entire tale after we've all had a good night's sleep. For now, know that they work for me. Cicero appointed me an apparitor and along with paying off the loan, I am here on official business. The soldiers are part of that." I pulled the medallion out of my tunic. "More troops outside of town will come here tomorrow afternoon if everything goes well."

For a moment, no one said anything. Then everyone started talking at once.

"Wait. Wait, people. We'll answer questions tomorrow. We've been traveling for three days and need sleep. Mother, we have to find a place for the soldiers."

She turned to Syphāx, who had just appeared with our luggage. "Syphāx? Can you take care of the soldiers, please?"

When Syphāx had left with the four soldiers, I looked over at Aemilia, who nodded. "One thing that we must do today, because it requires some planning." I took Aemilia's hand and turned to Epiphanes. "Epiphanes, I would like your permission to marry Aemilia."

Again, no one said anything for a moment. Then, for a second time, everyone started talking at once.

I raised my hands. "Please. Please, people… Epiphanes?"

He cleared his throat. "Aemilia, is this what you want?"

"Yes."

"Then of course. I think it would be wonderful."

Aemilia smiled and kissed his cheek. Everyone started talking again.

Vitruvia stepped forward and hugged Aemilia. "Welcome to the family, Aemilia."

My mother followed and wrapped her arms around Aemilia. She whispered into her ear and only released her after some time. When she pulled back, both women had tears in their eyes.

Another hour passed before we all made it to bed. Aemilia slept on pillows arranged on the floor in Vitruvia's room. This was the first time in weeks that I hadn't shared her bed, and I missed her.

***

I awoke just as the sun crowned the hilltops to the east. After dressing, I stepped out into the deserted olive groves and wandered along the neatly planted rows. The silver leaves whispered in the light breeze, murmuring the same reassurance as ever, but they no longer offered the refuge they once had. The orchard that had loomed so large in my youth stretched only as far as the creek that divided our farm from the next. My life had outgrown their reach. My gaze was pulled more and more to the mountains in the north and what lay beyond. I had work to do.

I walked back inside and into the tablinum, where I sat at the desk and drafted a letter to Gaius Gargonius requesting an audience. He would undoubtedly think it another stalling tactic, which suited me just fine.

"Syphāx," I called. He entered a moment later. "Please deliver this to Gaius Gargonius." When he took the scroll, I grasped his forearm. "It is good to see you, old friend. Now keep a straight face with Gargonius. I don't want him to know any of this."

He smirked and nodded.

I left the tablinum and walked into the atrium, which was filled with excited chatter. Aemilia was encircled and being bombarded with questions.

"I think you should all find a chair, and Aemilia and I will tell you our story from the beginning. It'll make more sense from the start."

Aemilia and I sat on a couch while everyone else found a chair. Cinna, Hanno, and the rest of the slaves crowded into the room.

We told the story of our adventure from the time I left Epiphanes's house that morning in the rain to when we arrived at the door last night. At various points, Aemilia added details of what she had seen, from her point of view. Her story included my various mishaps, which everyone but me found humorous. In fact, many years had to go by before I was able to laugh at my sickness, vomiting on her shoes after being hit on the head by the trio of thieves, falling down the rope, and my other painful experiences.

I told them about the ciphers, but I kept my promise to Caesar and didn't give them the specifics. I could tell by Epiphanes's glance that he noticed the omission, but he didn't pursue it. Aemilia added details of her meetings with Pompeia and Caesar, some of which I hadn't known. When we finished, the room was silent save for the murmuring of the water fountain.

My mother and sister were looking at us as if we had told them north was south and east was west. Epiphanes only nodded with a knowing smile.

My mother was the first to respond. "You talked with… you dined with, with them? And you, you *work* for them now, Caesar and Cicero?" she asked in a shaky voice.

"Yes."

She turned to Aemilia. "And you work for Pompeia?"

"Actually, I work for Caesar, too, but I will be directed by Pompeia."

Mother shook her head. "This is all too much for me to take in." She paused and then straightened. "Does this mean you will work in Rome? That you will have to return to Rome? When?"

"Yes. We'll work in Rome, or wherever Caesar says, I suppose. He is giving us a modest house there, the one he lived in until he became pontifex maximus. We'll have plenty of space for you to visit us. We have to be back in Rome by the first of the year." I looked over at Aemilia. "We'll have to marry as soon as we can."

"Then who will run the farm?"

"You will. You and Vitruvia. We will be debt free. That should make the operation here easier. You know more about olive farming than most around this town. If you need to, you can hire a manager. I could afford that." I knew this wasn't the answer she wanted, but I could see that she was thinking, considering it.

"I can help if you would like," Epiphanes said. We all looked at him. "Aemilia will be part of your family. I don't have anyone else and would be pleased to stay involved. I've grown comfortable here over the last month." He turned to face my mother. "Besides, you're one of the few people I can speak Greek with."

"Mother? That sounds like an excellent solution to me," I added.

My mother smiled. Her eyes lit up. "Yes, Epiphanes, I think that would work. Why don't you have Hanno move your things over. If Marcus will not be here, we have plenty of room to make your temporary arrangement permanent." That seemed to have settled things.

After midday, Gaius Gargonius's servant delivered his master's reply. He would receive me in the second hour the next day. That was all the information I needed. I wrote out instructions and had Syphāx take it back to the rest of the company, who were camping outside town. Tomorrow would be an interesting day, one I had rehearsed in my head many times.

***

We were up before dawn, preparing for my meeting with Gaius Gargonius. Accompanied by the money box and the four guards, I started for his house midway through the first hour. The money and the soldiers, wearing their caracallae, waited across the street as I knocked on Gaius Gargonius's door. The rest of the company lined up at the top of the street, just out of sight. They would move down to Gaius Gargonius's house after the guards were summoned to bring the money inside.

A servant I had met several times before greeted me. "Master Vitruvius, please come in and wait until the master is ready to receive you."

"Thank you." I was left to wait yet again. His treatment of me was such a childish thing, doubly irritating now that I was not beholden to him. I had briefed the company that this would likely happen, so I waited.

Gaius Gargonius didn't keep me waiting as long this time. Only an hour elapsed before the servant ushered me into the tablinum, where Gaius Gargonius, with ruddy cheeks, and small, dark eyes, sat at his table, pretending to read a scroll. Having now had the privilege of visiting the homes of truly great men, Sanga and Caesar among them, the overindulgence of vermilion paint in the room seemed pretentious. I could see no elegance in the decorations, no thought beyond conspicuous display. The home's design was rather more stingy than restrained. All this was like the man who occupied it. As I watched him strive to annoy me, all I could feel was disdain.

Finally, he looked up at me. "Well, young Vitruvius, I must tell you before you start, I will not extend the due date for your loans. I have been more than generous with your family. Had you been better at minding your finances, you would not be in the position you are. I will expect full payment, nothing less, by the end of the month. Nine days. Do you understand?"

I laughed, which caused him to squint his eyes to their utmost beadiness. "I understand. But you see, I'm here to pay back the loans. In full."

His mouth was agape; the look of disbelief was priceless.

"All of it? But that's…" He pulled a document from a drawer in the table and read the sum aloud.

"Yes. I know. All of it."

He glanced around, expecting to see denarii piled on the floor. "Well, where is it?" No doubt he thought this was some ruse.

"Waiting outside with guards. Could you have your servant call them in?"

He signaled his servant and told him to summon the guards. After a moment, the four men brought the money box inside and set it on Gaius Gargonius's table. I stood, unlocked it with the key from my tunic, and opened the lid to reveal the contents.

Gaius Gargonius stared. After a moment, he turned to me. "How did you get this?"

"Later. Right now, I need you to count it and sign this receipt." I passed him the receipt. In addition to acknowledging his receipt of the money, the document declared that he no longer had any claim to my family's property. He sat, and we watched as he counted every silver denarii in the box.

"Well, Vitruvius. I, I don't know what to say. It's all here." He put the coins back into the box, his disbelief warring with wonder.

"Sign the receipt, please." He read it and signed. "So, to be clear, I paid you in full, and you have no claim over any of our property, correct?"

He tilted his head, annoyed. "Yes, that's correct. I signed your document, boy."

"Yes, you did, but I have one more piece of business with you." I nodded to the soldiers. "Bring them in, please."

As one soldier left, the other three pulled off their cloaks, revealing their legionnaire's uniforms, armor, and the gladii at their sides. A moment later, the cavalry officer and four other soldiers came in, all in full kit. The officer nodded to me. A small crowd of the household servants and Gargonius's wife had entered the room and were held back by the soldiers.

I reached into my tunic and pulled out the medallion, and set it around my neck. "Gaius Gargonius, I am here on official business of the Senate as an apparitor for Consul Cicero." He stared at the medallion. "The Senate has named you a participant in the conspiracy of Catiline against the Republic. Specifically, your correspondence with Quintus Annius Chilo showed your actions to be in support of the conspiracy in furthering the conspiracy's communications. Therefore, the Senate has decreed that your property shall be forfeited to the Republic and you shall be detained pending a trial to decide your fate. The forfeiture shall include all lands, livestock, buildings, and any money in your possession."

"No!" Gargonius's wife cried.

I handed the document over to Gaius Gargonius. His face was ashen, and his breathing labored. He looked on the verge of fainting and was not even able to reach out for the document, so I let it slide onto the table. I locked the money box. It was part of the seized property. What I had worked out with Caesar was that it hadn't been Caesar's money at all. With Cicero's permission, he had borrowed it from the treasury, and now it would be returned.

"You, you cannot," Gargonius said. "How can you do this? How can you do this to me? I've known your family since you were born."

"How could you have set my father up to be murdered? I read the letter you wrote." I handed the cavalry officer the money box key. "He's all yours."

"My pleasure."

I walked outside. What I had waited for, had imagined for days now was done. I had my revenge, but it didn't bring me any joy. My father was still dead. I felt more disdain for the greedy fool who had done this to us than anger. Just knowing that we had obtained justice would have to suffice.

A small crowd had gathered outside, kept at a distance by the remaining soldiers. I heard a commotion off to the side. One onlooker was yelling at the soldiers to let him by. It was Gaius Gargonius, the Younger. Our eyes met.

CHAPTER TWENTY-SIX

AD MELIORA
Toward better things.

I didn't want a marriage ceremony. A marriage is a marriage if the couple publicly declares their intent to make it so. Marriage needs no ceremony. I was overruled, by everyone.

Since our announcement, Aemilia had spent an appreciable amount of time huddled with my mother and sister, working out the details. Even Epiphanes contributed. Mother advised me they would let me know all I needed to know when I needed to know it, and that was that.

But I came to admit mother was right. She drew me aside when I grumbled. "Marcus, the ceremony isn't for you. It's for Aemilia. She is leaving behind her home, her family, her identity. She is becoming a member of your family. Epiphanes is passing her to you. Her old life ends, and her new life begins. She needs to mark the transformation with ceremony, with ritual. The comfort of ritual opens one door and closes the other."

So three days after our return, I stood in Epiphanes's house in the late afternoon, waiting for Aemilia to be led into the atrium by her uncle. She entered dressed in the style of Roman brides. Her long hair had been separated into six locks with headbands and piled on top in a cone. Arranging her hair must have taken my mother and sister most of the morning, especially if they had followed the tradition of parting her hair with an iron spearhead to symbolize vitality. A wreath of wild flowers and marjoram adorned her head. Her dress was a simple, plain white tunic fastened with the knot of Hercules as a good-luck charm. Her eyes shone brightly beneath her veil, which was the feminine yellow-red of saffron, as were her shoes.

She looked beautiful, stately, elegant. And how perfect for Aemilia, as saffron is the woman's color, because it is used to treat women's medical issues. All the trappings provided tradition, symbols, connections to our ancestors, and Aemilia's unique gift.

Aemilia looked up at me, trembling. I had never known her to be nervous, even when facing robbers or kidnappers with knives. She inhaled deeply and then recited, "Where he goes, I go," the simple statement that cemented our marriage. My mother stepped forward and put Aemilia's right hand in mine, *manus in mano*.

I had remained in my own mind something of a spectator to the ceremony, even as a central figure, but with those words, my knees grew weak, and a rush of emotion came over me for which I was entirely unprepared. In an instant, I realized that my life was changing as completely as Aemilia's. I swayed slightly, but then a squeeze from her hand steadied me. I lifted her veil and kissed her.

What followed was a feast even Caesar would have applauded. Aemilia and I sat side by side in two chairs covered by a single sheepskin at a table heaped with the roast pig we had sacrificed that morning, and every other delight that was available in our little town of Fundi. We were surrounded by friends and neighbors, packed so tightly into Epiphanes's house that moving from where we stood or sat was difficult. In fact, my mother and sister seemed to have invited the entire village. Like my family, many had owed Gaius Gargonius money, and I guess they were rejoicing as much for his arrest as for our wedding.

Despite being a small town, Fundi had some very fine wine, good enough to need very little water to make it tolerable. Everyone drank, ate, and drank some more, taking time out occasionally to yell, "*Feliciter*!" before returning to their wine. Even Surius Publicius drank liberally and he was noted for his sobriety.

After the feast, everyone still standing joined a joyous torchlit procession, marching Aemilia and me to my family's home. Along the way, guests threw candied almonds at us and shouted the traditional wedding acclimation, *"talasse!"* They filled the night air with chorus after chorus of bawdy songs—the more inebriated the reveler, the bawdier the verse. At least two guests passed out along the route.

When we reached the house, Aemilia threw the wedding torch into the crowd of a number of willing guests, though the act of catching a flaming torch is a skill few of the guests were willing to attempt. The baker's daughter stepped forward and deftly caught it by the handle, a feat that supposedly granted her a long life. According to tradition, Aemilia was to rub oil and fat on the doorposts as an offering of domesticity and fertility, and then I was supposed to carry her over the threshold. However, we thought we should wait until we moved into our house in Rome to perform that part of the ritual.

Still, as Aemilia and I were to use my bedroom for the few days we remained in Fundi, my mother and sister had festooned it with flowers, greenery, and fruit to promote fertility. I had told my sister I thought the whole idea silly, but she cautioned me not to complain where Mother could hear. Mother, it seems, was already speaking of grandchildren.

***

Everyone slept in the next morning, as one would expect after such a celebration. The knowing smiles that follow a wedding night greeted us in the triclinium for breakfast with the family. Aemilia's face flushed, and I struggled to ignore the gazes as we picked at the remnants of the prior night's feast piled on the table.

Vitruvia put down her plate and embraced Aemilia. "Good morning, sister."

Aemilia's smile was wonderful, filling the room with light. All of her doubts about what my family would think of her had faded over the last few days as she worked with my mother and sister to prepare for the wedding. Perhaps that was also a reason to honor traditions. Our wedding not only marked the crossing of a threshold for Aemilia and me, but the time she spent with my family, even if but a few days, had brought all of us together. That was important, as it was unlikely we would return for quite some time.

The cavalry detachment that had accompanied us had taken Gaius Gargonius to Rome under guard a few days earlier. The eight legionaries who remained would escort Aemilia and me when we left in two days.

Rome now owned Gaius Gargonius's property. The Senate decree had charged the town magistrate with evicting the family and servants and securing the house until it could be auctioned. Traditionally, magistrates allowed the family time to find new accommodations. Gargonius only had his wife and son, and no one knew the whereabouts of Gargonius the Younger. Most in the town presumed he had followed his father to Rome. I wasn't so sure. He was so filled with anger that I couldn't believe he would just fade away. Such humility wasn't like him.

After eating, I pulled on a cloak and stepped outside for a trip to the livery to secure horses and a wagon for our return. The clouds piling up in the western sky suggested a covered wagon would be wise if one were available. Still, the journey would be miserable for the foot soldiers.

I had traveled no more than three blocks when a man stepped out of an alley, blocking my way. I recognized him as one of Gargonius the Younger's lackeys, the tall one with rotten teeth. Before I had a chance to react, he stepped forward and shoved me to the ground. Unprepared, I landed hard on the paving stones, hitting my head. He didn't advance, and I scrambled to my feet, having to take an extra step to catch my balance. My head was spinning, now a familiar feeling.

"Not so tough are you, without the soldiers to back you up?" came a familiar voice from behind.

I spun around to face Gargonius the Younger, who stood back a few paces. With him was another boy I knew to be one of his cronies. Both held clubs fashioned from thick pieces of wood. I took a deep breath and said as confidently as I could muster, "I wondered where you were. Three against one. How very like you."

"You shut—"

At that instant, the door to the house across the street opened and an older woman, the maidservant of the home, stepped out and turned a wide-eyed look at us.

"What are you looking at, slave? Go back inside if you don't want to be hurt," the prick sneered.

She swallowed, dashed back into the house, and shut the door.

I backed to the side of the street, facing out so I could watch all three of them, and pulled the medallion out of my tunic. "I'm on official business for the Senate. You earn a death sentence should you hinder or harm me." I wasn't sure of that, but I gave his companions a menacing glare. "Do you want that? Is he worth your life?"

The boy standing next to Gargonius the Younger licked his lips and hesitated. "Gaius, maybe this is not such a good idea."

"He's bluffing. He's nothing but a little shit who thinks himself better than us," the prick replied and took a step towards me.

I reached under my cloak and drew my pugio. I had put it on before leaving the house, anticipating that the prick was still somewhere in town and would try some trick.

As they took a few steps back, the door across the street opened again. This time the farmer who lived there stepped out bearing a long pruning hook. He had been a guest at the wedding, one of those who had passed out in the street during the procession. That he was standing now was a wonder. "I think you boys should leave here," he said to them.

Gargonius the Younger turned to face him. "Shut your mouth. This is none of your business."

"It's in front of my house. That makes it my business, you little toad."

Gargonius the Younger's hesitant friend threw down his club. "I'm leaving. This isn't my fight."

A crowd had gathered just up the street and had started to jeer at the three. The prick looked at them and then at me, and for the first time, he seemed unsure. His expression shifted to panic as he turned toward me and took a step. *Thump*. A rock hit his chest. Then another hit him in the arm, and another landed at his feet, breaking into pieces and showering him with fragments. The crowd threw more stones and brickbat at him, yelling all the while. His two companions were also being pelted. They tried to escape but were hemmed in by the crowd. Without his father's loans, he had no protection. I was close enough that some of the badly aimed stones were landing around me. I wondered if they would kill him or me first.

"Stop!" a commanding voice boomed over the rabble.

Everyone turned toward the voice as three of the legionnaires stepped out of the alley, followed by the maidservant I had seen earlier. The soldier in the lead, Ramirus, drew his sword and walked up to Gargonius the Younger. "If you don't drop that club, I'm going to stick this sword up your ass. Do you hear me?"

The prick went pale as the club clattered to the street.

Ramirus glanced at me. "What do you want to do with them, sir?"

Gargonius the Younger was even more pathetic than his father had been. He had grown accustomed to bullying others for his own gain. I knew, with some satisfaction, that his life as he had known it was finished, but I also knew he was like a trapped animal, still dangerous. I looked at his two friends, who stared at the soldier in terror.

"Let the two others go." I walked up to the prick. "If you ever threaten or harm anyone in the town again, I will make sure Ramirus here puts his sword where it will do the most good." I picked up his club and tossed it to the side. "Ramirus, take this prick to the magistrate and see if the magistrate can persuade him to leave town."

I sheathed my dagger and started again for the livery.

***

I squatted in a chair as Aemilia cleaned the new bump on my head. "Hold still. You're fidgeting again."

"I don't need all this. I'll be fine."

"Someone is going to have to follow you around. Every time you go out, you hurt yourself. You'd think you would grow out of this at some stage. And why is it always your head?"

Vitruvia stood in the doorway, laughing. "He always gets into trouble. I've had to bandage him plenty of times. He's your problem now."

When Aemilia was satisfied with her bandaging, I returned to packing. We were leaving in the morning and taking a wagon's worth of spare home items. The rest we would buy in Rome.

Syphāx and I carried boxes and bags to the stable yard and loaded them into the wagon I had brought back from the livery. The cavalry had taken Gaius Gargonius to Rome in the original wagon, but I still had one of Cicero's two servants to drive this wagon with Aemilia and me on the seat beside him when we headed for Rome the next day.

"Thank you, Syphāx."

"Yes, sir."

"I don't just mean about loading the wagon. I mean about everything, defending the house, looking after Mother and Vitruvia. You've done a good job. We'll miss you."

"Me, sir? You'll see me often enough when you come back home."

"No, Syphāx. I'm giving you your freedom. I've already completed the documents. You will be a freeman as of tomorrow when we leave. The whole family has agreed. You deserve it."

Syphāx stood rooted to the spot for some time before he spoke again. "You are really doing this for me, sir?"

"Yes, Syphāx, we are. The family is. You can go back to Crete if you wish, see your home. You are your own man."

He was quiet again for a moment. "Can I stay here and work, sir? Your mother and sister will need me and…" He looked down, uncomfortable. "You see, sir, Cinna and I have become… friends."

I had hoped he would want to stay, but dared not mention it. I smiled as relief surged through me. "Yes, we would be grateful if you would. I didn't know about you and Cinna. I guess I should have. We will pay you a laborer's wage and give you food and a place to stay. If Cinna is agreeable, I'm sure we could arrange something."

I reached over and hugged the mountain of a man as tears rolled down his cheek.

***

In the late afternoon, Vitruvia and I went for a peaceful walk in the groves. We stopped at the small covered area. Conversations I'd had with my sister under the old wooden roof were among my fondest memories. The area was empty now save for unused baskets, a bare table, and a set of scales. The old three-legged stool squeaked as she sat on it.

"So, you're off. I will miss you," she said.

"I'll miss you, too. You can always come up for a visit. We'll have the room."

"Perhaps, but I think I'll be busy here. I'll have to do most of the work, you know. Mother isn't as strong as she once was."

"Use Epiphanes if you need him."

She laughed. "Can you see it? A Greek scholar counting olives."

I had to chuckle at the image. No, it was not something I could imagine, either. "Use Syphāx. He's capable and wants to stay. Hire someone else if you need to."

"I am immensely pleased Syphāx is staying. I'm not sure how I could manage without him. The house wouldn't be the same." She paused and smiled. "I didn't know about him and Cinna. They must have been very discreet. I hope they can find some happiness here."

I studied her resting on the stool, my sister, who didn't seem to have a chance for a fulfilling life with children of her own. "Vitruvia, the farm is yours for a dowry. I doubt I'll be back here to live. If you find the right man, it would be a good start."

She gave me a look of shock. "Marcus, I couldn't do that. It's, it's—"

"Vitruvia, I'll never be a farmer. But you could be if you want."

"I don't know what to say."

"Just remember it's an option you have."

Footsteps approached, and I turned to see Tatian, one of the soldiers, jogging over to us. "Sir, this message just arrived from Rome."

I took the scroll. It bore Caesar's seal. I broke the seal and read it. Caesar wished Aemilia and me *talasse* and then commanded me to return at once. He had a project that *"requires your utmost skill and talents."* I took a deep breath and sighed.

"What is it?" Vitruvia asked.

"I think it is the beginning of the rest of my life."

And that was so. I, a staunch defender of the Republic, went into service to the man who would bring about its downfall. But I am old and must rest now. I'll write more sometime soon.

THE END

GLOSSARY

Abeona Roman Goddess of outward journeys.

Adiona Roman Goddess of safe return.

Aerarium Rome's treasury, housed in the Temple of Saturn and the adjacent tabularium in the Forum.

Alba Hills Volcanic area southeast of Rome. Because of their coolness in summer and the absence of malaria, the hills were a favorite summer resort of Romans.

amicus Friend or comrade.

animus Rational soul, life, or intelligence, from a root that means 'to blow' or 'to breathe.'

apparitor A servant of a public official, an attendant who executed the orders of a Roman magistrate.

Aquilo Name (personification) given to the north wind.

Aricia Town in the Alban Hills southeast of Rome where many of the proletariat of Rome had their resort homes.

calda Drink of hot mulled wine.

caracallus Cloak worn by Roman soldiers.

centurion A legion officer commanding a Roman century (about 100 men).

Cilician pirates Pirates that dominated the Mediterranean Sea from the 2nd century BCE until their suppression by Pompey in 67–66 BCE.

cognomen The third name of a citizen of ancient Rome. Initially, it was a nickname, but lost that purpose when it became hereditary.

colegium A brotherhood, fraternity, or guild of men.

consul The senior magistrate of the Roman republic, two of whom were elected annually, usually in July, to assume office the following January, taking turns presiding over the Senate each month.

curia During the Roman Republic, the building where Roman senators met together. It was on the northeast side of the Forum.

decani Roman soldier in charge of ten other soldiers.

Decennovium Canal A canal that ran parallel to the Via Appia for nineteen miles from Forum Appii to Teracina.

decuriae An association of apparitoris, a pool from which apparitoris would be drawn for employment.

denarii Ancient Roman silver coin, originally worth ten asses.

domus publica The home of the pontifex maximus, the chief priest of Rome.

Elysium The abode of the blessed after death in classical mythology.

fasces Bundle of wooden rods, bound together, sometimes including an axe with its blade emerging. It symbolized a magistrate's power and jurisdiction.

ferryman In Roman mythology, a figure whose duty it was to escort deceased souls from earth to the afterlife.

Forum Appii Town on the Via Appia, 43 miles southeast of Rome. The usual halt at the end of the first day's journey from Rome and the starting-point of the Decennovium Canal.

fullonica Laundry facilities in ancient Rome. The process of cleaning and whitening cloth was done in three stages. The first of which used water and nitrates (urine) to wash the cloth.

Fundi The main town of the Plain of Fondi, a small plain between the mountains and the Tyrrhenian Sea, halfway between Rome and Naples on the Via Appia. The plain includes three lakes and is agriculturally very fertile.

Furies The three ancient Greek goddesses of vengeance who lived in the Underworld.

fuumentarii Officials of the Roman Republic charged with wheat collection for the legions. They acted as the secret service for the Roman Empire in the 2nd and 3rd centuries.

garum Fermented fish sauce which was used as a condiment in the cuisines of Phoenicia, ancient Greece, and Rome.

Hepius The god of medicine in ancient Greek and Roman mythology.

hostes In Roman law, a public enemy to be shown no quarter.

ianitore A porter or doorkeeper.

imperium The authority held by a citizen to control a military or governmental entity.

Julii The gens Julii was one of the most ancient patrician families in ancient Rome, primarily remembered for Gaius Julius Caesar.

kalendas The first day of the month.

Lake of Nemi A small circular volcanic lake nineteen miles south of Rome, taking its name from Nemi, the largest town in the area, that overlooks it from a height.

Lares Roman household gods that protected home and family

Latiaris stairs Shortcut down from the Quirinal Hill, eighty-six flat stone steps about a span wide, cut through the hillside.

lictors Roman officials who acted as bodyguards to those magistrates who held imperium. They carried rods decorated with fasces and, outside the religious boundary around the city of Rome, with axes that symbolized the power to carry out capital punishment.

lingulaca Gossip or casual conversation.

Lucus Feroniae Minor town along the Via Appia.

macellum Indoor market building that sold mostly provisions.

medica Female healer, medical doctor.

medicus Male healer, medical doctor.

Minerva Roman goddess of both wisdom and war.

Miseria Roman goddess of misery, anxiety, grief, depression, and misfortune.

Mithras Roman god of soldiers, light, truth, and honor.

new man A man who was the first in his family to serve in the Roman Senate or, more specifically, to be elected as consul.

novus homo See *new man* above.

nundine A market day held every ninth day according to ancient Roman reckoning.

ostium The pathway leading to the main entrance hall of a Roman villa.

palla A woven rectangle made of wool that a matron put on top of her stola when she went outside.

patria potestas The "power of a father," in Roman family law, power that the male head of a family exercised over his children and his more remote descendants in the male line, whatever their age, as well as over those brought into the family by adoption.

peristyle A colonnade surrounding an interior court or garden.

pilus prior The commander of the senior century in a legion.

plebs Plebeian, an ordinary person, especially one from the lower social classes.

Pomona Roman goddess who was the keeper of orchards and fruit trees.

pontifex maximus The chief high priest and most important position in the ancient Roman religion.

popinae Cook shops that served "take-out" food. They had masonry counters inset with cooking pots, and customers might have selected their choice of porridge, ham, stew, and other culinary delights. The walls were often painted with frescoes bearing images of the available food items.

pozzolana A volcanic ash that is a natural siliceous or siliceous-aluminous material which reacts with calcium hydroxide in the presence of water at room temperature. Main ingredient in Roman hydraulic concrete.

Praeneste Ancient Roman city located 23 miles east-southeast of Rome on a spur of the Apennines, home of the great temple to Fortuna Primigenia.

praetor An ancient Roman magistrate ranking below a consul and having chiefly judicial functions, eight of whom were elected annually, usually in July, to take office the following January.

pugio Dagger was used by the Romans, sometimes passed on as a family heirloom.

Praefect of the camp The third in command of a legion who dealt with much of the administration and with command tasks that required technical knowledge of how the legion worked.

quaestor A junior magistrate, twenty of whom were elected each year, and who thereby gain the right of entry to the Senate.

Quirinal Hill One of the Seven Hills of Rome, at the north-east of the city center.

Reate An ancient town in central Italy near Rome.

rostra A long, curved platform in the Forum, about twelve feet high from which the Roman people were addressed by magistrates and advocates.

scriba armmentarius Engineer in charge of arms and siege engines in a Roman army.

scribae The highest in rank of the four prestigious occupational grades among the apparitores, the attendants of the magistrates.

tabernae A single-room shop or stall for the sale of goods and services, generally, on the ground level with one side open.

tablinum A room or alcove between the atrium and the peristyle of a Roman house for storing the family records on tablets, an office.

Tabularium The official records office of ancient Rome and housed the offices of many city officials. Situated within the Roman Forum, it was on the front slope of the Capitoline Hill, below the Temple of Jupiter Optimus Maximus.

Temple of Saturn Ancient Roman temple to the god Saturn in Rome, at the foot of the Capitoline Hill at the western end of the Roman Forum. It housed the Roman treasury.

talasse Wedding salutation.

triclinium Formal dining room in a Roman home.

Tullianum Rome's oldest prison, for many centuries a maximum-security penitentiary for the enemies of Rome awaiting execution.

vestibule Antechamber next to the outer door of a Roman home.

DRAMATIS PERSONAE

Aemilia Epiphane's niece who has studied to be a medica under Surius Publicius.

Aemillius Quintilianus, Lucius Roman senator known for his willingness to take new clients.

Annius Chilo, Quintus Roman senator with a bad reputation.

Caesar, Gaius Julius Pontifex maximus and praetor elect from one of the oldest families in Rome.

Caster Field slave for the Vitruvius family.

Catilina, Lucius Sergius Roman Senator best known for the second Catilinarian conspiracy, an attempt to overthrow the Roman Republic.

Cicatrix, Acaunus Former legionnaire and hired thug.

Cicero, Marcus Tullius One of two consuls. Known for his intelligence and oratory.

Cinna Slave, maid servant, and cook in Vitruvius's household.

Davus One of Quintus Fabius Sanga's guards.

Epiphane Greek scholar, Vitruvius's tutor, and Aemilia's uncle.

Gargonius, Gaius Unscrupulous land owner in Fundi to which many in Fundi are indebted.

Gargonius the Younger, Gaius Son of Gaius Gargonius.

Hanno Slave in Epiphane's household.

Hostilius, Narcissa Woman employed by Quintus Annius Chilo.

Lepidus Field slave for the Vitruvius family.

Marrius Scaevola, Lucius Name used by Marcus Vitruvius Pollio for a short time while in Rome.

Manlius, Gaius War veteran and close ally of Lucius Sergius Catilina.

Mia Youngest daughter of Pavo Tragus.

Mona Middle daughter of Pavo Tragus.

Nasus One of Quintus Fabius Sanga's guards.

Onyebuchi Nubian bodyguard and knife expert.

Pavo Tragus Bodyguard and cook, former Centurion with the rank of Pilus Prior.

Philona Mother of Marcus Vitruvius Pollio.

Placida Works at Quirinal Hill apartments.

Plautus, Titus Maccius Commonly known as Plautus, a Roman playwright of the Old Latin period.

Pompeia Pompey's daughter and Gaius Julius Caesar's wife.

Publicius, Surius Medicus who once worked for important patrician families, but now lives in Fundi.

Sanga, Quintus Fabius Roman senator and patron of the tribes in Gaul.

Regulus Owner of a small inn.

Sabrina Eldest daughter of Pavo Tragus.

Sejanus Terentius Thief and highwayman.

Scaurus Older son of Sejanus Terentius.

Syphāx Senior slave for the Vitruvius household. Originally from Crete and taken in Pompey's wars against the Cilician pirates.

Tiro Secretary to Marcus Tullius Cicero.

Trebius Younger son of Sejanus Terentius.

Trebonia Wife of Quintus Fabius Sanga.

Vitruvia Vitruvius's seventeen-year-old sister.

Vitruvius Pollio, Marcus Architect and engineer for both Julius Caesar and Augustus Caesar. He is the author of *De Architectura,* the only major work on architecture or engineering to survive from classical antiquity.

ABOUT THE AUTHOR

David lives with his wife in Seattle, Washington and now pursues his dream of writing after a long career as a research scientist and a US Naval Officer with a background in military history and theory.

He is interested in historical fiction, both reading it and writing it. He is fascinated by the "white space" of history, what happened in famous events or in the lives of famous people that was lost from history. Writing historical fiction is filling in the "what if" of those missing details.

The story, *The Vitruvian Man,* began with a question that was debated among friends at a pub; *how do you do engineering without algebra*? It led the author to research *De Architectura* and Marcus Vitruvius Pollio.

THANK YOU

I hope you enjoyed reading about Vitruvius as much as I enjoyed writing about him. Feel free to send me a note if you have comments or questions. In particular, I would like to know if there is any interest in continuing Vitruvius's story. I can be reached through my website:

https://teranovabooks.com

As an Indie author, reviews are much appreciated. Please take the time to review this book on the site where you purchased it

CPSIA information can be obtained
at www.ICGtesting.com
Printed in the USA
JSHW020309270623
43831JS00001B/51

9 781734 988949